Beneath A Bu

Dougie McHale

Azzie Bazzie
Books

Edinburgh

2018

Connections

A self-assured smile crosses the face of Jason Lavigne as he sits in Cadiz on George Street and orders a fillet steak.

Across the table, Rachel studies the menu. 'I can't decide.'

The waiter asks if she would like more time.

She puts a finger to her lips and hums. 'No. I think I'll have the mackerel.'

'Excellent choice,' the waiter says as he collects the menus.

Rachel sips her coffee and replaces her cup in the saucer.

'Have you been here before?' Jason asks.

'A few times. Friends' birthdays, that kind of thing.'

'It seems nice. I like the décor.'

'The food is lovely. One of the reasons I asked you to come.' Rachel smiles at Jason. 'It's been too long. We should see each other more often.'

'Life's been busy lately.'

'That's true, but it shouldn't be an excuse.'

'No. It shouldn't. You're right. So, what have you been up to?' Jason asks.

'Boring stuff like work. But I think I've found myself a new hobby. The other day, I was reading an article about the history of surnames, and I was amazed to discover there's a lucrative business growing up around them.'

'Really? What do you mean?'

'Historical tours, books, groups, societies, Facebook groups. In America, if you have a certain surname, you can spend an entire weekend at these clan gatherings. It's a bit like the Highland Games, but exclusive to your name. Having a Scottish or Irish surname is a big deal over there.'

Jason smirks. 'It's not called the land of opportunity for nothing; they'll bleed anything dry.'

'It's not like that. They take it seriously. Anyway, I was jealous. It sounded quite fun and there's little prospect of me ever experiencing that sense of belonging.'

'Why not?'

'Come on. *Clarke*. It doesn't exactly have an ancient ring to it.'

'You never know. Have you checked it out? There could be an annual gathering of Clarkes. Let's see, I'll Google it.'

Rachel looks at him with her large eyes. She is slim, with wavy strawberry blonde hair that falls over her shoulders.

They had known each other since high school, went to the same university and were part of a close-knit group that shared a common interest in politics, global warming, and environmental issues. Then, when they moved into the world of work, they remained close friends. There was always the rumour that there's was more than just the friendship others saw on the surface. Rachel secretly enjoyed the intrigue it produced, whilst Jason would never jeopardise the friendship they had. He loved her and she loved him and, for both, it was the essence of that love that was different.

She waits expectantly as Jason taps his mobile phone.

'Mm,' he frowns.

'That doesn't sound very encouraging.'

'You're right. The first thing that comes up is Clarks the shoe shop, a shipping container specialist, and… a Bognor Regis Estate Agent!'

'Ah! That's worse than I thought.'

'I'm pulling your leg. There's lots here. Here's one that says, Clarke is a popular surname in Ireland.' He looks up from the screen and smiles at her. 'Even I didn't know that. It goes on to say that the Irish version of the surname is believed to have come from County Galway and County Antrim, and spread to County Donegal and County Dublin. The name is derived from the Irish Gaelic sept Ó Clearing, meaning "clerk" And there's even a family crest. How about that?'

'I had no idea. Wow! I need to research that a bit more. I feel much better now. What about your surname? It's French and exotic. I bet it's better than mine.'

'Let's have a look,' Jason says. 'Here we are, Google says the history of the Lavigne family goes back to the Medieval landscape of north-western France, to the regions known as Brittany and Normandy. The name Lavigne is derived from the Old French word "vine," meaning "vine," and as such, it is likely that the first bearers of this name owned or worked on a vineyard.'

'I might have known yours would be more interesting than mine. My lot were pen pushers whereas yours grew bloody wine,' she laughs.

'Actually, they were French Polishers.'

'Really?'

'Yeah.'

'I never knew that. I knew your name was French, but didn't think much of it. And you know your family's history. I'd love to know mine.'

'Well, I don't know it all. On my dad's side, the French side, I just know as far back as my grandad. And on my mother's side, I know as far back as my great grandfather.'

'That's still a generation more than me. I've not a clue about mine. It was never really spoken about. Your dad wasn't French. Was he? He spoke with an Edinburgh accent.'

'He was born in France, and his dad, my grandfather, came from a line of French polishers in Nice in the south of France.'

'Really!'

'Oui.'

She slapped his arm. 'Stop taking the piss.'
'I couldn't resist it. Your face was a picture.'
'French Polishers, that's different. My dad was a painter and decorator.'
'There's nothing wrong with that.'
'I know. But French Polishing… come on, that's pretty cool.'
'I never thought about it. To me, it was just ordinary. It was what dad did. I was brought up with it. But saying that, it's a uniquely skilled profession. It takes years to master. My most abiding memory of dad's workshop was the constant smell of wood, oils, and varnish. It takes patience and dexterity; dad always said it was an art form. He spoke French too.'
'I never knew that.'
'Yeah, grandad made sure he was connected to that side of the family.'
'So, I'm intrigued now. Tell me about them, the French side of your family.'
'After all this time, you've just become interested in my family history?'
'It's my new hobby, remember, and to be fair, you've never asked about mine.'
Jason shrugs. 'You're right. I haven't.'
'I know I'm right. So, come on, tell me.'
'Okay. I know a little. So, my grandfather came to Edinburgh in 1964. He was just a young man at the time and a bit of a rebel.'
'I like him already.'
'The way dad tells it, he was determined to find his way in life and break away from the family tradition he was expected to follow.'
'The French polishing?'
Jason nods. 'I'm not sure how common it was, but he left Nice and arrived in Scotland to study at Edinburgh University. Obviously, his English was good enough to

study at that level and exhibit some charm, because after meeting a certain young Edinburgh girl, and the whirlwind romance that followed, he and my grandmother married within months. This didn't go down well with her parents, mind you. Anyway, not long after that, my grandfather's mother died, and so he took his new wife to France for the funeral in Nice and to meet his family for the very first time.

'It seems my grandmother fell in love with the country, the culture, the climate, the language; it was everything Scotland wasn't. She persuaded my grandfather to stay and that initial visit lasted four years and, during that time, she gave birth to a son, my dad.

'To make a living, my grandfather immersed himself in the family tradition of French polishing once again. When they eventually returned to Edinburgh, with an investment of money from my grandmother's father, whose apprehension about the marriage had by now thawed with time helped by the arrival of a grandson, my grandfather set himself up in a small workshop on Leith Walk.'

'That sounds amazing. Your grandparents must have been pretty resilient, and obviously loved each other very much.'

'To me, they've just been my grandmother and granddad. But you're right, it must have taken real guts to do what they did. And when they came back to Edinburgh, there was a need for the trade in Edinburgh and beyond, as both granddad and dad made a success of the business.'

'Wow! See, I never knew that about your family. I wish mine was as interesting.'

'What do you mean?'

'Well, look at your dad's history and then there's your mum. I read about her at Uni. Studying politics. We all did. She was an inspiration. Most of us, the females that is, held her in high esteem.'

'Really!'

'Sure. If you were a woman and politically minded, as we all were, your mum was who we all wanted to be like. She was a role model.

Jason shrugs. 'She was just my mum.'

'Of course she was, but she was more than that. A lot more. Your mum was political, she was a feminist, and a bloody talented journalist. She was one of us, went to the same University, graduated with honours in English and politics. All my friends at uni aspired to be like her. She even came to the uni as a guest lecturer. You couldn't get a seat for love nor money.'

'I spent many a day and a good part of school holidays in dad's workshop while mum exposed the dealings of bent politicians and bankers. I think that's what drove her to become involved in politics. She wanted to make a difference.'

'That's the reason most do. But they change their perspective and then become driven by personal gain. She never did. Your mum was different. She was a future leader of the Labour Party.'

'She was complex.'

'People like her are. That's what makes them do what they do. That's why they achieve more than most. I almost died when you told me who your mum was. Remember?'

Jason laughs. 'I do. It made me popular amongst your friends.'

'It's funny that we're talking about families and their history. Family was very important to her. I don't mean dad and me, we were, of course. I mean her family history. She was very passionate about that. It rubbed off on me, too. She would drum into me. We're all formed by a sense of place, where we have come from, by family, that these are the ties that bind us. It built character and substance. She believed in being that person you always wanted to be. I never felt she was ever missing in my life. She interweaved being a mum and her career seamlessly.'

'She would have been proud of you. I bet your dad is too.'

He smiled. 'Eventually. When I didn't follow him into the family business, and instead went to university, he was disappointed, but he hid it well. After a year or two when mum died, he sold the workshop. Eventually, it was knocked down and replaced by a modern development of upmarket apartments. That really got to him. The old giving way to the new.

'When I graduated, he said it was one of the proudest days of his life. A photograph of us both, outside the Usher Hall, me in my graduation robes, and dad in the suit he bought for the occasion, took centre stage in the gallery of family photographs on his mantelpiece. His only regret, my mother wasn't there to see it.'

'That's so sad.'

Jason's voice shakes a little. 'I'm glad I had time to talk to him. After his diagnosis, we got really close. With the little time he had left, we crammed in a lot. It's sad that it takes something like that to make you realise the important things, the things you need to say before it's too late. Even when the cancer was in stage four, it wasn't all doom and gloom. We had some great times together. We spoke a lot about the past, lots of it I'd forgotten about.'

Rachel reaches over and touches his hand. 'You got the chance to say goodbye and be with him, that's important.'

'I know. I was lucky. That's why we made the most of the time he had left.'

'Always hold that thought.'

Jason blinks away the tears. 'It fits quite well with what I was going to tell you.'

'Oh! And what was that?' Rachel leans forward.

Just then, the waiter arrives with their meal and sets their plates on the table. He fusses with the cutlery and Jason smiles to himself as Rachel struggles to conceal her exasperation.

'God, I thought he would never leave. So, what were you going to tell me?'
'It's something I've been thinking about for a while, I suppose.'
'What is?'
Jason looks momentarily embarrassed.
'You'll have to tell me now.'
'Its… well, complicated. Even I don't understand it.'
'Now I'm intrigued. You'll have to tell me.'
'It won't make sense…' He hesitates. 'If you're going to understand this and I want you to…' he looks at his feet under the table; then, with a huge effort, as though stepping into unfamiliar terrain, he says, 'I need to explain about my family.'
'I know your family. We've just been talking about them. We've been friends for years.'
'You do, but sometimes… there are secrets that… well, remain secret. It's like an iceberg.'
'An iceberg!' Rachel looks at him like he has gone mad.
Jason shifts his weight. 'What I mean is… remember the film 'Titanic'?'
'Yes, Leonardo de Caprio.'
'Well, not him, but what happened? The Titanic struck an iceberg.'
'Obviously.'
'The point is, it struck the part of the iceberg that everyone onboard could see. Underneath the water, there was a lot more to the iceberg.'
'Ah, I see. So, what you're trying to illustrate with your fancy concept is there is a lot more to your family than I know about. You could have just said that.'
'I thought you were going to take this seriously?' Jason's voice has an edge to it.
'I am. Sorry. Jason, I'm sorry. Really, I am. It obviously means a lot to you.'

His solemn face breaks into a smile. 'It does. I mean, it really does.'

'Wow! You're serious.'

Jason nods. 'It's weird, Rachel. I've never felt like this before.'

'I'm all ears.'

'Okay. It's best if I give you some background to all of this. That way, it'll make more sense.'

'Jason, the suspense is killing me.'

'Alright. When I was younger, every Sunday, mum dragged me and my sister to our grandmother's for lunch. My great grandmother, Ruth, was always there on a Sunday too. Grandmother collected her by car every Sunday. We soon learned about Ruth's habit of speaking about the past, always to the indignation of our young minds. It was a side effect of getting old. Mum often rebuked us.'

Rachel smiled.

'It was on these occasions, since Ruth had a captive audience, I learnt about the Scottish side of the family. Family scandals and mysteries, wayward relatives with dark secrets, the same stories repeatedly told word for word, as if she was revealing to us some great secret for the very first time.

'I was never all that interested until she spoke about my great grandfather, Marcus, and the stories about him during The Second World War. They intrigued me and stayed with me, you know, like the lyrics of your favourite song, forever stuck in your head. I couldn't wait for Sundays to come around and hear the next instalment of Ruth's stories about Marcus.

'By then, that's all I wanted to hear. My sister grew bored with it, so she spent most of her time in the playroom, or in the garden with the dogs. Mum insisted on only fifteen minute instalments, but I think Ruth loved recalling his life just as much as I enjoyed listening to it.'

'She sounds a character.'

‘She brought old photographs too, of her and Marcus. There was one of him in his army uniform. I loved that.’

‘What did he look like?’

‘Like a man of his time, I suppose.’

‘I bet he was handsome.’

He smiled. ‘Ruth thought so.’

‘Do you have a picture of him?’

‘I’ve kept them all.’

‘I’d love to see him… and Ruth, especially when they were young.’

‘When Ruth died, and mum and dad cleared the house, which by the way took weeks, it was such a big house, they found hundreds of photographs, from the forties onwards. Mum kept them all, which, of course, she would. It was part of the tapestry of our family’s history, she said. She had such an eloquent way with words. And now, I’ve got them all.’

‘That’s amazing!’

‘I should really scan them and catalogue them. Better to have them digitally.’

‘Definitely. You should. You could never replace them.’

‘I’ve thought about doing that with his journals too.’

‘Journals?’

‘Yeah. Mum found them in Marcus’ study when Ruth died. It was an amazing find. There were boxes of them. All dated with the days, months, and years. He was a perfectionist when it came to detail. They were stored in our house for years. I came across them when I was sorting out dad’s things in the house. When I read his accounts of the war, I couldn’t stop.’

‘Did he record everything?’

‘No. Not everything. Marcus was very sketchy when documenting his time in Cairo and Alexandria but, other than that, most of the journals that recall his war years read like a novel.’

‘Cairo! That’s in Egypt.’

'He was stationed there. It was classified, so there was not much detail. Most of it is full of stories and characters and undercover operations.'

'Really! It sounds like James Bond. So, he wasn't just any old soldier.'

'No. And that's what makes his journals special. He was a British agent with the Special Operations Executive.'

'Wow!' Rachel exclaims, not really knowing what it means, although she thinks it sounds impressive. 'Did he ever show the journals to anyone?'

'I don't think he did. Ruth maybe, but if she did, well…' he sighs. 'She told no one.'

'What is it?'

'Some of it wouldn't have been easy reading for her. But I'm just surmising. I'd like to think he told her.'

'I see.'

'You don't. Believe me, you don't. When I read them, they captivated me. That's the only way I can describe it.' Jason's voice strains and his eyes water.

This stuns Rachel. 'My God, Jason. I've never seen you react like this.'

There is an awkward silence.

'You'd never believe it. Honestly, Rachel. When I think about it, I saw everything through his eyes. That's what it felt like. It's hard to explain. Even now, when I think about his story, it feels like I'm experiencing and feeling the same things he did all those years ago. It was like I was seeing everything through his eyes. I feel invested in it. It's weird, I know.'

'I wasn't expecting that.'

'No. I've told no one about this. I don't know why, but it just felt right telling you. I suppose if ever there was a time to tell you, it's now.'

There is a pause.

'I feel stupid now,' he says evenly.

'Don't be. I feel honoured that you felt you could tell me. I'm not just saying that. I do. Actually, I feel jealous of you.'

'Now it's my turn. I didn't expect that.' He thinks for a moment. 'Why? Why would you feel jealous?'

'You have such a connection with your family's past, whereas I… well, let's just say, I wouldn't be too keen on knowing much about mine. There's not much to be proud of unless you can relate to drunks and believing everybody owes you a living. Most of mine never worked a day in their life.' The memories bomb Rachel.

'When I look at you, that's not what I see.'

'I was lucky. No. Let me rephrase that. I was determined never to use their example to live my life. And now, it seems, I'm too good for them. Well, that's what they think.'

'Even your mum?' Jason asks.

'No,' she says quickly. 'Not her.'

Rachel swirls her fork around the food on her plate. She attempts to change the subject. 'Ruth sounds nice. I'd like to have met her.'

'She was well into her nineties when she died, but her memory was as sharp as a knife. I wish I could, but I can't remember Marcus. He passed away when I was about three.'

Jason smiles to himself.

'What is it?' Rachel asks.

'Mum used to swear that when I was about four, one night, she woke up, and I was standing at the bedroom door and Marcus, who had passed away a year before, was standing beside me, smiling, and holding my hand. She said it had the quality of a dream about it, that's how she remembered it. Anyway, that morning when she awoke, I was in her bed and sleeping beside her.'

'Wow! Do you think…'

‘I’ve thought about it a lot. Of course, I’d like it to be true, but then I’d have to believe in ghosts.’

‘Or just life after death.’

‘And that the dead can visit the living. It’s a very comforting concept, but far-fetched,’ Jason says lightly. ‘Secretly, mum believed what she saw. She called him my guardian angel.’

‘That’s lovely.’

‘If I’m honest, I like the idea, the thought of it, that is.’

‘Who are we to belittle what we don’t know or what we don’t understand? That’s the problem with humans. We think we’re all omnipotent. Full of our self-importance, to the detriment of what might be just the simple truth. As a race, we’re a bunch of wankers.’

‘Present company exempt, hopefully?’ he asks, trying to sound light-hearted.

‘There I go, off on one of my rants again. Sorry. I didn’t mean you.’

‘You don’t have to apologise. Every good Catholic believes in guardian angels. The Pope tells them to.’

‘And you’re not?’

He smirks. ‘As you already know, I’ve not been for a very long time.’

She laughs.

‘It’s a comforting thought, though,’ Jason says.

For a moment, there is silence.

‘If there is something else when we die, I’d like to think Mum is watching over me. When she was dying, Dad said her world shrank to just the inside of the house and the garden. Yet, she told him, although she was seeing things for the last time, she was also seeing them for the first time. The simplest things in life exploded with meaning: the leaves on the trees, the blue of the sky and the heat of the sun. One night when dad had had a few drinks, which was rarely, he said you can’t understand the shape of a life until you witness the end. I found that statement extraordinary.

He thought he knew everything there was to know about the woman he loved, who he'd spent most of his life with. Yet, it wasn't until she was slipping away from him he saw who she really was. She had an insane love for her family. It was not dying that she feared, it was the thought of leaving us behind that caused her the greatest anxiety. She told him it was excruciatingly difficult dying: it was the hardest thing she'd ever done. If there was even the slightest chance that she could come back once she had died, that woman would have found a way. There's no doubt in my mind about that.

'I'll never forget her last words to me. She said, *Never forget your past, where you have come from. It anchors you. It hooks you.* Some things are just so momentous. I didn't know it but now, when I think about those words… with Dad gone too, God, how relevant are they now?

'I thought I knew everything there was to know about my family's past. That was before I read Marcus' journal. Now, I believe the past becomes our present. It shapes us, even when we are unaware of it. There is a physical link, even though that link is separated by generations. That's why I need to see it for myself.'

'Where? See what?'

Jason thinks for a moment. 'I'll put it another way. Can a person be homesick for a place they've never been to?' He asks over a cup of coffee.

She smiles with her green eyes and with her mouth. 'I have no idea what you're talking about. It doesn't make sense to me. This cup and the coffee that's in it, this restaurant with all the people inside, you sitting opposite me, that makes perfect sense because it's real. I can see you, hear people talking, and smell the food they're eating. This is the world I live in, the sensual world, so it makes sense to me.'

'I get that and, before all of this, I would think exactly like you. You see, Marcus was in Greece, during the war, in a village in Corfu.'

'You're going to go to this village, aren't you?'

'I know it sounds crazy, believe me, I've thought about nothing else.'

Although she can't pretend to understand what Jason is feeling, she can't conceal the light of intrigue in her eyes.

'There's one other thing.' He taps his forehead several times.

'What?'

'It concerns a book.'

'A book.'

'Not just any book. This is an old book.'

'That sounds mysterious. I like a mystery. How old is this book?'

'Ancient. About seven hundred fucking years old.'

Rachel's mouth falls open. 'Wow! That's an old book.'

'It's a religious book. It's gorgeous and full of decorative writing and colourful illustrations.'

'You have this book?'

His face breaks into a smile. 'I do.'

'Jesus, Jason.'

'I know. It's insane. In his journal, Marcus details very specifically the origin of the book, the author and its significance as a historical artefact.'

'Have you read any of it?'

'No. I wish I could. It's written in Greek.'

'Where did he get it from?'

'A monastery in Corfu.'

'If it's such a historical artefact, why isn't it in a museum?'

'That was Marcus' intention. He wanted to return the book to the monastery after the war. He feared that if he passed on the trusteeship to a museum, Edinburgh being the obvious choice since he worked for them, he might not get the book returned to him. He cited the Elgin Marbles as an example.'

'So, what did he do?'

'He considered putting it in a safe, his bank's safe. This was just after the war, remember. If he put it in the bank's safe, then the book would have to go in his will. It was like a legal requirement. That option didn't appeal to him. He had every intention of returning the book to Corfu. Putting it in his will would just have complicated matters so…'

'He dug a big hole in the garden and buried it.' Rachel suggests.

'He could have, but he didn't.'

'Surely, he had to write about its location. As you said, storing it in the bank's safe would have thrown up lots of unnecessary complications.'

'You would have thought so, wouldn't you?'

Rachel frowns. 'So, he left a cryptic clue?'

'Now that would be a mystery. I'm afraid not. It was less complicated than that.'

'That's a shame.'

'I was sorting out the stuff mum and dad had kept over the years, and I found it in a concealed drawer in a chest full of mum's letters and documents.'

'So, it's obvious your mum knew about the book, too; Marcus gave it to her.'

'I don't know. Maybe he did. The thought of dying and not telling anyone about the book maybe was enough for him to tell her about it so that it wouldn't be lost, forgotten about. Then I wondered, did he tell mum about what happened in Corfu during the war? Did he give her his journals? Or did she find them and read them? Either way, she knew about the book and what it meant to Marcus. That's why she kept it too, instead of announcing its existence to the academic world and the likely prospect it would spend decades in a glass case, hundreds of miles from the only place that had an eligible claim and right to its return.'

'The monastery in Corfu.'

'Precisely.'

'I don't understand why Marcus just didn't return to Corfu after the war and give the book back to the monastery? And aren't you forgetting someone else in all of this? What about Ruth? Surely, she knew about the book?'

'That's what I thought. But I don't think that now.'

'Why not?'

'It doesn't just represent memories of that time. It was more than that. A lot more. Marcus could never go back to Corfu and the book was the only tangible object he had of that time. That was a reminder of why he couldn't. It was all he had left. You see, Rachel, in a historical light, and the world of academia, the book was a once in a lifetime find. That's not what we're talking about. It represented something completely different. In a personal context, it had stopped being the find of a lifetime. It was more special to him than that. To Marcus, it was more precious than life itself. It was the only thing he had that still connected him to the love of his life.'

Corfu

1943

An Angel

He fell like a stone through the sky, accelerating rapidly with each passing second. The deafening rush of air pressed against him, filling his nose and lungs. He glimpsed the plane, dipping wings, dissolving into the cloud.

The clouds! Where did they come from? It was not meant to be like this. The forecast predicted good visibility, almost clear skies. Someone had seriously fucked up.

A river, raging with adrenaline, roared through him. He grabbed the cord, released the parachute and, in an instant, everything changed. His world turned to silence. He floated like a feather, but his senses were in overdrive. Below him, a dark mattress of cloud obscured the landscape. This was bad, very bad. He felt like a train entering a dark tunnel. And then he was through it. Dark silhouetted hills, specks of clustered lights, a village, and trees. So many trees. With each beat, his heart bruised his chest. He tried to guide the parachute, twisting and turning, but with each failed attempt, the dense mass continued to rush towards him.

He pulled his legs up towards his chest, bracing every muscle in his body. The sudden impact engulfed his cries of despair. Branches cracking like bone tore fabric, and sliced skin, searing feet, shin and thigh, like piercing blades. The noise was deafening, crunching. His head struck something solid like a wall and then nothing but darkness, silence.

When Andreas saw the man hanging from the tree, he thought it was an angel, like the ones in the paintings in the church that he was dragged to every Sunday morning. With each tentative step, excitement and fear rose in him. As he drew closer, Andreas stared at the motionless figure. It was not an angel, but a man. Andreas dropped the stick that only moments ago had been a sword cutting through the air. He assumed the man was dead. He had never seen a dead body before. The man's eyes were closed and there was blood on his face. Then, he saw the parachute above, torn and twisted, and Andreas hesitated just a moment and then turned and ran as fast as his legs would carry him.

He tried not to think of the bloodied face; the clothes ripped and torn, the lifeless limbs hanging like hens before their feathers are plucked. He willed his legs to move faster, through the puddles of rainwater and mud that splashed and sprinkled his legs. His mother had told him to wear his long trousers that morning and he wished now he hadn't ignored her.

He passed the olive grove and vaulted the stone wall.

At first, he saw the white shirt, sleeves rolled up along weather-beaten arms and then the black waistcoat.

'Patera! Patera!'

Andreas' father was in the garden, tending to his vegetables and herbs destined for the market and others to hang above the fire in the big pot that his mother said had been in the family for years, feeding each new generation.

None of that mattered now. There was a dead man in a tree.

Vangelis Bouzoukis straightened his back and peered through the morning light towards the tiny figure running towards him. Vangelis frowned, just as Andreas, his chest burning and struggling for breath, tried to speak.

'Who are you running away from now? Have you been stealing again?' His voice was stern but still laced with softness at the edges.

'No, Patera.' Another deep gulp to catch his breath. 'I was playing in the woods. There's… There's.'

'What? Take your time Andreas.'

'A man… hanging from a tree. I think he's dead.'

Vangelis rubbed the bristles on his chin. 'Is this another one of your games, Andreas? If my garden were as fertile as your imagination, I'd make a fortune at the market.'

'No Patera. He has a parachute.'

'A parachute. Are you sure?'

'Yes, Patera. It's tangled in the tree.'

Vangelis crouched, so that he was at eye level with his son. 'Is he dressed like a German soldier?'

Andreas shrugged. 'He wasn't dressed like the men that come to the village.'

Vangelis' breathing was deliberate and measured. He may have on a flight suit, Vangelis thought. 'Did the parachute have any markings on it?'

Andreas shook his head. 'I don't think so.' His father's serious face scared him. 'I don't know. Will the Germans take me away?' Tears welled up in his eyes.

Vangelis placed his hand on Andreas' head and ruffled his hair. 'No one's going to take you anywhere. You did a good thing coming straight home.'

'I did?' A relieved smile crossed his youthful face.

'Yes. You were very brave. Let's get you into the house.'

Helena was cooking lunch at the stove when she heard the door open. She turned to see her husband and son. She knew that look on Vangelis' face. He had his hand on Andreas' shoulder, who was staring at the stone floor.

'We have a problem.'

At first, she thought Andreas was in some sort of trouble again. She eyed her son closely. He seemed frightened, but he was not hurt.

'There's a young man in the woods.' Vangelis said simply.

'German?'

'I don't know, Andreas found him.'

She looked at her son. 'What do you mean, found him?'

'I saw him in a tree. There was a parachute.'

Vangelis turned to the door. 'I need to go. I'll be back as soon as I can.'

Vangelis knew the Germans were now using their own to infiltrate the resistance. They used airmen who spoke perfect English, without a trace of a German accent; often they spoke Greek too. The Germans, dressed in British uniforms, were well versed in the war from the allied point of view, and had the appropriate papers. They would gain the trust of their hosts, many sheltering in family homes, and accumulate knowledge and the structure of the networks before revealing the identity of the individuals who had protected them.

Vangelis had heard the stories of those men and women who were captured, tortured, mutilated, and eventually shot.

Not only did they want to spread fear and distrust amongst the networks, but the Gestapo also sought individual allied airmen, who were a more valuable acquisition, and in this way, the networks continued to operate, which often suited the Germans as it was not unusual for them to have Greek collaborators in villages and towns who would continue to infiltrate the network's cells.

Vangelis knew he had to be careful. He always had to be cautious. He trusted few. The consequences of being exposed and caught had left him with many a nightmare.

He had read about and heard on the radio of ruthless reprisals by the German; massacres, firing squads, hundreds of villages torched. Throughout Greece, they had left nearly a million people homeless.

In the kafenion, men drank strong coffee, played backgammon, and inevitably talked politics. Vangelis was a republican, anti-royalist, and socialist. The National Liberation Front (EAM) was his natural home in the resistance to the German occupation, as it was with the Italian occupation before them.

***

The two men sucked on their cigarettes, inhaling deeply.

'Why couldn't he have landed somewhere flat? My legs are killing me.' Petros complained.

'If we don't get to him quickly, it might not be the only thing that kills you. If he was seen by the Germans, this place will soon crawl with them. They might have even beaten us to him.'

Petros could sense Vangelis' mood and thought it better to remain silent.

They trudged through a forest of ferns, their senses alive with the sounds and landscape around them. A dark, damp line traced Vangelis' shirt. The sun had warmed the air, scented with wildflowers and herbs. They entered a thicket of trees: oak, pine and chestnut, their boots crushing acorns and needles scattered on the forest floor. Between the trees, the light faded. Above the two men, a vast canopy of branches and leaves stretched towards the sky.

'There's a clearing not too far, that's where Andreas saw him.'

They moved in silence now. Vangelis saw the clearing. It was a natural dip in the landscape, where a narrow stream gurgled and trickled below them. He gestured for Petros to stop and put his finger to his lips. They stood like statues as still as the tree trunks around them. When Vangelis was certain they were alone, he moved cautiously, his heart quickening with every step.

'There!' Petros pointed to a dark shape.

Although eager to get it over with, they hesitated, their eyes combing every inch that lay ahead of them. There was the possibility, instead of a rescue, they might have to bury the body.

'Poor bastard. Another few feet and he would have cleared the trees.'

The ladder they had brought rested against the trunk.

Vangelis, careful not to unbalance himself, tugged at the parachute strap and sliced at it with a knife.

'Do you think he's alive?' Petros looked up into the man's face. It looked like a frozen mask. The skin had gone grey, and the dried blood sent a shiver through Petros.

'I don't know. I can't reach him to feel a pulse.'

'Shit! We're going to have to bury him.'

Vangelis drew the knife backwards and forwards. The strap frayed, and then, to his relief, it gave way. The body swayed.

'Support him, Petros.' Vangelis worked on the other strap, the weight of the man's body making it easier to cut through the fabric. Petros wrapped his arms around the man's legs. He shut his eyes and braced himself.

'Just about there,' Vangelis warned but, when the man slipped from his confines, he was heavier than Petros had expected. The sudden weight buckled his knees and he stumbled forward, the body falling and landing with a dull thud.

Air escaped from the man with a groan. When Petros got to his feet, Vangelis was already kneeling beside the man.

'Did you hear that? He's alive,' Petros gasped.

Now that he was close to him, Vangelis pressed two fingers to the side of the man's neck. 'There's a pulse. It's faint, but it's there.' He shook his head. 'They seem to get younger every time.' Anger pulled at his heart. 'We need to get him out of here and quickly.'

He was not in uniform, but that was not unusual. He would have to blend in with the population if he was going to be undetected. Vangelis searched the man's clothing and pulled a wallet from inside his jacket. Inside, he found a photograph of a young pretty woman, a girlfriend perhaps. Or a wife? His thumb ran over a thick bundle of money, drachmas, enough to feed Vangelis and his family for months, a year perhaps. He took out a neatly folded sheet of paper and studied the writing on it. A few words were familiar to him. They were not German but English. He folded the sheet and placed it back in the wallet. 'He's British,' Vangelis heard the relief in his voice.

Petros lay the ladder on the ground. Vangelis rolled the man onto his side and they slid the ladder under him. Cautiously, they manoeuvred him onto the ladder. Petros unravelled a length of rope he had been carrying, and both he and Vangelis set about tying the legs, arms, torso, and chest to the ladder. They worked in silence, each knowing the danger they were now putting themselves in.

They secured the rope and each took an end of the ladder. Vangelis leading, they laboriously retraced their steps through the forest and scrubland.

They placed him on the table, his hair stuck to his head, bloodied and matted.

'Another one,' Helena whispered. Her fearful eyes swept over the figure lying on her table like a corpse.

'Towels and water, lots of it and boiled too,' Vangelis commanded. They removed the young man's jacket. With long shears Vangelis gently clipped at the trouser legs, first the left and then the right, exposing the torn flesh of the shins and thighs, like slashes from a blade. 'I'll need a bottle of Raki.' Vangelis instructed without looking up from his task. 'And something to dress these wounds.'

Helena disappeared into an adjacent room and appeared again with a white sheet. 'Petros, help me cut this into strips.'

Vangelis carefully removed pieces of fabric from the wounds. He cut away the rest of the clothes and inspected an open gash on the man's ribcage. He could see the white of bone against the torn flesh and blood. Vangelis studied the awkward angle of the left arm, badly swollen and bent.

'Morphine and a splint.'

Petros was uncertain if Vangelis was thinking out loud or giving him instructions

'Helena. We'll need Dr Iannis. He's in a bad way.' Vangelis turned towards Andreas, who was sitting in the corner. This was not the first time Andreas had seen a stranger in his house and lying on the kitchen table.

'Andreas, tell Dr Iannis to come. We need him. Tell him the wounds are deep, tendons will be damaged. He's lost a lot of blood.' Andreas nodded and ran to the door, glad to escape the blood and broken bone and breathe clean, fresh air.

Helena dabbed a wet cloth over the man's forehead and face, wiping dried blood and dirt with grim purpose. 'How old do you think he is?'

'Twenty-three, twenty-five, maybe.' Vangelis shut his eyes briefly. Helena heard an edge of weariness in her husband's voice.

'Is he going to die?'

'I think he'll live. He will take a long time to heal. He's not going anywhere in a hurry, that's for sure.'

'What will you do with him?'

'He's too ill to move.'

'So, he is our guest.'

'For now. There's no other way.'

'I'm worried. What about Andreas?'

'He isn't the first allied soldier we've had. Andreas found him for God's sake.'

'He's just a child.'

'If anything, this war will make him a man.'

'You mean it will rob him of his childhood.'

'I was working when I was his age.'

Helena sighed. 'It was different then.' She looked at the young man lying on her kitchen table, and she could not help but feel a sharp needle of pity. She noticed faint freckles blotched his cheeks and her chest tightened as she thought of a mother's anguish over a son fighting a war far from home.

The door sprung open, and the large frame of Dr Iannis filled its frame. From somewhere behind him, Helena could hear the rumble of an engine.

'How is he, Vangelis?'

'Not good. Broken bones, a deep wound.'

'Let us get to work then.' The doctor leaned over and inspected the wound. 'That's a nasty one.'

Helena understood the urgency that permeated the air in her kitchen. She wanted to recoil from the blood and opened wounds, her kitchen table now a butcher's slab.

Helena climbed the stairs and went to her bedroom, and it was not until she grasped the handle of her bedroom door, she realised she had been unconscious of the fact she had been holding her breath. Helena could scarcely believe there was a stranger in her house who may die. She stepped inside the room and crossed to the window, which she opened and inhaled the dry, undisturbed air. She moved from the window towards the dressing table and studied her reflection in the mirror. Her hair tied above her head would tumble to the base of her spine when released of its pins. Recently, she had noticed discrete strands of subtle grey appearing amongst her blue-dark hair. She was aware of a fleeting relief that Vangelis had not noticed, or if he did, he had never said. She felt disappointed and frustrated with herself. These things did not matter. Not now. There was a stranger in her house. She was angry with this stranger for coming into their life and with Vangelis for bringing him.

She hovered closer to the mirror. With a finger, she traced a shadow under her eye. She straightened her back and walked across the room, her shoes clicking the floorboards. Opening the oak wardrobe, she reached inside and pulled a heavy blanket, some linen, and a pillow from the shelf. Helena held them close to her chest. She inhaled the fabric, the comforting smell of home, and she thought again of the young man's mother. What would she feel?

She could hear the muffled voices of the men as she stepped down the wooden stairs. Dr Iannis did not seem to notice her presence as she walked across the room. Helena glanced at his face, serious and determined. There was an intensity about him as he leaned over the young man, his fingers nimble and delicate, almost weightless for a man of his age as he stitched a wound. Vangelis was sitting smoking a cigarette. Petros paced the floor, hands in his pockets, a cigarette clamped between his lips.

Sunlight speckled the space around them, brightening Vangelis' face, yet his eyes remained dark, strained and tired.

The mattress was still in the basement, left there when the last occupant, an Australian, hid for three weeks.

Helena found it hard to comprehend that young men, from the other side of the world, were fighting alongside her countrymen to rid her country of Italian and German occupation.

Helena spread the sheets over the mattress and made a bed. She stood to her full height and gazed at her work. At first, she didn't look at the neat and symmetrical bedding. She focused on the fact that she was powerless to alter what fate had given her.

Soaked in the anguish of her dilemma, she clenched her eyes and then opened them. They were all in stupendous danger. Their days would ache with fear. Trepidation formed around her throat. An involuntary shiver coursed through her. She crouched down and ran her hands through her hair. She wanted to curl up into a ball, only her breathing escaping her mouth disturbed the silence around her.

When she regained her senses, she straightened herself and flattened the fabric of her dress. There was no electricity in the basement. She must remember to get candles.

'Can we move him? I mean, it won't open the wounds?'

Dr Iannis wiped his brow. 'He won't wake for some time. He might even sleep for days. That is a nasty wound on his head, there may be lasting damage.'

'Damage? What do you mean?'

When Helena entered the room from the steps that led to the basement, the men's voices were distant, words floating from their mouths. She looked at the young man, and instinctively her eyes moved to his chest and the sign of life immediately soothed her. He looked awful, swaddled in bandages, broken and battered, his thick dark hair matted with blood, and her guilt stroked her then.

The doctor gathered his things and packed his small bag. 'It's difficult to be certain, but the trauma to his head could have caused… debilitating damage to the brain. As I said, it's difficult to be certain, but it's something you need to be prepared for.'

Helena tried to shrug off the feeling of despair, but the room shrank and the look on her husband's face sucked the breath from her.

Vangelis and Petros awkwardly manoeuvred the young man down into the basement and placed him under the sheets on the mattress.

31

The Englishman

The Englishman, as they now referred to him, had been sleeping for two days, drifting in and out of consciousness. Outside of Helena's household, the only two people in the village who knew about his existence were Dr Iannis and Petros. Vangelis had contacted the resistance, whose instructions were to keep him hidden until he had recuperated.

Each morning, Andreas asked to go down into the basement, to see the man he last saw hanging from a tree in the woods. Vangelis forbade it.

'What if he dies? What will we do with him?'

'He won't.'

'How can you be so sure?'

'Dr Iannis never mentioned that as a possibility.'

'Maybe he doesn't want to worry us.'

'Helena, he won't die, but if he does, Petros and I will bury him in the woods… deep in the woods.'

She tried to push away the images Vangelis' words had formed in her thoughts.

Sometimes she watched him as he slept. Helena wondered what his name was, this man who lay disembodied in her basement. His colour was deathly. It reminded Helena of her mother, lying in her open coffin. His jawline was straight, and when she thought of him speaking, she pictured his mouth revealing symmetrical white teeth. She imagined the colour of his eyes, the timbre of his English accent, deep and resonating. She liked his face; it was an attractive face. Was there a girlfriend or a wife waiting on his safe return?

She had never felt herself thinking like this, and she found it impossible to decipher its meaning.

When she reached the top of the basement steps, the smoky caramelised aroma of coffee met her.

Vangelis was sitting at the table, staring into his cup. He looked up when Helena crossed the room. 'I've made you a coffee. How is he? Is he awake yet?'

She shook her head. 'No.'

'He will have to drink and eat soon. Maybe we should try to wake him.' Vangelis' eyes tightened.

'When is Dr Iannis coming?'

'Today.'

'Then we should wait.' She took a sip of coffee and savoured the strong bitter taste.

His face was severe, and Helena looked away. At night, she had heard him cry out as he lay beside her, his nightmares sharing their bed. When she asked him about them, he seemed to shrink inside himself.

He scraped the chair on the stone floor as he stood. 'I'll see Dr Iannis. I'm not happy about this. I've got a bad feeling inside me, Helena. He should have woken by now.'

Helena's fingers wrapped around her cup, its warmth seeping into her, comforting her. 'He's probably too busy to see you. He'll come when he has the time,' she suggested, more hopeful than certain.

'We need more kerosene. I'll get it at the store. We can light the basement with a lamp, not candles. It will be one less thing to worry about.'

When he was gone, Helena sat in the silence of her house. For the first time, she considered Vangelis was maybe right to be worried. What if he never wakes? It was one thing removing a dead body, but what do you do with one that is still alive and does not speak or move or open its eyes? Dread spluttered in her stomach.

Just then, she became aware of a sound. She stood up, her hand clutching her chest. Again, a low muffled sound. He was awake!

Tentatively, Helena descended the steps. The Englishman's eyes were open, and he turned his head slightly to look at her. She should have brought him some water, she thought as his crack lips moved, but no sound came from them.

She noticed a presence behind her. Andreas stood at the top of the stairs.

'Get me some water,' she instructed and knelt beside the mattress.

A glazed look covered the Englishman's eyes, and there was no recognition that he could see her. She wondered if he was blind, then dismissed the thought. It would be the morphine Dr Iannis had left, which Helena had injected into the Englishman's vein at intervals as Dr Iannis had instructed. She thought perhaps he was over anaesthetised. Had she administered more than she should? No, she had followed Dr Iannis' instructions to the letter; she was sure of that.

Andreas appeared at her side, staring at the Englishman with wide eyes. Helena took the cup from her son's hand and, lifting the Englishman's head, his hair damp with sweat, she gently fed him cool sips of water. She was sure that more had run down his chin than his throat but, with an effort that seemed to steal the little strength he had, the Englishman swallowed and continued to do so until the last drop and the cup was empty.

She placed his head against the pillow, and he attempted to speak. His voice, but a whisper, cracked inaudibly. He swallowed, and, as his lips moved; she heard him this time.

'Efcharisto.'

Still clutching the empty cup, Helena turned to Andreas.

Andreas, as well, had heard the word in his language. 'I heard it too,' he gasped.

'He might only know a few words,' Helena said as Vangelis scratched his stubble.

'No. It makes sense. What would be the point in sending someone who could not converse with us?'

'But the others could not speak Greek.'

'This one is different.' Vangelis paced the stone floor.

'How can you be sure?'

'They're coming to see him.'

'Who?'

'Someone from the resistance.'

Helena took a deep breath. This new and unexpected disclosure unnerved her. 'When?'

'Tomorrow.' Vangelis lit a cigarette. 'He is different from the others.'

'We are taking a risk. We are putting ourselves and Andreas in terrible danger.' She felt the tight beat of her heart.

'As are they as well coming here. It will be nighttime. It will be dark when they visit. It will be their camouflage. Their identity must be concealed.' His face, serious and determined, squashed her concerned look, and she averted her eyes and said no more.

The Resistance

In the absolute darkness there are only outlines, blurred and soft, forming shapes that lurk in the corners. He drifted and slept, and when he broke the surface of the fog in his mind, her face lingered before him, staying long into the night.

She had leaned towards him, and he had caught her perfume, inhaling her fragrance, sweet and rose-like as she pressed the cup to his lips.

He felt her fingers against his hair and his head resting against her palm. Long hair like sheets fell in front of her face. She rose quietly and left him, a boy by her side.

There was no window, only the seeping light from under the door at the top of the stone steps. He knew it must be daylight as birdsong permeated the surrounding walls. He shifted and the pain in his leg forced the breath from him.

The air was stuffy and hot. He pulled the sheets from him and saw that he was wearing a man's shirt. He felt every pore secrete sweat like condensation running down a windowpane.

He remembered the vastness of the dark sky, drifting clouds, and falling through space. Empty darkness.

They came at night, just as Vangelis had said they would. There were two of them or, if there were more, only two entered her house.

She offered them a coffee; the water had just boiled on the stove. They looked at Helena as if she had insulted them and, turning to Vangelis, the shortest of the two removed his hat and asked for anything with alcohol in it.

Vangelis poured two glasses of Raki and handed them the drinks. They sat around the kitchen table and lit cigarettes.

'Has he spoken yet?' the short one asked.

Vangelis shook his head. 'Only to say thank you.'

'For what?'

'I gave him water to drink,' Helena said.

The short one tilted his head, an acknowledgement, but his eyes were expressionless.

'Has he said anything else?'

'No. He sleeps most of the time.'

'Who knows he is here?' He aimed the question at Vangelis.

'Petros and the doctor who treated him.'

'Who is Petros?'

'A friend. He helped me bring the Englishman here.'

'Can you trust him?'

'Of course.'

'There was a boy who found him.'

'Yes, my son Andreas.'

'So, Andreas knows about him.'

Vangelis knew instantly what he was referring to. It was an unsaid accusation.

'Yes, yes, Andreas as well.'

'We need to trust you Vangelis,' he said casually and looked at him in silence. He took a deep draw on his cigarette. 'Do you understand?'

Vangelis rubbed his hand over the stubble of his chin and nodded slightly.

Helena wanted to shout at them and tell them to get out of her house. She did not like to think about what they did or had seen, but she knew it was as far removed from her own life that their presence in her home instinctively made her feel threatened and scared for her family.

'If you are caught, you know what the repercussions will be. You will be interrogated, not just you, but your wife, your son… the reprisals will be severe.'

'He is not the first we have looked after.'

'No. He is not.' He took another long draw on his cigarette. 'He is not important; it is the information he has that is important, that is of value to us. We need him to talk.'

Helena stood, turned away from them and walked to the stove. She busied herself with making coffee. Her hands trembled. The Englishman's presence was a death sentence and then, unexpectedly, she thought about the colour of his eyes, the softness of his voice.

There was nothing they could do now but wait. She felt numb.

Once they emerged from the basement, Vangelis walked with the two men outside. A few minutes passed before he came back into the house. He slumped into a chair and poured himself a Raki, emptying the glass with one swallow.

'I should have left him in the woods.'

'What you did was the right thing to do.'

Vangelis tried to force himself to agree with Helena, but any willingness to do so slid from him. 'Sometimes doing what is right can be the wrong thing to do.'

A Question

Once a week, Helena would take a trip into Corfu Town. The journey by bus was hot and uncomfortable. Before the war, she would sense the chest filling breath of pleasure as she ambled through the labyrinth of narrow lanes and cobblestoned streets that curled around buildings, where patches of masonry crumbled from walls of vivid colour: limestone, reds, salmon, shades that softened in the glow of the early evening sun. Helena would saunter past crates of tomatoes, aubergines, and cucumbers, spending idle time in shops, exploring the new fabrics and fashions that came from Athens, discussing with the shopkeepers the news of the day, the latest gossip and scandals. She always enjoyed a coffee at a café in a square or hidden in a lane, sitting outside, and watching the world go by.

Now it was different. Everywhere there were German soldiers, and everyone was looked upon with suspicion, as the eyes and ears of the resistance. Vangelis had aired his concern around these trips that Helena refused to stop taking. Although on many levels they had lost their freedom as an island and as Greeks, the occupation would not take away her right to choose what she wanted to do on a personal level. Vangelis had often raised his voice when countering his wife's stubbornness. He asserted that was exactly what the Germans were doing. The curfews and restrictions, the disappearances, the imprisonments, and executions were the outward expressions that the Nazis and their occupation of the country defined and policed all civil liberties. Such confinement raised Helena's contempt for each German soldier she saw.

She knew it was only a matter of time before she could no longer indulge herself in the activities she had once taken for granted, and she knew she no longer had the will or strength to argue with Vangelis. These days, they hardly spoke to each other and, when they did, it concerned the mundane existence of daily life. And she thought how easy it was to continue in such a way, hiding from the truth of what they had become; strangers to one another. There was a time when it was different, and she blinked the memory away. It provoked the question: Why was she living this way?

She heard him. The words were not of her language. Was he talking to himself? Had he gone mad? Andreas was eating his breakfast, and he looked up from his bowl to see if his mother had also caught the sound emanating from the basement. A look passed between them, and Helena forced a smile.

'Stay here. I'll check on him.' Helena ruffled Andreas' hair as she passed him. She left the stucco walled surroundings and watchfully made her way down the steps and into the breeze-block interior of the basement.

Helena had never liked this part of the house and only entered it if she had to. It left her with a heaviness that could only be shaken off once she had left. Helena proceeded more cautiously now. Perhaps she wouldn't experience it this time. So, she thought of the washing hanging in the garden, the stone wall adorned with crimson roses, sweetening the breathless air. She heard the clatter of an engine. These days, only German trucks and jeeps rumbled past.

The air was still and as thick as water. Even though the morning light infiltrated the house above, Helena's eyes struggled in the surrounding gloom. She bent over the lantern and turned it on, immediately dispelling the subdued light.

She gazed at the man lying in front of her and wondered what would happen to him. She stood, looking at him for a long time. He was silent now, his shallow breathing the only sound that lay between them. As she studied him, Helena shifted her feet. Sweat coated the man's forehead and his skin had not returned to its normal colour.

He had hardly eaten since he arrived. This was the fifth day, and a shadow of stubble needed a razor's attention. She had dressed the wounds, following Dr Iannis' instructions, inspecting and cleaning each wound before applying new dressings and, as she worked, Helena hoped the Englishman could hear her apologies, as he groaned but did not awake into the world.

Andreas was still sitting at the table when she returned from the basement.

'You haven't eaten much. Are you unwell Andreas?'

'No.'

'Then what is it? Usually you're asking for more.'

Andreas stared at his abandoned breakfast and without looking at her said, 'I want to kill the Germans.'

Helena's hand covered her mouth, the words stealing her breath. 'Andreas! What has made you say such a thing?'

'Everything has changed. Everything is different. I hate them. I hate what they have done. The Germans will come and take the Englishman away and then it will be your turn and father's and I will have no one. I will be alone.'

She rushed towards him and threw her arms around his small body. 'Nothing is going to happen to us. In a few days, he will be gone, and everything will be back to normal.'

'Even you and Dad?'

Helen's stomach dropped. 'What do you mean?'

'I've heard you arguing with each other at night when I am in bed.'

Helena combed her fingers through his soft hair. 'Oh, Andreas. Adults argue sometimes. It's nothing for you to worry about.'

'Then why does he shout at you?'

'Because… because he…' Helena turned Andreas' face towards her and kissed his forehead. 'He is not angry with me. He is angry with the Germans, with the war.'

'Does he want to kill them too?'

'Look at the time. You will be late for school. And remember…' Helena nodded towards the basement door. 'He is our secret.'

'I know. I'm good at keeping secrets.'

***

He heard her voice, now familiar to him, and her footsteps descended towards him.

'I've brought you soup. You must eat if you are going to recover and leave here.' Her voice was soft and comforting.

Helena placed the tray with the soup and some bread on the floor and knelt before him. She leaned over him and arranged the pillow so that he could eat the soup without it spilling down his chin. He could smell her fragrance, reminding him of an eruption of flowers in a garden he couldn't quite place. In those seconds, she hovered over him. She gently propped him up and her hair brushed his cheek like strands of silk. Floating over him, his eyes drank the detail of her face. Drawn to her mouth, he lingered over the fullness of her lips, the curve of her jawline, and when he met her eyes, they were soft and translucent.

She sat for a moment, and then, combing her hair behind her ears, she held the spoon to his mouth and brought it to his lips; Marcus sipped the hot soup.

Half smiling, in Greek, he said, 'Thank you. You make a delicious soup.'

'You're welcome. Now eat it all, and the bread too.'

Helena watched him as he ate in silence and then, after a minute or two, he said he would try to eat from the bowl. She handed it to him, and with both hands, he concentrated on bringing it to his lips. She tore a piece of bread and handed it to him. Balancing the bowl on his chest, he dipped it in the soup and smiled satisfyingly at this small achievement. Chewing on the bread, he asked. 'Did you make the bread?'

'No. We have a baker in the village.'

He realised it was the first time he had seen her smile.

'Ah, I see. Well, that explains why it's not as good as your soup.'

He saw her hesitate.

'Your Greek is excellent. How did you learn to speak it so well?'

'I studied theology and history at St Andrew's University. We had to learn Greek, Hebrew and Latin.'

'And you can speak the others too?'

'Not as well. Before the war, I visited Jerusalem and Athens. By then, I was working for the university, researching ancient biblical text. My Greek improved a lot then.' He tore another piece of bread and dipped it in the soup. 'How long have I been here?'

'Five days. My son, Andreas, found you and then, Vangelis brought you here.'

'Vangelis?'

'Yes. My husband. He and Petros cut you from your parachute and brought you here. Dr Iannis has been visiting when he can. He dressed your wounds and gave you medicine to help with the pain.'

He fingered the dressing on his head. 'My head still hurts, like a bad migraine.'

'You have been lucky. Not only are you alive, but you can still talk. Dr Iannis said there might be lasting damage. He wasn't sure…'

'I can remember everything. Jumping from the plane, the parachute opening and then realising I was heading for the trees and then wakening up in your basement.'

'Do you remember why you are in Corfu?'

'Yes. I know why I'm here.'

He realised then; he didn't know her name. 'What is your name?'

'Helena.'

The sound of her name soothed him as if time itself had stopped.

'And you are Marcus, if that is your real name? We found your wallet,' she explained.

Marcus nodded. 'Who knows I'm here?'

'Only a few trusted people and the resistance.'

'I need to speak with them. I have a name, someone I need to meet.'

'They already know. They have already been here. They will come again.'

Marcus nodded. 'Have there been others before me?'

'Yes. There have been others.'

'You put yourself in danger for others you don't know.'

'We do what we have to do,' she said, simply.

Marcus smiled briefly.

'You're doing the very same and your country has not been invaded, not like ours. We're all making sacrifices. Hopefully, you will be back home in England soon.'

'Edinburgh is home.'

She thought a moment. 'You are not English?'

Marcus smiled. 'I hope not.'

'I'm sorry.'

'Don't be. We're all on the same side.'

'I've seen photographs of Edinburgh. It looks like a delightful city and a good place to live.'

'It is.'

'I would like to travel and see other countries.'

'Maybe after the war is over, you could?'

'I don't think so. Vangelis would not go. Anyway, we could not afford it,' she said defensively.

'Have you always lived in Corfu?'

'Yes. I've been to the mainland a few times.'

'Have you been to Athens? I never tired of it.'

'Only once.'

'I'd like to go back there, sometime.'

Helena smiled. 'After the war, maybe?'

Marcus grinned.

'There was a photograph of a woman in your wallet.'

'Her name is Ruth.'

'She is pretty. Your wife?'

'No. we're not married.'

'A girlfriend, then?'

‘Yes. We’re going to get engaged after this is all over.’

‘A lot relies on the war being over. Do you think the Germans can be defeated?’

His eyes fixed on her. ‘Yes. They have to be, otherwise the consequences will be unthinkable.’

‘You need to rest. I’ll leave you now.’ Helena took the empty bowl and placed it on the tray. ‘Is there anything you need? More blankets, it can get cold down here at night?’

‘I’d love a cigarette.’

‘I’ll bring you some.’ She smoothed her dress and, taking the tray, she stood up. ‘There’s colour in your face now. That is good.’

He shifted his weight. ‘I need to get up and walk.’

She shook her head quickly. ‘It is too soon. Dr Ianins is coming tomorrow. It is better that you speak to him about such things. You lost a lot of blood and your wounds have still to heal.’

He was about to speak, to protest, when she continued.

‘You need to stay hidden for now, for all our sakes.’

He rested his head on the pillow, sighing, and watched as she climbed the stairs, the smooth skin of her leg, the last thing he saw as she disappeared.

Confessions

Marcus looked closely at her face as Helena lay the bowl of water beside the bedding. She had brought Vangelis' shaving brush and blade.

Marcus rubbed the stubble on his chin. 'You don't have to do this. I can do it.'

'You don't have a mirror and you've bled enough already.'

'Are you sure?'

'Don't worry, I've shaved a man before when my father was too ill to do it himself.'

'Ah, I see.'

'I'm glad he didn't live to see these times.'

'I'm sorry.'

'It was a long time ago. I was only thirteen.'

'Was he ill?'

'It was an accident. A horse trampled him. He lived for several weeks. It was a painful death. I remember thinking at the time that I wished the horse had killed him there and then. It was dreadful seeing my mother waiting for him to die. So, he didn't die from my shaving.' She smiled and Marcus realised he had rarely seen her smile.

He adored her smile.

She knelt beside him and dipped the bristles into the water and brushed the hard soap into a lather. Marcus leaned on his elbows and shuffled up the mattress, Helena steadying him until he could sit upright.

She hesitated before shifting her weight, and then leaning towards him, she reached over and applied the soap to his face with delicate strokes. He concentrated on the movement of her hand as it bent at the wrist, the angle of the elbow and the smooth skin of her arm where the sleeve of her dress rested.

Satisfied with her work, she brought the blade to his face. With a delicate finger, she pressed and stretched the skin of his jaw and, when the sharp steel grazed his skin with the tenderest of strokes, she removed his whiskers.

He had nowhere to look but upon her face and watch her eyes train along the line of the blade. He wondered if she would blink, such was her resolute focus. She was methodical and efficient in her task. He studied her mouth, the curve of her upper lip, the fullness of her lower lip; her foreignness mesmerised him. He could not explain it specifically, but when he was with her, he felt complete.

When Helena finished, she handed him a towel.

'How does that feel?'

'Much better. I feel more like myself.'

'You look different.'

'I do?'

'Yes.'

'How?'

'Younger.'

'How old do you think I am?'

She crossed her arms and shrugged. 'Twenty-two.'

Marcus put his hand to his mouth.

'Don't mock me.' She found herself embarrassed.

'I'm not. I'm enjoying the compliment. I'm twenty-five.'

'I'm older by a year.'

'I wouldn't have asked you.'

'Is this a custom in your country?'

'It's how we were brought up, I suppose. Vangelis is older?'

'Only in age.' She avoided his eyes.

There was a long silence between them.

'I know it is hard for you. I've heard that in some parts of Greece, people are starving.'

'It is different in Britain?'

'There is rationing but nothing like what is going on in Europe.'

'The British fly over us and drop supplies.'

'For the villages?'

'If we get to them before EDES (National Republican Greek League) does. They make us feel like we're thieves.' There was a wobble in her voice.

'I'll eat less.' His chest tightened.

She shook her head. 'Then you would take longer to get better. It is not an option.'

He regretted ever landing near the village. But then, he would never have known this woman, which now seems incomprehensible to him. When he looks upon her face, it feels like he has known her all his life.

'Vangelis can still set traps; he is sometimes lucky. The bakery is running short of flour, but the trees still bear their fruit.'

It is not so much the words that weighed on him but the way she said them.

Then, as suddenly as the daylight turned to night, his shame gave way to a paralysed ache.

'Tell me about the girl in the photograph.'

This surprised him. Marcus hesitated. 'Ruth?'

Helena nodded. 'Yes. Ruth.'

The sound of her name from Helena's lips inexplicably felt like an intrusion.

'There's not much to tell. I met Ruth at university in St Andrews. We enjoyed each other's company. We went to the cinema, took long walks in the countryside, along the beach, that kind of thing. When my work took me abroad, we stayed in touch by letter. I was recruited by the intelligence service. She works at the museum in Edinburgh. It has been difficult. I haven't managed to get back to Edinburgh. We haven't seen each other for quite some time now.'

Marcus enquired about Vangelis. Helena told him they had known each other since they were youngsters. Vangelis, being older, showed no interest in her. He left the village when he was sixteen and didn't return until he was twenty-one. He had gone to Athens, joined the Greek

Merchant Marine and only returned because of his father's death; his mother died two months later.

'By then, I was sixteen, and I looked very different from the girl he remembered. By the time I was eighteen, I had been married for a year with a newborn baby to care for.' Helena managed a smile but there was something in her expression. She looked drained.

'I think Vangelis resents my presence.'

Her silence answered his question.

'I don't blame him.'

'It is difficult for him.'

He sensed she was holding back. He wondered if she was afraid.

'He is a good man. A good father.'

He risked asking her, but he needed to. 'A good husband?'

She averted her gaze. 'What do you know of marriage?' Helena gathered the shaving objects and, in her hurry, the brush fell. Marcus retrieved it and handed it to her.

'I shouldn't have asked. It was reckless of me. I've offended you. I'm sorry.' Helena's response had told him all he needed to know.

Small Steps

Dr Iannis adjusted his spectacles and inspected his handy work, nodding with satisfaction. 'You're healing well. There's no sign of infection or inflammation.'

As Dr Iannis continued his examination, he asked Marcus if he was suffering from headaches? Did he ever slur his words? Was his vision blurred? Could he remember events as they happened before his accident? Satisfied with the answers given, he checked Marcus' pupils and pulse, lifted the ill-fitting shirt and, with his stethoscope, listened to Marcus' breathing.

'There's nothing I can do for your ribs. You've broken a few and they'll take time to heal. My medical advice would be try not to sneeze.' Dr Iannis grimaced.

Once he packed his small bag, the doctor stood stiffly and rubbed the base of his spine.

'Thank you. I'm indebted to you. I wish I had some way of repaying you,' Marcus said.

Dr Iannis took his spectacles off and wiped the lens with a cloth retrieved from his pocket. 'Just make sure you accomplish what you came here to do. That will be payment enough.'

When Dr Iannis left, Marcus lit a cigarette and enjoyed its taste. Pleased with the rate of his recovery, he needed to feel strong enough to walk. The doctor had encouraged him to stand and initially take a few steps around the basement. He advised Marcus to start each day this way and accumulate his steps and his strength.

With an effort, he extricated himself from the bedding. With a hand, he held onto the wall for balance and, bracing himself, he pushed himself into a crouching position and again with effort finally he was standing. His legs shook with involuntary spasms, and a sharp pain took the breath from him. He leaned against the wall and swore at the desperation of not being able to put one foot in front of the other.

Small steps, he told himself. With a hand against the wall, he tentatively put his weight on one foot and then on the other. As the pain eased and, reassured with his progress, Marcus removed his hand from the wall, managing some more steps. Realising he needed to retrace his steps to get back to the bedding, he felt heartened with his accomplishment, and Marcus reassured himself tomorrow would bring further improvement.

To be released from the confines of the four walls around him, his rehabilitation would need to be such that climbing the steps on his own or with assistance, was the only way he would leave the confines of the basement.

St Andrews

1939

The Fragility of Happiness

The horizon and the sea merged into one another, and it was impossible to see where one ended and the other began. The rocks glistened with seaweed and corn-coloured reefs swayed in ripples where dunes rose like miniature mountains.

With each step, their shoes sank into the sand as they strolled the mile-long beach. The wind whipped at her hair that trailed around her face before she brushed it away with a gloved hand. Walking towards them, a man, heavyset, with flushed cheeks, passed by. He nodded a 'hello' and smiled at them. Ahead, his dog barked, chasing the crashing waves.

'We're going to be at war with Germany within weeks.' Marcus said and, seeing the concern in Ruth's watery blue eyes, he put his arm around her, and she buried her head into his shoulder.

'I've never liked that little man. He makes my skin crawl.' Ruth took a long breath and let it out.

Marcus looked towards the sea. 'He's a very dangerous little man. It seems he's convinced the German people they are invincible.'

'There was another little man who also thought he was invincible.'

Marcus' eyes narrow and she can tell he is trying to work out who she is referring to.

'Napoleon!' Marcus said, pleased with himself.

Ruth nods. 'The very one, and it didn't work out well for him.'

'At least I've got some news to tell you. I was going to tell you tonight at the restaurant, but I can't wait that long.'

'Is it about the job?'

Marcus raised an eyebrow.

'Well. Did you get it?'

Marcus smiled. 'I did.'

'That's wonderful. I'm so pleased for you. You deserve it after all the work you've put in.'

He looked at his feet. 'There is just one thing.'

'What's that?'

He stopped walking and drew his hand through his hair. 'It seems they want me to take part in their research programme partnered with The Hebrew University of Jerusalem. They want me to go, Ruth. I wasn't expecting that.'

'No. I suppose you weren't. Jerusalem's another world away. When?'

'In two weeks.' The catch in his voice was clear.

Ruth's smile had completely disappeared. 'For how long?'

He takes a deep breath. 'Six weeks.'

The fragility of happiness stares him in the face.

'Six weeks!'

'I know. It came as a shock to me too.' He took her hand. 'Before you know it, I'll be back. And anyway, you'll be busy at the museum. And you'll be in Edinburgh with your friends. You won't even notice I'm gone.'

'You think I won't miss you?'

'No. Not at all. I just meant if you keep yourself busy, time will pass quicker. That's all.'

'I'll miss you terribly.'

Marcus pulled her close to him. He kissed her forehead.

'Are you hungry?'

'How can you think of food?'

'I'm hungry. Let's have lunch at that little pub on Bridge Street.'

They sat in a corner of the pub, enjoying the heat from the coal fire. Marcus ordered steak pie and battered cod with chips for Ruth. After they had eaten, Marcus supped his beer and Ruth nursed a white wine.

'Jerusalem is so far away. You'll have to write to me.'

'I will. I'm sure I'll have lots to tell you.' It enthralled Marcus, the prospect of working with The Hebrew University of Jerusalem and although the prospect of being away from Ruth was not ideal, it didn't dampen his enthusiasm. He kept this from her. He had hurt her enough.

'You'll be able to explore the city. I can imagine how you'll be.'

'A child in a toy shop.' He grinned.

'Exactly.'

'While you're there, what will happen if we're at war with Germany?'

'I'm sure they'll have thought of that. They'll be some sort of contingency plan. And anyway, Jerusalem is a long way from Europe.'

Ruth sighed and then nodded. 'I suppose so.'

Marcus placed his hand on her thigh. 'Let's finish up here and go back to my place.'

Ruth raised an eyebrow. 'Was that a proposition?'

'We've only got two weeks. I'd like to make the most of it.'

'Well then. What are you waiting for?' Ruth smiled enthusiastically.

The Detachment of Strangers

The version of herself she saw each morning was incomplete. She wondered if her face had changed. Did it give her thoughts away? And if it did, could Vangelis see it too? If so, he had kept it to himself.

The house was full of memories. Their first night together as man and wife. The joy of being pregnant. She gave birth to Andreas in this house. She remembers the birthdays, his first day at school. This was where they became a family. Now it was a place of haunting. It imprinted her memories on its walls.

She felt the familiar ache rise behind her rib cage. She had wondered what the term 'growing apart' had meant, or how it felt in real life. Now she knew. They were strangers to one another. Terms of affection had died in their tongues. The intimacy of wanting to touch and be touched was no longer an urge that satisfied their need for one another. Vangelis' eyes had changed. They were cold, stonelike when he looked at her.

His expression fixed, far away, not of the here and now. He barely looked at her. There was a darkness about him. A detachment. Something was different about him now. He was lost to her.

A flicker of guilt turned to anger. She was invisible to him.

So much had changed. Vangelis left the house most evenings, just as it got dark, and he seldom returned before Helena went to bed, lying in its emptiness, waiting on his return. He never discussed the details of these meetings with the resistance or the undertakings, she knew he was now involved with. She often thought perhaps this would be the night he would not return. What would she do? What would become of her? Her mind looped and circled at such a prospect. She willed him dead and immediately willed him alive. The Germans would imprison him, torture him even. What if he was already dead, shot by a German soldier? She baulked at the horror this would inevitably bring, but also, she felt ashamed of the relief that spilt over her.

How long can this go on? That was the question that filled her thoughts.

A Sense of Relief

With each visit to the basement, Vangelis grilled Helena about her conversations with Marcus. Had he disclosed information about his mission? What did Marcus ask about? What interested him? Did he give her any reason to doubt him? Spies were everywhere, he warned her. All Marcus had to do was infiltrate the cell, win the confidence of the resistance, and expose them. They would be in danger.

Vangelis had only gone to the basement a few times, either when Helena could not do so or to see for himself the rate at which Marcus' health was improving. But that was as far as his involvement stretched.

He had met the two men from the resistance again, at an agreed location close to the village.

'What did they want?' Helena asked.

'It is too dangerous to move him just now. They want us to keep him a while longer. I told them he is too ill to be moved anyway.'

'I've heard people are talking. The parachute was found.'

'It was tangled in the tree. There was no time to cut it loose and bury it. It was a mistake, but we had no choice. I didn't know if he was going to live or die on us, and we had no way of knowing if the Germans knew about him.'

'You know, there are those in the village who will tell the Germans about the parachute. They might already have done so.'

'We have nothing to worry about.'

'How can you say that. They will search houses.'

'They would have done that by now. Darius has assured me, according to their intelligence, there has been no mention of a parachute.'

'Who is Darius?'

'He is from the resistance. He was the one that came to see the Englishman.'

'I told you he's Scottish.'

'Does it matter what I call him?'

'His name is Marcus.'

Vangelis shrugged. 'Darius was the one that did all the talking.'

'He is not a likeable man. I don't trust him.'

'It doesn't matter what you think of him. It's what he does that's important. He puts his life on the line for us, for Corfu, for Greece.'

'And we don't?' She recoils as if struck by a physical blow.

'They strike the Germans where it hurts, they ambush trucks, they use explosives, they destabilise the Germans with every soldier that is killed, every vehicle that is blown up.'

'You sound envious, Vangelis.'

'Maybe I am. Why wouldn't I be?' He ran a hand through his hair.

She stared at him. 'What do you mean?'

'I need to be doing more than this.'

'What we're doing isn't enough? Every minute he stays here, our lives are in danger.' She felt unease coil through her stomach.

'I'm suffocating. I can't stand by and let others do what I am also capable of. I will no longer be made to feel a piece of shit under the heel of those Nazi boots.' The fierceness in his voice was so unexpected she felt herself shrink from him.

'You wouldn't? You haven't?'

He reached out to touch her hand, but she swiped it from him.

'What have you done, Vangelis?'

'I have no self-esteem. I am worthless. I need to be worthy of the name that is my birthright, to be Greek. I can't stand by any longer, Helena. I cannot just do nothing.

I want to build a better world for Andreas, and I can't do that by tending to vegetables and animals.'

She felt despair, revulsion. He felt like a stranger to her. Suddenly overwhelmed, her eyes blazed with fury. She clenched her fists, and the urge to strike him was overpowering. But what would that achieve? A reprieve from the shock, only to be replaced by the fury that struck at her heart.

'You could be killed. You would make me a widow. What about Andreas? Have you thought about him in all of this? Imagine the pain you would be responsible for. Is that what you want? Is it worth that?'

'I can shoot a gun just as good as any man.'

Helena gasped. 'That's not the point.'

Vangelis slumped into a chair. 'Helena. If you want the man you once knew to return, let me go.'

'And what will I do? Wait each day for word of you and wonder if I'll ever see you again? She glanced at the basement door. 'You would leave me knowing that each second he stays here, I am in danger of being found out.'

'They have told me they will come for him soon.'

'How can you be so sure?'

'They need him more than they need me, it would seem.'

Helena turned from him and leaned both hands on the sink. She wanted to scream, even as the tears blurred her eyes.

'So, there it is. You're jealous of a man that can't even walk out of here. That's what this is all about, isn't it? It's not about patriotism. It's not even about the German's. My God. This is all about you.'

Immediately, she wanted to grab the words back. 'I'm sorry, I shouldn't have said that.'

He looked away, and that surprised her. Helena expected a volley of words in retaliation. His silence was more disconcerting. She would rather face his normal retribution. She could answer that, rise to it, but not this. His face was impassive, his lips immobile. Vangelis eased himself out of the chair and, without looking at her, he crossed the room.

'Vangelis!'

It seemed her voice brought him to a standstill as he stood motionless in front of her. He rubbed his brow with his palm. 'What?' His head remained turned away from her. At that moment, she knew something had changed.

'Stay.'

'I have to go.'

She felt herself softening. 'What will I tell Andreas?'

'Tell him… tell him I love him.'

'Then tell me where you're going? What are you going to do, Vangelis?

'You know I can't tell you. You know that.'

'Why won't you speak to me? If not for me, then stay for Andreas. Don't go.'

'I have to. I want to and that's the difference.'

Even though she knew it to be true, the reality of his words impaled her.

Watching him reach the door, he hunched his once broad and straight shoulders as if he carried the weight of events yet to happen.

And then he was gone. She sat amongst the memories that filled the space around her and suddenly her whole body was shaking and then, something suddenly occurred to her, it was not sorrow she was reacting to; the impression left on her was a sense of relief.

She sat beside him as he ate a breakfast of bread and a little cheese she had brought him. Marcus was aware he had not heard Vangelis or seen him for several days. He asked her about this.

‘He thinks if he doesn’t tell me what he is doing, he is keeping me safe.’

‘Maybe it’s better that way. You would only worry more.’

‘I’m worried now.’

‘How long has he been gone?’

‘Two days.’

‘Is that normal?’

‘No.’ She shook her head firmly. ‘He has not done this before. He has always come home.’

‘If he has been caught by the Gestapo, it’s only a matter of time before they come here.’

‘I know.’

‘What will you do?’

‘If the others have not been caught or killed, they will send me word and tell me what to do. I thought I would know if he was dead. I would somehow feel it, but I feel nothing.’

‘Then you must still think of him as alive.’

‘We are married. But we don’t live as husband and wife. Not anymore. The war changed him…it has changed us all. Everything has changed.’

‘I’m sorry, Helena.’

‘Don’t be. It’s not your fault. We were like this before you came. Vangelis is already dead. He died when he walked out and left me for the resistance.’

‘I’ve heard a radio.’

‘Yes. I listen to it.’

‘Do you get the BBC?’

'Of course. Sometimes I listen to that as well. It helps to improve my English.'

'I didn't know you could speak English.'

'I try, but not very well. It's nowhere near as good as your Greek. I'd prefer to speak to you in Greek.'

'Could I listen to the radio? Is it possible?'

'It's heavy, but I could carry it down here.'

'I'd like to hear the news.'

Set in a rectangular wooden case, the radio had three circular dials. It had a leather strapped handle that Helena did not trust to bear the weight, so she carried the radio into the basement. She placed it on the stone floor and sat by the bedding, curling her legs under her, self-conscious of how small the basement had suddenly become. They waited expectantly for the valves to warm up and then eventually it hummed into life. Helena turned the dials until the unmistakable English accent of an announcer emerged from the crackling and hissing and Marcus lent forward, eager to catch his words. Marcus and Helena listened absorbedly.

They learnt that the German army in North Africa had surrendered to the British and Americans. The announcer gave details of General Montgomery's congratulations speech to the soldiers in North Africa.

Marcus rubbed the short stubble on his chin. 'This means the British and Americans will invade Italy. Mussolini's days are numbered.'

Helena raised an eyebrow. 'And then it will be Hitler's turn.'

'Unfortunately, that will be a very different fight.'

Helena averted her eyes, aware of the hollow sensation Marcus' words induced.

'It means the war from an allied perspective is heading in the right direction, for now at least.'

'Then that is good.'

Marcus reached under his pillow and found the packet of cigarettes Helena had brought to him. He offered her one and, taking the cigarette from him, she flicked her hair behind an ear before lighting it. She took a long pull on the cigarette and Marcus watched her as she inclined her head and blew the smoke towards the ceiling.

'You must be proud of Andreas; he is a credit to you.'

'He knows we all have to be careful. The war is stealing his childhood. We do what we have to do.'

'I can't imagine being in your position. I feel I'm a burden to you. You're putting your family at risk. If I could, if these legs would let me, I would leave and disappear.'

'And go where?'

'Anywhere. As long as you are no longer in danger. It doesn't matter to me. You and Andreas would be safe.'

She was silent. 'What you talk of is madness. You would be caught, imprisoned, and tortured. It is safer for us all that you remain here and that you heal. You need to regain your strength.'

There was an intensity about her as she spoke. It unhinged him, but he knew she was right. In a way, they were all prisoners.

The Bomb

The sharp crack of thunder roared overhead, shaking walls and window frames, and sucked the heart from Helena's chest. The cup fell from her hand and tumbled towards the stone floor, fragmenting into pieces. She rushed outside. A dark malicious cloud curled towards the blue sky and suddenly, Helena knew what had happened. The realisation knocked the breath out of her body. Men and women, old and young, scampered along the only road that led to the centre of the village. Helena's mind emptied of any thought she had been occupied with as the horrifying reality soaked in. She, too, joined the procession of panic and fear. She passed an old lady struggling with an inexorable hobble, mumbling a relentless prayer.

Finally, she reached the square. To her relief, everything was as it should be.

'The school! The school! They've hit the school.' The words fell upon her like a shockwave. She heard them then, the screams and wailing, the unearthly shrieks and immediately, she was hurrying in their direction.

Where the school stood, a wide crater had appeared. Where once there was a classroom, there was now obliteration: mounds of bricks, and stones, and beams of scorched wood. Part of the school still stood, which gave the impression that the bomb had ripped the rest from it.

Several men, panic-stricken, scraped at the debris with clawing hands, shouting the names of children that went unanswered by their silence.

A group of women clung together, some burying their stricken faces in their hands, lips trembling, wailing uncontrollably, pleading with God to have saved their child.

The unrelenting horror overcame Helena. Her weakened knees forced her to stagger in helpless dismay. A tremor of panic surged through her heart. 'Andreas! Andreas!' She put her hand to her mouth and, paralysed with grief, she dropped to her knees and sobbed.

Later that day, the shocking reality that eight children and their teacher died when the bomb struck the school numbed the village in a mist of perpetual mourning.

The sound of sobbing punctured the air, wakening him, pulling him from sleep into a disoriented state. He lay motionless, perplexed and confused, trying to make sense of the sonorous wailing and lamentations, the guttural moans not of this world. His head reeled. An unpleasant sensation shivered down his spine. He heard the tramp of boots. He distinguished a voice. Helena? It was her and it was not. He strained to pick out a word, any word he could identify.

He lifted himself onto his elbows. A pain shot through his side.

Another voice, deeper this time in tone, Vangelis. The scrape of a chair on the stone floor. Again, he tried to listen, to concentrate. He pushed his hand through his hair and exhaled. He leant back into the pillow, more sobs muffled through the walls.

Marcus lay staring at the ceiling. Something had happened, something terrible. It was now late in the day, his stomach cramped with hunger.

It was Helena he heard crying. He gave a long sigh and felt a sudden surge of pity for her.

He raised his swollen hands in front of his face; he saw that were peppered with slight cuts as he turned them, inspecting them. His side felt like a hot poker had scorched his skin. His legs were heavy and weak, useless. He felt a shadow of the man who had jumped from the plane into that dark forbidden sky.

Then, the door that separated him from the outside world opened. The footsteps were heavy on the steps. Vangelis appeared, holding a tray. He stepped into the basement and leaning forward; he set the tray on the floor and pushed it towards the bedding and gestured towards the bowl of stew.

Vangelis stared at the bowl. ‘It’s rabbit,’ he said without looking at Marcus.

Vangelis’ visits had been few and brief. There had been an awkwardness between them. Marcus felt that as the days passed, although he had always been polite, Vangelis had grown to resent Marcus’ presence in his home. Marcus understood this and the circumstances embarrassed him. To his relief, it was a feeling he had never detected or sensed from Helena.

‘It’s fresh. I caught it in the trap yesterday.’

‘Thank you.’

Vangelis raised his head and, as he opened his mouth, Marcus thought he was going to speak again, but no sound came from him.

Although the desire to ask about Helena was potent, Vangelis’ detachment inhibited Marcus from doing so. Vangelis turned and headed back up the steps.

After his meal, Marcus lit a cigarette and drank the bitter-tasting coffee Vangelis had also left. He turned and twisted in his thoughts what could have caused Helena’s grief. Vangelis’ face was pale and taut, with dark patches under his eyes. He was different, diminished even. He looked like a man who had seen so much suffering that it had eaten away any sign of life in his eyes.

Had the resistance abandoned them, left them to their devices? Would they do such a thing? Only if the Germans discovered their cell. They would vanish and regroup once it was safe to do so.

He remembered the terrific noise that seemed to crack open the sky, the profound roar, and then when it ended in nothing but silence, the ever-present stillness in the basement resumed.

He knew it had been a bomb. He hadn’t seen Helena since that morning when she brought him his breakfast. She had on a new dress, pale blue like a clear winter sky, he hadn't seen her wear before. She had tied her hair back from her face and it hung in lustrous waves down her back.

Although he tried, he found it impossible not to notice the light curvature of her waist and hips, the outline of her breasts against the fabric of the dress. He found the curve of her top lip irresistible; he could not stop himself from gazing at it.

It was unusual not to hear Andreas. The boy talked continually when he returned from school and Helena always asked him questions enquiring what he had learnt that day in class. Then, always to his protestations, Andreas had chores to undertake before dinner.

Marcus thought about the blast. His thoughts circled before finally settling. With increasing comprehension, he now knew what had accounted for Helena's distress and weeping, and his chest burned with the horror of it.

They lay a procession of small coffins out in the church, side by side before the altar. The air, infused with the scent of the many flowers placed around the coffins, was a reminder of the infinite innocence lost. Washed in sunlight that filtered through the church, each coffin represented a family cloaked in darkness, shadowed by loss and tragedy. The pews bulged with what appeared to be the entire village and those that could not sit inside stood outside, shaded under a canopy of branches from two large trees.

Helena clung to Vangelis' arm, her eyes puffed with tears, her throat raw with sobs. When they cleared the rubble, they found Andreas. Remarkably his face was untouched, unblemished, and smooth, unlike some children. Most had been sitting at their desks when the bomb struck. They found Andreas in what would have been the corridor outside the classroom. He was always being reprimanded. The teacher had told Helena that he often thought of moving Andreas' desk and chair out into the corridor as he spent so much of his day there.

He had died alone. It haunted Helena. My beautiful Andreas. She knew there would never be closure. She would never heal.

The priest warned of the swift retribution that would follow if they took revenge against the Germans. Vangelis, stricken by grief and outrage, widened his eyes and, hammering his chest with a fist, he ordered that it was their duty as Greek citizens to avenge the sacrifice of the innocent. Every patriot, royalist and communist would gain the support of the populace with insurrection against the Nazi occupiers, who, he reminded them, they should hate with every fibre of their being.

Some looked at him in astonishment, while others nodded their agreement. Appalled by this, the priest stepped backwards, winded and punched in the stomach by Vangelis' words.

He raised a hand in protest. 'Enough!' Spittle flecked his beard. 'Vangelis, you are here to mourn the loss of your child along with these other families, your friends and relations. The entire village feels your grief and anger. This is not the time nor the place for in inciting what would only bring even more pain and suffering.' He stretched out his arms. 'Is this not enough for you?'

Vangelis slumped to his knees and sobbed. With the slightest of movements, Helena touched his shoulder and straightened her back. Fresh tears came to her eyes and slid down her cheeks.

She only had two photographs of Andreas. One taken by a professional photographer, Vangelis standing stiffly and uncomfortably in a dark suit, his hand resting on Helena's shoulder who sat with Andreas, a toddler in shorts and boots, sitting on her lap. The other, taken at a cousin's baptism where Helena remembers having to tuck Andreas' shirt into his trousers several times.

After the funeral, Vangelis would not sit with her and look at their son in these photographs. She told him she needed to; she wanted to. Helena's frustration boiled over into anger; he was shutting her out. He told her she expected too much from him; she replied, he gave too little.

There was a desert between them.

To mourn his son, they gave Vangelis two days leave from the resistance's activities and, in that time, he and Helena no longer slept nor spoke to each other as husband and wife.

Vangelis' face lit up when he explained there were plans already in motion that would inflict an immense blow to the Germans. It would strike at their jugular and avenge every child, woman, and man who had died in the name of Greece.

It shocked Helena that Vangelis could speak of such things when all she longed for was to have Andreas in her arms. She had never felt so crushed.
Helena was sitting drinking coffee when he told her he was leaving. Her hand shook when he said he didn't know when he would return. That was if she wanted him to. She did not reply.

The Heart's Conditioned Reflex

There were mornings when she awoke that even though the sun was shining, darkness encompassed her. She cursed every breath she took. She did not want to live any longer when Andreas was lying in the ground. How could she? A mother should not have to endure the death of a child. It was inconceivable, unnatural; it went against everything. But unspeakable horrors were the oxygen of war. It was a fact that had ripped out her heart.

She had nightmares. She couldn't stop thinking about Andreas. All she could see was his terrified face. Did he hear the bomb at the very last second? Was fear the last thing he felt? What was his last thought? She hoped it was a happy one, innocent and comforting.

It filled her days and thoughts, the ghosts that lurked in the corners of her mind, numbing her, reminding her of the unthinkable. She felt an overwhelming sensation of violation. From now on, she could only exist. *It should have been me that the bomb fell on. If only she hadn't taken him to school that morning. There was no longer a God. How could he have allowed this to happen?*

Her heart felt crushed, a heavy, unbearable weight squeezing her chest, leaving her gasping for breath. The pain was sharp; the emptiness overwhelming. Life was no longer intact; a haze had fallen over her. Just the minimum of tasks was a struggle. She felt exhausted just trying to focus on retrieving a cup from the kitchen cupboard.

She could still hear him call her moumia (mummy). She could smell him on the soft toy dog he cuddled and went everywhere with, tucked safely under his arm. And later, when he thought he was too old for such childish things, he could not resist taking it to bed each night.

Each morning, the sun grew bright and warm, and each evening faded into the horizon. Everything around her was still in its permanent state, yet her life had changed insurmountably.

How could she live with the loss of Andreas? Such things were incomprehensible. The enormity of it overwhelmed her. She did not know it but given time, she would fold her grief within herself, and it would become part of who she was. It was the heart's conditioned reflex.

The smell of his cigarette turned her mind to Marcus. It had been a week since Vangelis left. She had been alone in the house with Marcus. Petros had visited, checking in on her and offering to do whatever he could to help. He told her that Vangelis must have gone mad. He couldn't understand how Vangelis could have just abandoned her, especially after the bomb. She had borne so much pain and he could not stand it if he thought she was lonely.

Helena was grateful for his concern and thanked him for his kindness. She had enough to do to keep her busy and not dwell on her thoughts. Petros asked if she had heard when the soldier would be leaving. She had not, but was sure the resistance would send word when the time was right.

Vangelis' warning played on her mind, and it perplexed her that even Petros, with his concerned and mild manner, could be an informer. Her heart sank. She hated the thought of thinking suspiciously of someone like Petros, who was a friend and who she was fond of.

Helena felt more vulnerable than ever. She could trust no one. She had never felt so lonely.

As the days passed, Marcus' physical ills had abated significantly. He could now walk once around the perimeter of the basement without leaning on the walls for support before his legs tired and protested. His body was no longer failing him. His balance had improved and the routine of walking daily lifted his mood with a sense of elation and triumph.

Helena's visits were becoming more frequent too, and he looked forward to her company. Helena had noticed Marcus' eyes now gleamed with the prospect of possibly replacing the dimness that had been there before.

Helena could not describe it specifically, but there was something about him. He smiled more, and she liked the way it lifted his cheeks and creased the corner of his eyes. Marcus' voice was unique to that of the other soldiers she had looked after. His words seemed to dance from his lips. His voice was soft but also resonant. She thought of her voice and wondered how it sounded to him.

The Garden

The rising grey thread of his cigarette smoke curled between them as Helena brought Marcus his evening meal. She asked for a cigarette and smoked as he ate. They settled into a conversation and Marcus enquired about her day. She told him there had been more Germans than normal passing through the village, trucks full of soldiers with weapons and heavy equipment. She visited Andreas' grave as she had done every day. Often, there were other mothers there also, and they had found strength and comfort from one another. Marcus had heard her crying during the night, but he didn't tell her this. He already felt awkward, uneasy about intruding upon her grief.

When he finished his meal, he told Helena he had something to show her.

A flicker of surprise lit up her face as Marcus pulled himself to his feet and, initially unsteady, with each step his confidence grew, and he made his way around the periphery of the basement.

'That's wonderful. Look at you, you're walking.'

Marcus grinned. 'I've been practising.'

'I can see that.'

Since his arrival, Helena had never seen Marcus stand, and it surprised her he was taller than she thought.

'Now all I've to do is get up those stairs.'

'Are you sure that's a good idea?'

'I don't have a choice. If the resistance can't come to me, then I'll have to go to them.'

'No!'

Marcus stared at her in disbelief. And the assertiveness in her voice even shocked Helena. 'It's too dangerous. Someone will come when it is safe to do so.'

He knew she was right. Staring at walls all day had distorted his ability to think rationally, increasing the knot of dread in his stomach.

He was not confident that Helena would agree, but he had to ask her; he had thought of nothing else for days.

'I know it's risky, but I need to feel the sun on my face, smell the air and see the sky, just for a few minutes, that's all.'

Helena thought for a moment. 'I have an idea.'

'Will I like it?'

She inclined her head slightly. 'I think so. Are you sure you can walk up those steps?'

Helena stood and followed behind him as Marcus, leaning his hand against the wall for support, slowly but gradually, climb each step.

'You've made it!'

Marcus felt lightheaded but also at the same time exhilarated. He was no longer confined like a bird in a cage. Marcus remembered the hours he had dreamt of this and, even now, as he held onto a chair, catching his breath, he glanced around the room, and he still couldn't believe it. He saw the range where Helena had prepared his meals. The sturdy wooden table he lay on as Dr Iannis cleaned and stitched his wounds. Marcus thought of the times he heard Andreas' voice. He owed him his life. Marcus would have surely died in the forest if it was not for Andreas, and the irony weighed heavily on him. Helena's grief had been a constant reminder.

Helena walked across the room to the kitchen area and reached into a cupboard. She turned to face him, with a bottle of wine in her hand.

She placed it on the table. 'It was for a special occasion. I think being able to walk again counts as one.'

From the same cupboard, Helena retrieved two glasses and a corkscrew from a drawer and then asked him to follow her out of the house.

In the garden, she led Marcus to a bench beside a bulbous tree trunk and beckoned him to sit.

He would have liked to view the garden, but it hid in the surrounding darkness. The village also, but for many windows with soft light flickering behind them.

Helena unscrewed the cork. It sprung free with a deep pop, and she filled the glasses, giving one to Marcus.

'You might not be able to feel the sun on your face, but I think the moon will do.'

The moon hung brightly in the night sky. A silver light, like molten metal, spread across the ground in front of them.

'It's perfect.'

'No one will see us.'

He tilted his head. It always surprised him how big the night sky was. 'The sky is amazing. I've never seen so many stars. They just keep appearing.'

'But in Edinburgh, surely you're looking at the same night sky.'

'That's true, but there's too much light. It blots out the stars. You would have to go far into the countryside to see a sky like this and, even then, it would come second best.'

He breathed in. A hint of something was in the air, possibly from the garden. He had never been any good at identifying the scent of flowers or herbs, but this had a tone of pine and possibly lemon. Yes, he could smell lemon.

Marcus turned to her. 'This was a good idea. And the wine too.'

There was a second's hesitation. 'I'm glad you think so. This bottle has always been a reminder that Vangelis and I were…'

'You don't have to tell me.'

'We were blessed with Andreas. How can imperfection, because that's what we were, how can it make something so wonderful, so perfect? Am I being punished for not being a good wife? I tried to be a good mother.'

'You are the most unselfish person I know. Look what you are doing now. You don't have to do this. You are putting yourself in danger, risking your life for someone you don't even know.'

She shook her head. 'I have no choice.'

'There is always a choice. You did not ask for this, Helena. Vangelis has abandoned you. I wouldn't think anything less of you if you asked me to leave.'

'I couldn't do that.'

'Why?'

'You've also been abandoned. You're in a foreign country on your own. It's the same for you. You don't know these people, yet they see you as a liberator. We do what we have to do.'

'I just want you to know you've been in my thoughts. I didn't know what to say. What can I say? What good are words at a time like this? I just wanted you to know.' He dropped his gaze to the ground.

She closed her eyes. When she opened them, Marcus was looking at her.

'I'm not the first to lose a child in this war and I know I won't be the last. There are other families whose children were in the school. Everyone in the village knows someone who was killed that day. We are all suffering. I can't believe I will never see him again. I've tried to remember the last moment I saw him, what he spoke about and the things he did. I can't even remember kissing him before he left for school. My mind won't let me.' There was an ache at the back of her throat. She wiped the tears from her eyes.

'Do you want to go back inside?' Marcus asked.

She answered him by filling his glass and then her own. 'What I want is for you to enjoy being outside under the stars and not to feel guilty about it. Going inside won't change anything.'

He offered her a cigarette and held it out to her. 'It's my last one.'

'Then we'll share it.'

He lit the cigarette and passed it to her. Helena drew on the cigarette and inhaled. Marcus could not help himself. His eyes swooped over the fullness of her lips as Helena exhaled a plume of smoke. She had inclined her head and her eyes, dark and ornate with thick lashes, gazed at the night sky. Marcus regarded the contour of her forehead, the slender outline of her nose and the arc of her chin. She wore little makeup and, in the silver light of the moon, her skin glowed; at that moment, he longed to reach out and run his fingers along her face.

Reluctantly, he slid his eyes from her as she handed him the cigarette. He placed his lips where Helena's had been only seconds before and, as he drew on the cigarette, he wanted to sigh in pleasure, the intimacy of it astounding him.

From somewhere in the village, he could hear a dog bark. It had been the only sound to puncture the air around them.

'I think it's time to go back inside,' Marcus said, taking a last drag on the cigarette and as he stood it fell to the ground, where he crushed it with his foot. 'We should do this again.'

Helena smiled. 'I'd like that.'

Saving Herself

The sound of knocking loudly and persistently on the door woke Helena. She sat up and threw the covers from her. She could see daylight seep through the shutters as she wrapped herself in a cardigan and walked unsteadily downstairs in her bare feet. Her mind raced. Have the Germans come to take him away? Or could it be the resistance? Either way, each terrified her? She swept her hair from her face. 'Who is it?' she asked tentatively. She stared at her feet, cold against the stone cladding.

'Helena, it's me, Petros.'

Helena opened the door a crack and, seeing Petros, sighed with relief and unlocked the door. The room flooded with light, and Helena covered her eyes.

'I'm sorry for wakening you,' Petros apologised, as he stepped into the house.

'What time is it?' Helena pulled the cardigan tight around her.

'It's about seven.' Petros swallowed. He looked tired and nervy.

He pulled out a chair and sat down, breathing hard. He took a deep breath, then said, 'I'm sorry, Helena. I'm really sorry, it's Vangelis. The Germans have him.'

Helena's stomach tightened. She had so many questions, but they fell over one another. She sat opposite Petros and put her head in her hands. He reached over and touched her arm.

'I only know this because one of them managed to evade capture. Aristotelis, do you remember him? We were all at school together and he left the village and worked in Corfu Town at some hotel.'

Helena nodded.

'He's here in the village. I spoke to him last night. They were setting explosives; their intelligence had uncovered that the Germans were moving a large convoy of trucks and armour. They were to pass through a ravine and that's where the ambush would take place. There were enough explosives set to sink a ship, but not one of them went off in anger.'

Helena stared at him, her eyes wide. 'The Germans knew it was a trap.'

'They have a spy in their ranks. The Germans even knew where they were waiting. They didn't stand a chance. Aristotelis said they killed a few of the Nazi scum,' he said without enthusiasm. 'Most of his comrades were killed. Aristotelis was the only one to evade capture.' Petros leaned forward. 'There's something else I need to tell you.'

Helena took a deep breath. 'Tell me.'

'Vangelis was wounded, but he's alive.'

'For now.' Helena felt blood pumping in her ears. 'They will torture him. He is as good as dead. It would have been easier if the bullet had killed him. I pleaded with him not to go.'

'What choice do some of us have? Maybe, if Andreas hadn't died, he would not have gone.'

She swiped her arm from his hand. 'At least Andreas has been spared this. Vangelis knew what he was doing, and that he had put me in terrible danger. What has the resistance ever achieved? What have they done for us? They have brought violence, death and fear amongst the people they are supposed to be fighting for.'

'It is not the world we asked for, but it is the world we have to face. There is always a risk.'

'Don't lecture me on risk. I know the meaning of it more than most,' Helena said abruptly.

'I know. I know. You know as well as I do, there will be reprisals, house searches, arrests. The escape routes are still open, for now at least, but it will not be safe to move the Englishman.'

She almost corrected him, but stopped herself. Such things were trivial compared to the dread that had overcome her.

Petros looked at the door to the basement. 'How is he, anyway?'

'He's walking now.'

'That's good. He will need to if he is to get out of here.'

'What will happen now?'

'I'm not sure.'

Helena leaned back and stared at the ceiling. 'Has he been abandoned?'

'Helena, things are changing quickly, but I know, with the few conversations I've had with Vangelis, the Englishman is important to the resistance. They will come.'

'There must be something we can do?'

'You are already doing it, Helena. You too are helping the motherland in her hour of need. As long as the swastika flies on the Acropolis, Greece will never be free of oppression. The Greek government is Hitler's puppet. I've heard there are curfews in Athens now and those that demonstrate in the streets against the Germans have been fired upon. There is no such thing as freedom of speech in Greece anymore.' Petros swiped his hand through his hair. 'In Athens, people are starving. There are soup kitchens on the streets while Hitler sends Greek livestock to Germany. They're squeezing our country dry. We no longer have industries; economically the country is in ruins. The only thing that flourishes now is the black market.

'Every day there are reports of the bastards burning villages, executing men. They do not spare even the women and children. I've even heard the Jewish community in Athens has been banished to Nazi labour camps and those that are in hiding fear for their lives. Families have been torn apart. Their family members have even betrayed many ELAS (Greek People's Liberation Army) supporters and handed them over to the police. Fascism runs thicker than blood, it would seem.'

'That's terrible. What have we become?' The words stuck in her throat.

'There are many Nazi sympathisers who blame ELAS for the atrocities, even though it's the Germans who are murdering ordinary Greek people. Can you believe that? The Russians are closing in and the fear of communism blinds those bastards to Nazi atrocities.' He added emphatically.

'After all that's happened, we have to be optimistic. The Germans are not unbreakable.'

'Something will happen. I don't know what that will be but, whatever it is, I know for sure it will be people like you and me who will suffer because of it. ELAS now occupies a large area of Northern Greece. Right-wing and left-wing resistance forces are fighting each other.' He shakes his head. 'Greeks killing Greeks and, at the same time, they're putting us all in danger.'

When Petros finally left, Helena was still sitting at the table. She brought her hand to her mouth and stared at her feet. She heard the basement door open slowly and, when she lifted her head, Marcus was standing there looking at her.

'You heard it all?'

He nodded. 'Enough of it to know I can't stay in this house any longer.'

Helena looked at him seriously. 'You are safer here.'

'If they can't come to me, I'll go to them.'

She shook her head despairingly. 'And how will you manage that? You haven't walked for more than five minutes.'

Marcus looked away from her. He knew she spoke the truth. He was still weak, and his leg was often painful. 'I feel useless.'

She smiled sadly. 'I understand.'

He made his way into the kitchen and sat beside her at the table. 'I'm sorry about your husband. He saved my life and even now, he might be risking his life, and at this moment, being tortured. He knows that if he told them of my whereabouts, this would also expose you, risking your life as well.'

Helena lifted her eyes to him. 'He felt useless too, just like you. It drove him away from me. That's why he joined the resistance. You're thinking that you are responsible for this, that I am not safe because you are in my house and if you weren't here, I would no longer be in danger. But this is not true. I would still fear the knock on the door. I too, could be a suspect. They might arrest me and use this to weaken Vangelis, to break him, to get their information. So, even if you hadn't fallen from the sky and you weren't hiding in my basement, the bomb would still have hit the school, Andreas would still be dead, and Vangelis would still have been shot and captured.'

'I admire your courage, even if I struggle with its logic. You still want to save me, after all that's happened?'

'It's myself I'm saving,' she said gently.

He looked at her and nodded slightly, knowing it was all she had left.

Closer

At night, in the basement's darkness, he would often lie awake. What was it about her? He had never met other women like her. He had only known her a short time in the expanse of his life, but when he looked upon Helena's face and heard her voice, they were both so familiar to him; it seemed he had known her forever. It was an astonishing thing, this feeling, a sensation so rare, he had tried to search for an explanation for it, but it rendered him wordless.

He could not help imagining touching her. It was like an electric surge of expectation flowing through him. It was instinctive and intoxicating, for it would be heaven and it was an endurance not to do so.

Before this, the desire of wanting another woman would have been an illicit one, unthinkable even. The thought of Ruth had not even passed into his consciousness. Where was the anguish? Why did remorse not tug at him? Why did this not disturb him? He blinked such thoughts away. He would never intentionally hurt Ruth and yet, astonishingly, the calmness of his mind banished any such demonstration of wrongdoing.

Already, he could not imagine the thought of not seeing her each day, and that suggested a future yet, their time together was limited within the tragedy unfolding around them in which they had no control.

Some mornings, bread, cheese and milk wrapped in paper wait at the door, but always hidden from sight. Helena was grateful for these small offerings. Marcus, concerned that his presence was now common knowledge within the village, relied on Helena's assurances. It was a charitable gift of support from villagers who sympathised with the resistance fighters.

Now that there were only the two of them, Marcus ate breakfast and his meals with Helena in the kitchen. It felt a natural convention that brought a habit of civility to the horror that the consequences of being discovered would bring.

Over the coming days, they spoke to each other in ways that dismissed formality and restraint. There was a casual equilibrium about them.

They conversed more freely, sharing experiences, personal uncoverings of what they liked and disliked. They divulged the landscapes of their past, and Marcus listened intently to Helena's account of her childhood. The house had been her mother's dowry and Helena had grown up knowing no other home; it was where she and her brother Nikolas played as children, where the air was fragranced with the aroma of food that was always a temptation to taste as it cooked upon the stove. As they grew into young adults, Nikolas became unsettled and felt cut off from the modern world, denied the prospects it could offer. This led him to resent the restrictions he felt that living in a village placed upon him. He became obsessed with the American movies he avidly absorbed at the cinema in Corfu Town, and his fascination grew with the fast pace of life and skyscrapers that towered towards the sky. He discovered everything there was to know about New York, and life in America, and on his eighteenth birthday, he boarded a ship in Athens to the land of his dreams. Helena didn't know if his dream had come true. She had not heard from him since.

When she married, Vangelis had no dowry to give her, so they lived with her mother. It was difficult at first, but as time passed, and with a baby, life took on a new meaning and perspective. It was not just about them anymore; they had become a family and with that came the responsibilities of parenthood. Marcus had listened with rapt attention.

'Tell me about you, your life in Edinburgh.'

Marcus offered Helen a cigarette and lit one for himself.

'I've been fortunate compared to most,' Marcus said.

'My father's family made their money in business; they own several factories in and around Edinburgh. We lived in a well-to-do area, and I went to a private school. Most of the boys had to stay and were only allowed home on the holidays.'

Helena's eyes widened.

Marcus smiled. 'It was not that bad for me. I lived close by, so I got a reprieve. I remained at home, but my father still had to pay for the full school fees.'

She nodded and clasped her hands, resting them on her lap. She struggled to fathom such a life. How could she? For it was a life as far from her own as was possible.

'And your girlfriend, you must miss her?'

Marcus shifted in his chair, his eyes sliding from her face. 'Ruth. Yes.'

Helena waited for him to say more but he did not. Instead, he tapped ash from his cigarette into the ashtray.

There was a strained silence.

'She works in the Royal Museum.'

'Yes, you told me that. Is she a guide?'

Marcus ran his hand through his hair and took a long draw on his cigarette. 'She's an…' he struggled to think of the word in Greek. Instead, he said it in English, 'An archivist.'

'Oh!'

'It means she's responsible for maintaining the museum's collection of artefacts, art, objects, documents, historical items… that kind of thing.'

'It's an important job then.'

'Yes, I suppose it is.'

'You must love her very much.'

'The truth is…' She looked ethereal sitting opposite him, her hair tumbling over her shoulders in waves and even though her eyes were tired, she looked astonishing, sensuous, and adoring. He wanted nothing more than to reach out and touch her, taste her, and lace his fingers around her neck. Marcus rubbed his face. 'Yes. After all, she's my fiancé.'

Helena heard this as if someone else had spoken them. She could not speak. Instead, she nodded. She had half expected it. He had already told her this. He had a distant expression about him, but she couldn't read it.

They washed the breakfast plates and cutlery, and Helena stored them away inside the dresser.

When she had finished, Marcus stood back and focused on the dresser. It was immense, probably the biggest he had seen. He stepped around Helena and tried to push the dresser along the floor. Stubbornly, it didn't budge. It stuck solidly to the floor.

'What are you doing?' Helena stared at him blankly. 'Have you gone mad?

Marcus walked around her again and stood before the opened door of the basement. 'It's easily big enough.' He turned to face Helena. 'The dresser!'

She knew immediately what he meant. 'My mother's dresser.'

They removed the contents of the dresser piece by piece until it was empty, and then slid it across the floor, manoeuvring its great bulk until the dresser was flush against the plaster of the wall and covering the entrance to the basement.

'Perfect,' he said in English with a self-satisfied smile across his face. 'At least now we have a plan. If they search your house, the basement and I do not exist.'

'What about my crockery? We can't leave it on the floor?'

'We can only put some of it back. Otherwise, it will be too heavy for you to position the dresser once I'm in the basement. We'll need to test it out. I need to know the dresser will not be too heavy for you to move on your own.'

Finally, after replenishing the dresser with crockery and, several attempts later, Helena could move the dresser so that the gap was wide enough for Marcus to move through and Helena could return the dresser to its original position. They stored the remaining crockery in a cupboard, and Helena filled a pot with water to boil on the stove.

Marcus glanced out of the window. A track from the house led to the village where the paint peeled from cracked walls, but the buildings still gleamed in the morning sun. They oozed character and dignity and he had a definite sense that if he could stay long enough, he would eventually know this place and its soul. He imagined narrow lanes snaking in and out of tightly compact houses leading to a square with a tall tree in its centre. His eyes fell on the belltower of a church, and it occurred to him then he had still to hear the pealing of its bells.

Around the village, dense woodland covered magnificent hills with summits rolling against a cobalt sky and Marcus wondered if this was where Andreas had found him. This thought caused him to scan the village for a cemetery. When his effort was fruitless, he imagined it would be next to the church.

He saw two cats dozing in the shade and an emaciated dog in a frenzy combing the ground with its nose.

He felt a burning desire to be outside, to explore the village, and be amongst people again.

Helena watched him. 'I will have to go out soon.'

'To visit Andreas?'

She nodded. 'I'll pick some flowers from the garden.'

'I wish I could come with you.'

She managed a smile, but looked drained. 'We both know that's not possible, but it's something I would have liked.'

'He saved my life. I hope to visit him and thank him properly.'

Helena fought back tears.

'I'm sorry. I didn't mean to upset you. What was I thinking? I'm an idiot.'

'Don't be hard on yourself. I want his name to be spoken. Just because Andreas is not here doesn't mean we shouldn't talk about him and remember him. It's the only way I can keep him alive. I couldn't cope otherwise.'

'I wish I had got to know him.'

'He would have liked that.'

'You must wonder why I'm here?'

'All I know is what Vangelis has told me. I know you are important to the resistance. Other than that, I know nothing.'

'It's probably best that way.'

Helena nodded.

'I was meant to contact my superiors once I'd met with the leaders of this particular cell.'

'What will happen now?'

Marcus smiled slowly. 'They'll either think I've been captured or I've been killed.'

'What will they tell your family and Ruth?'

'That I'm missing in action.'

'They will be worried.'

'Yes. They will.'

'It must be dreadful for you too.'

'Both Vangelis and I share this. That's one thing we have in common.'

'What do you mean?'

'Ruth doesn't know if I'm alive or dead, and you don't know what has happened to Vangelis, either. I know how that will make him feel.'

'Can't the men you are supposed to meet tell the British you're alive?'

'There are ways, but it would be very risky for them. They're not going to do that.'

'How are you to return to Britain?'

'In due course; it would have been organised. The little you know Helena, the better it will be for you.'

'I'm not sure about that.'

'What do you mean?'

'If the Germans caught me and I gave them the answers they were looking for or I didn't, it wouldn't matter in the end. Either way, my fate would be sealed. I've heard what has happened to others. My life is worthless to them, but because they'll use me as an example to others, I'll be executed.'

Heat and colour crossed his face. 'I'd give myself up. I'd never let that happen to you.'

Helena reached over and touched his forearm. 'You might not even be here Marcus.'

He loved the way his name sounded on her lips. *You might not even be here, Marcus.* He could not speak.

Helena could not imagine what it must have felt like, falling through the sky like that, in the dark, and seconds away from disaster. Knowing that there was nothing he could do to stop the inevitable, and knowing what was about to happen, must have been terrifying. It filled her with dread. She wondered if Marcus remembered the actual impact, and it was then, she thought, he had never spoken to her about it. When something like that happened, did the mind close itself down? Like some kind of survival reaction, maybe?

These thoughts stayed with her as she walked briskly, with her basket in her arm. She had already bought bread at the bakers, and she was hoping there would be something of substance to be had at the small store.

Helena proceeded cautiously, her head bent, avoiding the possibility of speaking to anyone, careful not to draw attention to herself. Even though her heart pounded in her chest, it was exhilarating to be outside again and feel the morning sun on her face and warming her arms.

She entered the store and glanced around. To her relief, Helena was the only customer. Margarita had her back to her, as she straightened a few tins on the shelf, lately, almost customarily bare.

'Kalimera,' Helena offered.

Margarita turned to face Helena. 'Helena. How lovely to see you! How are you, my dear? I was just thinking about you this morning and here you are.' Her concern was genuine.

Margarita was in her fifties, widowed for over a year. She wore the black colours of mourning that highlighted her silver streaks pulled tight from her face in a bun.

Helena averted her eyes. She swallowed and caught her breath. 'I'm surviving.' It was all she could say.

Margarita moved around the counter and, with outstretched arms, embraced Helena. She cupped Helena's face in both hands. 'Be strong. You have suffered more than most have in a lifetime.' Margarita mentioned her pain at the hearing of Andreas' death and confirmed she knew of Vangelis' arrest. This did not surprise Helena; she knew, by now, this would be common knowledge.

'If you need anything, you come to me, do you hear? I've got to know a lot of people over the years in my little shop. It's not like it used to be, but there are means and ways, even if the Germans steal everything.'

'That's kind of you.'

'Nonsense. And I wouldn't do it out of pity. I respect you more than that. The Kafenion is full of men who debate politics, those who hanker for the days of Metaxas, the royalists and patriots and then there are the communists. Their ideologies are like fruit that falls from trees and rot. They accuse each other of not being true Greeks and then sit back and play backgammon, smoke each other's cigarettes and drink coffee together.'

Margarita held Helen's arm. 'Be careful, Helena,' she insisted. 'There are traitors amongst us and they're invisible.'

Helena thought of Marcus, and her stomach spasmed. 'I have to go, Margarita.'

'Of course, of course. What is it I can get you?'

'Some pasta, a little meat, if you have any. I see you have oxtail.'

'I can do better than that.' Margarita went behind her counter. As she did, Helena glanced out of the window. The street was quiet.

Margarita wrapped slices of bacon, a small piece of lamb and cheese in wax paper and handed it to Helena.

'Don't say a word. It is the least I can do.'

'But I don't have the money to cover this.' Helena opened her purse.

'Put it away,' Margarita insisted. 'That won't be necessary. And there is enough for two.'

Helena wanted to reply, but the words froze on her lips. In the end, there was no need for words, as Margarita could see the glow of gratitude behind Helena's smile.

Helena's heart raced as she hurried through the tangled lanes, where houses, although stacked together, had asymmetry that was pleasing to the eye. Soon, she found herself out of the shadows and on the road, which was merely a widened track that bent and twisted towards the next village. A breeze stirred the leaves of a plane tree as Helena neared her house.

Her eyes were immediately wary, darting from window to door, to the garden and beyond. There was nothing to suggest anything had changed since she left the house.

Helena's cheeks flushed as she emptied the contents of her bag onto the kitchen table. She could feel the trickle of sweat on her neck as she unwrapped the groceries. At that moment, emanating from the basement the voice of a radio announcer diverted her attention. The dresser moved from the wall, exposed a gap wide enough for someone to pass through. Her throat tightened as she strode across the room and slipped through the gap.

Marcus raised his eyes from the radio and watched Helena negotiate her descent into the basement at a determined pace. She wore a white dress that fell to her mid-calf and flat shoes that clicked with each step.

He smiled. 'Helena, I hope you don't mind.' He nodded towards the radio. 'I wanted to hear what news there was.'

Helena glanced at the radio. She touched her head with her fingertips, and Marcus wondered if she had a headache. Then he noticed her eyes. They were intent, pulsing with exasperation.

'What possessed you? I could have been anybody, a German soldier, the Gestapo. You moved the dresser and didn't put it back against the wall. You didn't hear me, but

I heard the radio. How can you be so stupid?' The ferocity of her tone was so unexpected it dazed Marcus.

'I'm sorry. I'm sorry. It was stupid of me, reckless even. It was just a momentary lapse. I suppose...' He searched for the words. 'I've started to feel... to feel safe in the house with you, in a way protected. I know it was wrong. It won't happen again.'

'You're not safe. I'm not safe. I feel vulnerable in my own home. Every time I leave this house, I wonder if I'll return. Every second, I'm frightened I'll be arrested. Do you know what it's like to feel like this, to live this way? Everyone I have ever cared for and loved has been taken from me. I don't have to die to know what hell feels like and I don't need a cell to know what it is to be a prisoner.' By now, her anger had dissolved into tears that pricked at her eyes.

Marcus wanted to hold her and tell her everything would be alright, but it would not be the truth and such sentiments would be belittling for she would know this too. He felt a weight descend upon him. He hated himself for the nightmare he had caused, the impossible situation Helena now found herself in.

'I'll put the radio back.' It was all he could think of saying.

'Leave it.' Helena wiped her eyes, turned on her heels and in a few seconds all that was left was the distinguished tones of the radio presenter announcing in the Queen's English. *'On the 17th October 1943, Communist ELAS partisans captured 81 German soldiers from I Battalion 749 Jaeger Regiment of the 117th Jaeger Division near Kalavryta in Greece. Treated initially as prisoners of war, they were detained at Mazeika south of Kalavryta but later all were executed.*

'On 4th December, unaware of the killings, three thousand German troops were deployed from Patras, Aigion, Tripolis, Corinth and Pyrgos to crush the partisans

and free the German prisoners. Sources have confirmed that the German commanders learned of the execution of the prisoners on 8th December and General Karl von Le Suire gave immediate orders for savage reprisals, calling them "atonement measures".

'Eyewitness accounts describe the males of Kalavryta over the age of twelve being taken to an area known as Kapi's Field, where they were executed by machine guns. 463 men and boys were murdered, and the town set on fire.'

Before being parachuted into occupied Greece, Marcus had heard rumours of the brutal reprisals and atrocities the Germans had inflicted upon the Greek populace. Like everyone, it shocked Marcus to hear of such barbarity, but it did not interfere with his daily life. It did not affect him day to day and soon faded from his thoughts. Greece was a country far from home and unconnected by the distance of sea and land, which bred an indifference that now shamed him to his core.

His hand trembled; his chest inflated with anger. He had heard the cries of mourning, the wailing of insurmountable loss. His eyes had fallen upon the tortured mask of grief. He had looked into eyes that had seen too much suffering and pain.

The abrupt change in Helena startled him, but he understood it. How could he not? Now, alone in the basement, he longed to be near her.

Stepping From the Shadows

The following day, Marcus awoke early. He filled a basin with water from the jug Helena left each night. Washed and shaved, he left the basement. In the kitchen, Marcus prepared a breakfast of boiled eggs and bread that he toasted, spreading it with a scraping of butter, a luxury found in the parcel deposited by the door from benevolent neighbours.

He boiled water on the stove and stewed some coffee, setting the table to the creak of a floorboard above him. He was pouring the coffee when Helena appeared in a navy-blue dress and white-collar. She crossed the room and sat at her usual place at the table.

Marcus sat up straight, cleared his throat, and smiled.

'Good morning.'

'Is it? I hadn't noticed.'

If Marcus hoped Helena had forgiven him, he found his answer in the residue of her anger that filled the space between them. She glanced at the breakfast, her arms wrapped around her chest.

'Not only can you fall from the sky and land in a tree, but you can also boil eggs too.'

Marcus adjusted himself in his seat. 'It's my way of saying sorry. I hope you like your eggs runny?'

With a knife from the table, Helena sliced open the top of an egg, exposing the creamy yoke inside. She nodded approvingly.

They ate in silence and, all the way through, Marcus had a wild and desperate desire to reach over the table, pull her towards him and kiss her. He imagined how her lips would feel and his stomach leapt at the thought.

Helena dabbed her mouth with a napkin. 'You should have only used two eggs. Four is a luxury we can't afford.'

'But was it a satisfying luxury?'

'It was.'

If she had been concealing her rage, it was now thawing.

Marcus took a long breath.

Helena rose and took her plate and cutlery to the sink. She turned to face Marcus. The words flowed from her lips like a breached dam and, when she started, she could not stop.

'You have to be more careful. I have to be more careful. I have to go out to buy food. I have no choice. It's a risk I have to take. The shops are getting emptier by the day. Meat is scarce. Soon we'll be eating the last of the vegetables from the garden. I'm terrified they will find you, but it is not safe for you to leave. The Germans are searching villages, arresting anyone they suspect of helping the resistance. For one German soldier killed, a village will burn. The men, women and even children are executed. I have heard stories of bodies being found hanging from trees. It's only a matter of time. They will come, but they can't find you. It would be more than I could bear.'

Marcus stood, scraping the chair on the stone floor. He reached for her and daringly settled his hand on hers, soft and warm to the touch. Her breath warmed his skin like a gentle breeze, and his heart raced. He had crossed a line and there was no way of going back, not now.

At that moment, there was a knock at the door. Marcus stepped back, Helena's hand falling from his. She peered at the door, her eyes wide and alarmed.

Helena walked briskly to the window and cautiously moved the net curtain, revealing a slight gap, wide enough to squint through.

'It's Petros.'

'I'll go to the basement.'

'No. Whatever he has to say, you need to hear it too. It's not as if he doesn't know you're here. He brought you, after all.'

Momentarily startled, Petros could not disguise his shock when his eyes fell upon Marcus. ‘You look much better now than when I last saw you,’ he said, finally.

‘I need to thank you Petros for helping me.’

Petros nodded. He paused and lit a cigarette without offering one to Helena or Marcus. He sat down heavily on a chair and inhaled and exhaled loudly. Marcus noticed nicotine stains yellowing Petros’ fingers.

‘Would you like a coffee?’ Helena asked.

Petros waved his hand. ‘I’m fine.’

Helena raised her eyebrows. ‘So, Petros. It’s not that I’m not glad to see you but is there a specific reason for your visit? Do you have something to tell me?’

Petros crossed his legs. Marcus felt unsettled. He decided he was overreacting as Helena did not seem overly concerned. But like an ache, he couldn’t get rid of it.

‘I think I’ll have that coffee after all.’

‘I’ll get it.’ Marcus poured some coffee and placed the mug on the table in front of Petros. He took a mouthful and sat back. ‘Where did you get this? It’s better than the shit masquerading as coffee at the store.’

‘On my last trip to Corfu Town. There’s not much left now.’

‘You won’t be going back there anytime soon.’

‘No. I miss my visits.’ Helena’s voice cracked as the memory of it felt another life away.

Petros removed a tiny shred of tobacco from his lip, looked at it and flicked it from his finger.

‘What can we do for you?’ It came out more harshly than Marcus wanted.

‘I have some news about Vangelis.’

‘What? Is he alright?’ Helena asked nervously.

‘They’ve moved him to a camp on the mainland. He would be dead by now if they had no interest in him.’

Marcus looked at him suspiciously. ‘How do you know this?’

'Let's just say, not everything is at it seems.'

'I don't understand.' Helena frowned.

Petros' demeanour had changed. He was more confident, self-assured, and Marcus had noticed this. 'You're part of the resistance.'

Petros inclined his head, his mouth curling at the corners, answering Marcus' question. 'I'm more than that. I command this region.'

Helena looked at him in shock, her eyes wide and confused. 'How can this be, Petros? Did Vangelis know this?'

'No. It is safer to be in the shadows. It is necessary. Only a handful of my closest men know who I am. It has to be that way.'

'How do we know this to be true? I can't believe this, Petros.' It was not so much humiliation Helena was feeling but a nervousness that concerned trust. What else, apart from this seismic revelation, was hidden from her? She had not foreseen this. She had been so preoccupied with Marcus' and her safety that it had not occurred to her the resistance had been close by, all this time, waiting and watching.

'There are informers everywhere, especially amongst people you would least expect. It's best to remain in the shadows.'

Marcus breathed in tightly. 'How do I know you are who you say you are?'

'That is for me to know and for you to believe.' Petros took another long drag on his cigarette before reaching into his shirt pocket. He handed Marcus a folded piece of paper.

Marcus unfolded it.

Petros smiled at him.

'There are only a handful of people who know this word.'

'The codename of your mission,' Petros affirmed.

Marcus folded the paper and gave it back to Petros. 'Yes. Aetos (the eagle).'

'I always wondered about that. Why Aetos?' Petros held the piece of paper between his finger and thumb and lit it with the end of his cigarette, watching it disintegrate.

'In Greek mythology, the eagle was the sacred creature of Zeus who turned into an eagle when he abducted Aegina. Eagles also carried the god's thunderbolts. It was a favourite of my superior officer.'

Petros sucked in his breath. 'Touching. It's a pity you didn't bring some thunderbolts with you; we could use them right now.' Petros pulled a packet of cigarettes from his pocket and lit one with the stub of the cigarette. He offered the packet to Marcus, who shook his head.

'So, what do I call you?'

'Marcus. I'm a British agent with the Special Operations Executive, SOE Middle East, Force 133. But you knew that already.'

Petros extended his hand, and Marcus shook it.

'I'd just about given up on you when I saw the state you were in.'

Marcus slumped into a chair. Helena stayed standing. 'I've Helena to thank for that.'

'Dr Iannis saved you, not me.' Helena breathed in deeply to still the hammering inside her chest. Who was this Petros sitting in her house? It looked like him, yet it was not the Petros she had known all these years. It was like a dream she could not make sense of.

'The situation has changed dramatically. I've seen intelligence that the Germans are aware of your presence on the island. It would seem the informer has been busy, yet I'm convinced they're unaware of your location or why you're here. That can change very quickly.'

'I need to contact SOE HQ in Cairo. They need to know I'm still alive.'

'I have already arranged it. We're going to have to be very careful. We need to find a way of getting you off Corfu.'

'But my mission? I'm feeling better by the day.'

'Is someone going to tell me what is going on? Or do you want me to stand here with my fingers in my ears?'

Petros pursed his lips. 'She has a right to know.'

There was a pause as Marcos digested the request. He hated keeping it from her. She deserved to know.

'I'm part of the British Government's Special Operations Executive, S.O.E. Its purpose is to inspire and assist in resistance against the Germans. There's a department in Cairo where I was trained. Agents have been sent into Greece and Yugoslavia to help the resistance organisations with arms, explosives and even money.

'I was to meet with the leaders of the resistance. It had all been arranged. With the help of a radio operator and armed partisan personnel, we were to scout the island. The aim was to identify isolated locations suitable for airstrips. I would then radio the map references to Cairo and wait on their approval. If it was given, with the help of the resistance and the local population, I would organise the construction of the airstrip, which would admittedly be rudimentary but, more importantly, fit for purpose.' Marcus looked at Petros.

'Carry on,' Petros urged enthusiastically.

'Very well. These airstrips would deliver arms supplies to the Greek resistance and distributed throughout the region and the other Ionian islands. Once achieved, the next phase of the operation was to repeat it all over again in the Southern Peloponnese. Build landing grounds from where allied fighter bombers could attack the Germans on the mainland. Lake Kaiafa has already been identified as a suitable seaplane base. Soundings and measurements need to be taken, map references and such, and the information passed on. Reconnaissance planes would be sent in and then it would be a case of waiting for approval.'

As Helena listened, a sense of being profoundly moved by an inexplicable emotion gripped her, suggestive of greater things occurring beyond her reality. She did not know this other Marcus. She only knew the man who had lived in her basement these last few weeks. As she listened to him speak, he had opened the door to another world and let her in. At that moment, he had changed. Marcus spoke of a life she did not know. This was the world where Ruth and Marcus were present with unknown histories. He had dropped into her life, blown off course. His time with her was just an interlude, an interruption to a greater intent. The reality they moved in had its limits. It was moving to a conclusion, an end. It was just a matter of time.

Helena had grown used to Vangelis' absence. She had dared to think she had rid herself of the life she shared with him, the ties of the obligation of a wife, the restraints imposed, and the misery endured that only Andreas could ever ease and melt. In her moments, she gave way to the dense weight of grief, and the sheer uncertainty of not knowing if Vangelis would ever return. The tricks of the mind and her vulnerability had intoxicated her in assuming she could ever be happy again. Had she allowed herself to think in such a way? To assume she was moving towards a release from this imprisonment by the hope Marcus brought?

When Marcus finished speaking, Petros rose from his chair. 'Your mission has been compromised, Marcus. I know it's not what you want to hear, but you can no longer stay in Corfu. We will make arrangements to get you off the island. In the meantime, I have a piece of shit to find, and we will, believe me, eventually. The piece of shit will make a mistake and expose himself. He will pay with his life for jeopardising our victory and liberation over these fascist pigs.'

Helena said nothing and, for the first time since Marcus arrived, she felt the panic of loneliness.

Elation and Relief

Sleep deserted Marcus as his mind raced in the thick darkness around him. What gripped him was a sense of failure. His mission had ended before it had begun. He now knew that, within days or weeks, the resistance would take him off the island. He tried to imagine what it would be like to leave Helena. The thought alone crushed him.

He raised himself from the mattress and pulled his hands through his hair. Tentatively, he made his way up the basement stairs and through the narrow gap of the dresser.

The house was silent and still. The stove, such a presence in daylight, hovered in dark, haunting shadows. He walked to a window and pulled back the net curtain. The village seemed to have slipped into a somnolent blanket and was hushed by the night. Only a few starlike lights flickered in darkened windows.

He could just about make out the outline of trees, many trees, giant shapes towering towards the velvet sky.

He could leave her now. He would reach the trees in under minutes, be amongst the hills in a couple of hours and, in the morning, she would be free of him, her life, once again, her own. Her nightmare would be over. It was unbearable to think that he was the one who had endangered her. He had heard about the brutality of the Germans interrogation: the torture, the beatings, the mind games, the killings. Every day he spent in her house, moved her closer to an unimaginable hell. He wanted nothing more than for her to be happy, and he was the last person in her world who could give her that happiness. He would leave, he must. The thought of Helena being safe would impel him and make living without her bearable.

He turned from the window and Helena was standing at the bottom of the stairs, her feet bare, her arms wrapped around her nightgown.

'You can't sleep?'

Marcus nodded an affirmation.

'Me neither. So much is changing and so fast. I thought I knew Petros. I've known him most of my life and yet I don't.'

'I'd imagine there'll only be a few people who'll know what Petros does. It has to be that way.'

'Do you think Vangelis knew?'

'Probably not.'

'I didn't even know Vangelis. He hid so many things from me. And look at him now. I don't even know if he is alive or dead. What I know is that what we once felt for each other has died.'

'I know how hard it has been for you, Helena. I could not live with myself if you were harmed because of me. That's why I have to leave tonight.'

'It's not possible.'

'I have no choice. Every second I stay, I put you in grave danger.'

'Where would you go?'

'As far from here as possible. If I can contact SOE in Cairo, they'll find a way to get me off the island.'

She raised her hand. 'You don't understand. If you're caught, there will be reprisals. The Germans will use you as an example. There will be no bargains. They will burn villages, people will be arrested and people will die. Women and children will die as a reminder of what happens when we shelter and protect their enemy. It is a gamble you cannot take. You cannot assume. There is no honour or morality involved in this. None.' She hesitated. 'They will torture you.'

'I would never tell them about you. Never.'

'You would. Eventually, you would.'

He shook his head. 'I'd rather die.' Marcus took a step towards her. He stood motionless and then raised his hand to her face. He traced the outline of her lips, which were inches from his. Marcus felt a tension in her ease as a sigh escaped her. He bent his head and glided his lips along her mouth, an echo of where his finger had been and, when he kissed her, he felt an extraordinary combination of elation and relief.

Helena took his hand and, without speaking, they made their way up the stairs.

Threads of sunlight filtered through the shutters as Marcus watched her sleep. He had been awake when it was still dark, listening to her shallow breathing. And now, as sunlight pushed into the room, she lay on her side facing him. Shadows dissipated, dissolved by a milky light that glazed her face, becoming visible to him. He studied her, drinking in every detail, absorbing every feature, every curve and shade of her skin. Her hair lay like sheets at the side of her face, and he recalled its feathered touch upon his skin.

Marcus thought of Vangelis. It was hard not to, lying next to Helena in their bed. He did not want to think about what had transgressed between them as man and wife. Marcus did not want to picture this. He pushed the image from his mind as his insides tightened as if a snake had crawled over him.

Such thoughts polluted the exquisite and sensual feeling of their lovemaking. He had experienced nothing like it before, not even with Ruth. He wondered if what they had done was wrong? It did not feel like a betrayal. How could it be? Nothing had ever felt so right. Every second, every minute, was thrilling. It was miraculous. It was enthralling and exhilarating. How could one regret such intimacy? She consumed him. He loved her.

It astonished him. Only a few hours ago, Marcus was preparing to leave her and now, he realised with an inner jolt, he could not, he would not, contemplate such action. The thought of never seeing Helena again tightened his chest.

They had only a short time left. His thoughts fluctuated between the emotional turmoil of what had to happen, and the fresh memories and thrilling imagery of last night.

With a tentative hand, he slipped the fine straps from her shoulders and let her nightdress fall from her. He never took his eyes from hers as she undid the buttons of his shirt and fanned her hands along his chest, gliding the fabric from him. He could smell soap on her skin as he kissed her neck and curled her hair between his fingers.

The sensation had such a pull that he reached over and brushed Helena's hair from her face and she opened her eyes and smiled.

Connected

It had been twenty days since his arrival. He had remained in the house and, in that time, he had watched as Helena's life imploded around her. There had been no word of Vangelis and he knew that in her mind Helena thought of him as being dead. That way, she was no longer a captive to false hope. Marcus thought it probably true. Vangelis was dead and, if not, it would be better for him if he were.

She seldom spoke about Andreas, but Helena continued to visit the cemetery every day. He often watched her from the window, walking briskly, before she disappeared from his view. The times he had seen her return, her steps were lethargic, weighted by loss and unimaginable pain. She would often go straight to her bedroom and Marcus would hear her crying; her agonising sobs penetrated him like a knife.

Marcus could not imagine living a single day of her life. He had never known such fortitude in another, and her resilience amazed him. He liked to think he had brought her some comfort, but he doubted this. His presence in her life could never fill her emptiness and ease her grief. Marcus was in admiration of the way he had watched her grow into a personal and moral force with each new day. He hated himself for changing her life. He felt embarrassed that he could only disappoint her. Yet she had changed him with an exquisite mix of fear and happiness.

He remembered the first time he saw Helena. His eyes fastened on her as she tended to him, cleaning and inspecting his wounds in the basement. Helena's touch was soft, her voice gentle. Her face was close as she leaned over him. Her fragrance filled the small space between them. In those first few days, he relied on the sensitivity of his senses to give meaning to and distinguish the details of the confined world he had woken into.

She had been a constant presence in what had now become his world. A world that had shrunk its perimeter within the walls of the house he awoke to each morning. It was a world of contradiction. It protected him, but he was also its captive. The fear of being discovered and the deadly aftermath that would befall Helena was often too much for him to contemplate. Yet the weeks he had spent with her was time so precious and cherished, it was the happiest he had ever been. She brought a golden light to his day and, unlike the sun he seldom felt, she encased him in a warmth that, if he could taste it, would be delicious and satisfying.

He was a foreigner, but he had never felt so connected. He wanted to stay and never leave. Could that be possible? How easy would it be to shed his identity and become invisible? Would such a life be possible? Maybe Petros could arrange it. He will undoubtedly have connections. Forging a passport and inventing a new life with a past would not be too tasking for someone like him. He would have done this before, Marcus was sure of it.

But what of Ruth?

He had stopped looking at the photograph of Ruth. She lived in a world that Marcus no longer felt part of. He wondered if she still thought of him as alive. Selfishly he wanted to be dead to her and, immediately, prongs of shame stabbed him. If Ruth still loved him, she loved the man he had been, not the man he had become.

An Unexpected Saviour

When Marcus awoke, Helena was already up and, when he went downstairs, he could see she had busied herself with cleaning the stove and washing linen.

From the shadowy kitchen, Marcus peered through the window and saw Helena hanging sheets on the washing line. The sun hovered over the village roofs, its soft hue and delicate shade casting everything in its dreamy light. His eyes followed the curve of her back as she bent towards the basket, the movements of her arms, with their taut skin and a hint of muscle, as she draped the sheets over the line, her long and slender fingers securing them with pegs.

Helena rubbed the back of her hand over her wide brow and, as she turned, he knew something had changed. He saw her mouth set tight, her worried almond-shaped eyes, her demeanour hesitant.

He stepped away from the window, rubbing the bristles on his chin. When she entered the house, she avoided his eyes and hastened towards the table, lifting a knife to cut a loaf of bread.

Marcus took her arm. 'Let me do it.'

She dropped the bread knife.

'Something has happened. Tell me what it is.'

Helena brought her hand to her mouth. Marcus could not help thinking she had heard some news of Vangelis and if so, it was not good, or was it simply he was alive and returning?

'Is it Vangelis?'

She shook her head.

'Helena!'

'No. It is not Vangelis.' There was a wobble in her voice.

'Then what?'

'This morning, someone had slid a piece of paper under the door.' She rubbed her temple. 'It was handwritten.

Petros is dead! Shot. He was betrayed. The Germans tried to arrest him. He killed two of them before he died.'

'Jesus. Poor Petros. The informer has given the Germans a lot of intelligence about the resistance. If they knew about Petros, what else do they know? They'll be able to cripple them. They'll cut off the routes for the resistance's supplies, arms and explosives. It will be like clamping an artery to the heart.'

'It's already started. Yesterday, they hanged three men in Corfu Town. One of them was just sixteen. A boy.'

His mission was to help the Greek resistance, and he had failed. How many more would die? There would be no makeshift runways for allied landings. The prospect of defeating the Germans had died with Petros.

'There's more.'

Marcus took a deep breath.

'They're going to move you. To another location. You're not safe staying here.'

'When is this to happen?'

'Within days. It just said, be ready.'

'I'm not ready to leave. I won't leave without you.'

'You don't have that choice to make. It has been decided.'

'Then you must come with me.' He looked at her desperately.

'It's impossible.'

'Nothing is impossible.'

'My life is here.'

'This is not a life. This is not living, it's just existing.'

'It's all I have. It's all I know.'

Marcus struggled for something to say. He wanted to tell her she would be safe with him. He would never leave her. He would make everything all right. His throat burned and his voice left him. He reached for her face and clasped it in both hands. He kissed her brow and inhaled the heady scent of her hair. She leaned her forehead against his chest and the warmth of her breath crushed the misery in his stomach. He held her tight against his chest. She pulled her head back, her face wet with tears.

'We are alive and, for now, together. That's all that matters. I can't think beyond that.'

'I'd like to sit outside tonight and breathe fresh air for a change, with you beside me.'

She looked into his wet eyes and smiled.

That night, they sat outside on the bench, drinking red wine, and eating a lump of bread and goat's cheese that Helena had sliced into small blocks. She discovered them that morning, wrapped in a parcel and strategically placed near the front door by another sympathetic villager.

Helena cast several glances around the track, and then towards the village, and its whitewashed houses, less distinguishable now, their roofs obscured in blackness. She tried to remain calm and told herself to just enjoy the moment.

'I've not tasted cheese like this for… well, for a long time. I wish I could thank whoever left it.'

'That would be old Theodore. He has several goats. Before the war, he made cheese and sold it in the markets.'

'Well, old Theodore.' Marcus raised his glass. 'Here's to you and your wonderful goats and long may your cheese prosper.'

Helena laughed. It was the first time he had heard her laugh and his heart sprung with the sound of it.

'It suits you. You should do it more often.'

Helena looked away. She felt her cheeks flush.

'I'm sorry. I shouldn't have said that. It was insensitive of me.'

'It's fine. Honestly. And you're right, I should.'

'I can't help thinking that my presence here has made things worse. I need to do something. I need to be useful. I was sent to make a difference, not hide away like some frightened animal.'

'Is that how you see yourself? It is not what we think. Just being here sends a message to every Greek man, woman and child that we're not alone, that the world hasn't forgotten us. You're willing to risk your life for those you have never met. These people are strangers to you, yet you put your life in danger for them. That is why you are a hero to them.'

It was a preposterous notion. 'What. A hero. I'm no hero.'

'Your country is not occupied. If it were, then you'd understand.'

He closed his eyes.

'Everyone has suffered. The war has seeped into the lives of even those who have not lost loved ones. We are lucky that we're not starving like some. So, every time they leave a parcel, that is an enormous sacrifice, but they do it freely and with gratitude.'

'Let's go for a walk. It's such a simple everyday thing to do, yet I've never walked with you.'

'We can't. What if you're seen?'

'It's dark. We'll be careful.' He rose from the bench and reached for her hand.

Helena's eyebrows arched. 'Has the wine gone to your head?'

He smiled. 'I may not be able to thank them personally, but I'd like to see the village, the houses, the streets, the square and the church.'

They walked hand in hand. Helena knew it was a kind of madness, but she could not bring herself to refuse him. He had not seen the outside world for six weeks now and soon he would leave her, and she would never see him again. Their time together was ending. How long did they have? A week, a day, hours even? Helena squeezed his hand, and he looked at her and smiled. She wished she had a photograph of Marcus. She feared with time, the image of his face would fade from her mind. The thought terrified her.

They kept to the shadows and the narrow road twisted and turned, climbing higher as they progressed. Periodically, on each side, through wooden shutters, lanterns flickered in yellow light. Sometimes as they passed an opened window, a radio played, they could hear voices, a baby cried. They passed a small garage, a grocery store, and an ironmonger. The further they went Marcus could feel a growing pain spread through his thigh. With each step, the steep incline suppressed his enthusiasm as his face flinched. It had been the furthest he had walked since his injuries, and he had overrated his recovery.

They rounded a corner and a square emerged. In the centre, a large tree dominated Marcus' view. Behind it, a church's white walls stood out in the darkness. A few tables and chairs sat neatly outside a café. Marcus longed to sit outside in the sun and enjoy a drink with Helena. It was now a luxury to think of such things, like indulging in a fantasy.

An unexpected rumble of tyres on flagstone accompanied the mechanical drone of guzzling engines as clunking tappets rose towards the dense night sky, a fearful warning loud in their ears. They could hear boots kicking down doors, the guttural tones of German soldiers, barking commands and striking heads, mere boys in the theatre of war.

Helena's heart grew large in her chest. She yanked Marcus' arm, pulling him into a narrow lane and underfoot a cat scurried, it too desperate to vanish. She glanced at Marcus and saw he was limping.

'Your leg!' Her breath was tight in her throat, her heart pounding.

'Keep going,' Marcus gasped, gritting his teeth in pain.

They heard sharp voices, a woman's scream, a dog barking. Marcus' face was a mask of pain, anger, and grief as they stopped to catch their breath. Ahead of them, the lane merged with another. Marcus glanced around, the air eerily quiet in stark contrast to the melee of only a few minutes ago.

Helena cautiously peered left and right. She leaned forward to get a better view as the moon cast a silver light in front of her. They moved on; their progress was slow, the pain in Marcus' leg grew and it felt like he was being dragged along. Marcus glanced nervously at a balcony above them. He gripped Helena's hand tight and cursed his stupidity for putting her in danger.

Headlights appeared, animal-like eyes in the dark. They sank further into the lane, the darkness engulfing them. They waited, each breath loud in their ears as a truck ladened with soldiers rumbled past. Marcus took her arm, 'We have to keep moving.'

He felt her hand slide into his and his heart jumped. They kept close to the buildings, making their way along a narrow lane. An old woman in widows' black stood in a doorway, her mouth tight, her face wrinkled in a map of lines. She looked Helena up and down and then gestured to them. Helena breathed deeply to still the hammering in her chest. Then, the familiar sound of heavy boots and German voices panicked Marcus into a decision. 'We don't have a choice.'

Helena felt a reluctance to enter the woman's house but, once inside, the old woman's face softened, a pronouncement which Helena felt was an acknowledgement. The room they found themselves in was lit by a single lamp. Above the fireplace, the image of Christ looked down on them in radiant and glorious colour, in stark contrast to the darker shades of the room. Four wooden chairs stood at each side of a small table and the old woman beckoned them to sit.

Helena found her composure and sat down, relieved to feel walls surround her. The old woman shuffled to a cabinet and, from a bottle, she filled three cups. She pushed the cups towards them over the grain of the table and stiffly lowered herself into a chair.

'Drink.' She gestured towards the cups with a thin and vein tattooed hand. 'It's Ouzo, it won't poison you.'

Marcus took a drink and welcomed the heat in his throat.

'Thank you for the drink and for taking us in.'

'The German's were almost biting your arse; you would not have got very far, especially with that leg.'

Marcus smiled briefly. 'You're right,' he said, another misgiving that confronted the fact it had been stupid and dangerous to venture into the village.

'Your Greek is excellent, but that's all. You still look very British.'

Marcus' mouth dropped. 'It's that obvious?'

'Do you want my honest opinion?'

'You know who I am. I suppose that answers my question.'

Helena said nothing. She looked above the fireplace and felt the eyes of Christ upon her.

'And you must be Helena. I'm sorry for your loss. No mother should lose a child. My heart goes out to you.'

Helena swallowed a rock in her throat. She felt touched by the old woman's sentiment and tears brimmed in her eyes.

'You're welcome to stay.'

Helena sucked in her breath. 'That's kind of you, but we need to get back to the house once it's safe to do so.'

'Of course. You know there is a curfew. No one should go out after dark. If the Germans catch you breaking the curfew, the penalties are severe. This was not unexpected. The Germans have been coming every night for days now. It will only get worse. If you stay, the chances are they will find you.'

Marcus looked at Helena and not for the first time did he curse his survival.

'If you knew who I was, then our situation is worse than I thought.'

'My name is Christina. I only know because I'm the mother of the doctor who saved your life.'

'Dr Iannis.' Helena could feel an instant relief sweep over her.

'Don't worry. There are only a few of us who know about you. Trusted people. They are the ones who leave the parcels for you. They will not betray you. It would be like handing over a son to the Germans. I knew who you were the moment I saw you. It wasn't as if I had to crack a code.'

The full impact of what she said struck Marcus in the stomach.

The old woman leaned on the table and rose to a standing position. 'When you get to my time of life, the days are full of ghosts and there is not much to look forward to, but there is something I can do to help.' She shuffled over to the kitchen. She returned and handed Helena a parcel wrapped in paper. 'These days, I have little of an appetite. Most of the food I have just goes to waste. There is cheese and some meat there too.'

'Thank you, but you don't have to,' Helena said, trying not to sound ungrateful.

'I know I don't have to. I want to.'

She turned to Marcus. 'Take this. It was my husband's. You'll have more need for it than I ever did.' She handed him an object wrapped in old cloth. Marcus felt its weight between his fingers. When he peeled away the cloth, Marcus' eyes widened.

'I know it's old, it hasn't been used in years but, as you can see, it's a good-looking gun. The bullets are in the box.'

Marcus held the pistol and inspected it. 'I hope I never have to use it.'

'In war, the luxury of choice is taken from us. If you use it, it will be because you have to.'

It was past midnight when they left the house. Above them, the sky was a large velvet curtain and, around them, the lanes and houses seemed cloaked in an eerie silence, unnerving their heightened senses. At the edge of the village, they hesitated at a track that cut through a clearing eventually leading to Helena's house. They stood entombed in the shadows. It felt safe compared to what lay in front: wild grass, sparse trees and shrubs that would expose them to any German patrol that was passing.

'Almost there,' Marcus said cautiously.

Helena nodded and bit her lip. Marcus took a deep breath. He moved forward and pulled at Helena's hand. They had only taken a few strides when, from the corner of his eye, Marcus noticed a moving shape and two milky eyes.

'Get down!'

They hit the ground in unison, air rushing from Helena's lungs, her knees trembled as she spat particles of dust from her mouth. Marcus raised on his elbows. They could hear laughter and voices, the crunching of gears breaking through the darkness and then, Marcus saw the rifles, the distinctive helmets, and the dark silhouettes of German soldiers sitting in the back of a truck, the glow from their cigarettes like fireflies.

'Don't move.' He lay his arm over Helena's shoulder. 'Are you okay?'

Helena nodded.

The moon slid from the clouds and its ghostly light caught Helena's eyes. Even now, he wanted to stare into their depths forever.

They lay like that until the sound of the truck was but a murmur and then fell away. Helena let out her breath as she realised she had been holding it and Marcus could feel it glide over his lips softly like a feather. He looked at Helena for a long time, his face inches from hers, and then he kissed her.

That night, they made love and Helena fell asleep in his arms. His love for her shimmered from every pore. His need for her ran so deep he luxuriated in the pleasure it brought, yet it also terrified him.

He remembered the astonishing care and comfort she showed him when, recovering from his injuries, she patiently nursed him. He recalled the shapeless despondency that seeped through him. How trivial that felt now.

She radiated a dignified and delicate dignity that was even more extraordinary in light of the way the drama of the last few weeks had played out.

Marcus couldn't imagine how Helena's life had changed, her child was dead and her husband at the mercy of the Nazis. Her world had shattered beyond comprehension. It was now unrecognisable and he, in part, was to blame. It made Marcus feel very uncomfortable and he felt a sense of loyalty towards her.

Sometimes he wondered if he filled a sense of absence in her. He thought more and more about it, and he concluded he needed to feel that he did.

He despaired at the confusion in his thoughts. He wanted to be free of the weight of anguish but one thing was clear, he loved this woman more than he had ever thought possible.

With the tremor of the unequivocal truth, he knew he could not leave her.

'I want to know about Ruth.'

Marcus looked at her curiously. 'Why?'

'Tell me more about her.'

'There's nothing much to tell.'

'I don't believe you.'

'Are you sure about this?'

'I'm not jealous if that's what you mean.'

'I didn't mean it like that.'

Helena stroked his face. 'How can I be jealous of someone who is not here?'

Marcus closed his eyes and sighed. When he opened them, Helena was smiling, her hair falling in front of her face. She sat back against the headboard and lit a cigarette, still smiling.

With an effort, he said, 'Very well then…'

St Andrews

1939

Ruth

In winter, St Andrews, on the northeast coast of Fife, suffers from petulant storms and gales, blowing in from the North Sea. In summer, its stretching sands are a beacon for families and couples, dog walkers and day-trippers. It's the little town with the big name. Education, history, and golf, such is its reputation. It is world-renowned in all three, and Marcus was happy there.

Twice a week, Marcus walked the length of the West Sands Beach, a two-mile expanse of uninterrupted sand. It was here he first saw Ruth. It was a windy day and she and a friend were talking to a young boy who was flying a kite. Marcus watched her as she spoke, her hand clamped to her hat and her coat flapping around her boots. The boy must have said something that amused them as both women laughed and Marcus could not resist the indulgence of inspecting Ruth's face and immediately it drew him to her. When he passed them, his fascination got the better of him, and he turned his head just in time to see her glance at him.

The following Friday evening, he saw her again, sitting a few tables from him, in a bar which was a favourite haunt for the town's student population. A fire flickered yellow and orange in the corner, the low ceiling capturing its heat along with the trailing blue plumes of cigarettes. She was with the same girl she had been with on the beach. He recognised the jacket, resting over Ruth's knee-length navy blue skirt, as the same one she wore that day on the beach. Her hair, now let loose from her hat, tumbled unrestricted to her shoulders and over her white blouse. Her red lipstick stressed her lips, giving them a full appearance that suited the shape of her chin, Marcus thought.

'Get the drinks in Marky, it's your round.' Gary drank the remnants of his pint. 'Same again if you don't mind.'

'Sure.' Marcus still had half a pint left. 'You're sinking them quick tonight.'

'I've got some catching up to do. That bloody flu floored me. I've been dry for two weeks.'

'Keep this up and I'll be carrying you out.' Marcus grinned, rising from his seat.

Gary's brow furrowed. 'I can hold my drink.'

Marcus leaned on the counter and ordered two more pints. In the next hour or two, the queue at the bar would be too deep, and it would be like a market trying to get served. As Marcus watched the barman pour his drink, he became conscious of someone standing next to him. He knew it was a female. He could smell her perfume, sweet but not overpowering like some.

'Hello.'

Marcus faced her. 'Hello.'

'It's quiet tonight.'

'It is. It usually gets busy around nine.'

'When the cinema comes out.'

'Exactly. Have you seen it?'

'Seen what?'

'The film.'

'Ah, I see.'

'Have you?'

'No. I find Charlie Chaplin annoying.'

'You do? Don't you think he's funny?'

'I prefer films that are more serious.'

'I see.'

'Do you walk on the beach a lot?'

'I do.'

'Me too. Although, I've only seen you once.'

'I remember.'

She smiled then.

'Are you at the University?'

'Yes. And you?'

Marcus nodded.

'It's a wonder we haven't bumped into each other before now. I'm Ruth, by the way.'

'Marcus.'

'Sorry to interrupt but you'll need to pay for these.' The barman smiled, nodding towards the drinks on the counter.

'Of course.' Marcus took his wallet from his jacket pocket. 'Let me get you a drink. What are you having?'

Ruth hesitated.

'I insist.'

'Very well. I'll have a red and Shirley's a white wine.'

'Why don't you join us?'

'Oh! I wouldn't want to impose.'

'You wouldn't be. I wouldn't have asked otherwise.'

'What about your friend?'

'Gary! I should think he'd be delighted, and Shirley?'

'She would be too, I'm sure.'

'Good. I'll bring the drinks over.'

Marcus learned that Ruth came from Edinburgh. However, his spirits dampened as she explained she was in her final year of study and would leave in three months to begin a job at The Royal Museum in Edinburgh.

Marcus warmed to her as the night progressed and Gary kicked Marcus' leg under the table and knowingly smirked. It was almost last orders when Ruth announced she was starving. 'I always get an insatiable appetite when I've had a few drinks.'

They finished their drinks and went out. In the cold air, they stood in a queue for fish and chips.

With their fish and chips wrapped in newspaper, they ate while they walked through the streets as the pubs emptied with men and women making their way home. Gary wiped his mouth on the sleeve of his jacket. 'These have to be the best chips I've ever tasted.'

Marcus smiled. 'Since last week and the week before that.' He looked at Ruth. 'He says that every time we go to a chip shop.'

Ruth and Shirley laughed.

'I like chips,' Gary said, depositing several into his mouth and chewing them enthusiastically.

They wandered along South Street and soon entered the grounds of St Andrew's Cathedral.

Despite there being not much left of the original cathedral, there remained enough evidence on display to echo what was once a grandiose building.

The moon was bright and its silver light illuminated the skeletal structure of the ruined walls and tower. Gary and Shirley sauntered off in another direction, leaving Marcus and Ruth on their own.

'This must have been pretty impressive in its day,' Marcus enthused.

'It was the centre of Catholicism in Scotland in the Middle Ages. Like all of history, the people were shaped by their time and not our twentieth-century morals and ethics. You have to put yourself in their skin and understand what it was like to live in those times, how people thought, what they believed and how that shaped their world.'

'I suppose you're right. We tend to judge history from a modern-day perspective.'

'You've heard of the preacher, John Knox, haven't you?'

'Yeah. The guy with the big beard that fell out with the pope.'

'That's him. Back then, in the 1500s, John Knox's condemnation of the Catholic Church was very influential, as was his view that it didn't represent the teachings of the New Testament and that made it evil and a heretic church. He preached several sermons with the theme of 'Cleansing the Temple'. I'm sure he preached in the cathedral as well.

Anyway, a mob, fired up by the anti-Catholic feeling, ransacked the cathedral and surrounding monasteries. That was the start of the Reformation in Scotland. The cathedral fell into disrepair as it wasn't used as a place of worship any longer. As time passed, they used its stonework for buildings in the town and what we see now results from that.'

'A bit like the Colosseum in Rome.'

Ruth nodded. 'Exactly.'

Marcus turned to her. She lifted her face to him, and he fixed his eyes on hers. He moved his mouth to hers and encouragingly she kissed him, her mouth wet, warm and inviting.

'I've been wanting to kiss you all night.' Marcus ran his fingertips along her cheek.

'I've been waiting all night for you to kiss me,' Ruth replied.

They wander around the ruins hand in hand.

'I wonder where those two have got too?' Ruth said, looking around her.

From behind a wall, they heard the distinctive sound of protracted moans and heavy sighs.

'They're getting on well together. I think they're busy.' Marcus winked at Ruth.

They walked along North Street when it drizzled slightly.

'We'd better get a move on before it pours.' Marcus increased his pace, and Ruth followed suit.

'Here we are. This is it. I share it with Shirley. It's small but snug.' Ruth said, flicking a tendril of hair behind her ear.

'When can I see you again?' Marcus asked, a hopeful look crossing his face.

'I'm not doing anything tomorrow.'

'And even if I were, I'd cancel it. Pick you up at one? We could have some lunch and see where the rest of the day takes us.'

‘That would be nice. I’ll look forward to it.’

Marcus leaned into Ruth and kissed her. She snaked her hand around his neck and when his lips left hers; she pulled him closer, finding his mouth again.

The next day, Marcus and Ruth were drinking tea from a silver teapot and eating lemon drizzle cake in a café on North Street. Ruth dabbed her mouth with a white napkin.

‘The cake is delicious.’

‘I believe it's freshly made on the premises. Their baking has a bit of a reputation around the town.’

‘I can see why.’ Ruth sipped her tea.

She cocked her head and looked at Marcus. ‘Isn’t it weird that we’ve never met before this? St Andrews is not a big town, and the university is quite compact. We must have walked past each other at some point.’

‘I’m sure I would have noticed you,’ he told her.

‘It’s possible that you haven’t.’ She smiled.

‘Well, you’ve got my full attention now.’

‘I’ve only a few more weeks left. I can’t believe how quickly time has passed, four years of my life, just like that. I’ll miss this place.’

‘You’ve got your new job to look forward to. That must be exciting?’

‘It is, but I’m also nervous about it. When we were waiting to get interviewed, I spoke with one of the other girls and she had bags of experience working in museums in London.’

‘You must have been what they were looking for. It was you who got the job, not the one with all the experience.’

‘I suppose.’

‘If you like, I could visit you on weekends. I’d stay at my mum’s. She’s always complaining that I don’t visit her often enough. That doesn’t sound right. I didn’t mean…’

‘I know what you meant, and I’d like that.’

‘You would?’

'Yes. I would.'

'That's settled then.' The corners of his lips curved into a smile.

'The first thing I need to do is find a place of my own.'

'What about your parents' house?'

'I'm going to have to live with them until I find somewhere suitable. I've lived self-sufficiently for the last four years. I love them, but the thought of going back to stay with them fills me with dread.'

'Have you made enquiries?'

'I have, but I need to make it a priority. I want a place that is near to the museum, within walking distance would be perfect. The rent in that part of town is on the high side. I suppose I could stretch to a bus ride away and save some money. What about you, Marcus? Where would you like to work?'

'Somewhere abroad. For a time, anyway.'

'And what would you do?'

'Well, given that I don't want university to have been a waste of time. Ideally, I'd want to work for an institution that offers theological and historical research. There's a lot of universities keen to develop their reputations and standings in the archaeological business, and the biblical period is an area rich with possibilities when it comes to research and archaeological significance. It's not like law or medicine, which both have a competitive job market and an abundance of opportunity, it's more of a niche market. Which isn't a bad thing. They'll be fewer applicants applying for the same jobs.'

'But not as many prospective jobs available. Less opportunity, I should imagine. Won't your options be limited? It's a very specific and narrow area.'

'Well, yes. That's the downside to it.'

'Well. If anything, you've still got time on your hands,' she said optimistically and sipped her tea.

‘Another year, by which time you’ll be an expert archivist.’ Marcus smiled.

Ruth laughed. ‘I doubt that very much, but your optimism is appreciated.’

Marcus lifted the teapot. ‘More tea?’

‘Yes, thanks.’

Once he had filled their cups, Marcus lit a cigarette, sat back in his chair, and crossed his legs. He thought for a moment. ‘Tell me, do you believe in fate?’

Ruth’s eyes narrowed. ‘I’m not sure. It’s not something I’ve given much thought to. Why do you ask?’

‘Oh, I was just curious. Why have we just met each other now? We’ve both been living in St Andrews, studying at the university, probably drinking in the same pubs, going to the same shops, yet it’s not until now that we’ve met and only weeks before you’ll leave.’

‘It’s slightly odd I suppose, but not unusual.’

‘My point being, if we had not met at the bar and struck up a conversation, we wouldn’t be sitting here today together. You would get on with your life in Edinburgh and, likewise, I’d do the same here. But now all that has changed. So, whatever happens from now on, was fated to happen.’

‘Was it?’ she asks with a smile. ‘Only if you believe in such things. Otherwise, it was just coincidence.’

‘Either way, I think my life has changed for the better.’

Ruth pulled a face. ‘You’ve just met me. We haven’t had our first argument yet,’ she said dismissively.

‘And who’s to say we will? I’ve never felt like this about anyone, Ruth. I think you're amazing, I do.’

She felt the heat rise in her cheeks. ‘You’re embarrassing me now.’

‘I’m sorry. I didn’t mean to.’ Marcus lowered his voice. ‘But the truth is, I haven’t stopped thinking about you since last night. I’m not even in control of my thoughts anymore.’

Ruth's eyes gleamed. Marcus took her hand across the table. There was an intensity in his eyes she found so profound she couldn't look away.

'What I'm trying to say is, I think... no, I know... I'm in love with you, Ruth.'

She caught her breath. 'This is all a bit sudden, Marcus.'

'I know, but I wanted you to know. I hope I haven't scared you off?'

Ruth smiled. Marcus still held her hand in his, and she raised it to her mouth and kissed his fingers. It was all the confirmation he needed.

'I've never believed in love at first sight. I found the concept only worthy of romance novels.' He looked into her eyes. 'Do you think it's possible?'

'I didn't think so either,' Ruth replied quietly. 'But I've just changed my mind.'

Helena lit another cigarette and handed it to Marcus. They took to sharing them now. Like the food from the sparsely populated shelves in the village shop, cigarettes had become a luxury. Unlike most, Helena could cook with the vegetables from the garden, but even those were running low.

'You love her?'

Marcus shifted his weight. 'I thought I did.'

'How can you be so sure you don't?'

'This is what love is. It was never like this. I love you.'

She was silent. It unnerved him.

'She is waiting for you.'

'Maybe.'

'What do you mean?'

'When I last saw her, we argued.'

'It's normal to argue.'

'It depends.' In his mind, he went over it again. 'I could have stopped her, but I didn't.'

'What do you mean?'

Edinburgh

1940

They made their way along The Mound, through a relentless downpour, crossing over to North Bank Street that rose and curved into Bank Street. They hurried on, over George 1V Bridge, where Saturday night buses and taxi cabs sprayed dark menacing puddles over unsuspecting pedestrians rushing and huddled under umbrellas and long overcoats. Turning left, they kept a steady pace down the slope of Victoria Street, where rain hurled against the walls of imposing 19th Century buildings.

Once they reached the Grassmarket, Marcus held open the door to a bustling pub and Ruth, thankful to be inside, peeled her gloves from her fingers and smiled in relief. Marcus shivered as he shook his umbrella free of rainwater. Then, with his hand resting at the base of Ruth's back, they walked through the bar, thick in plumes of smoke and condensation-streaked windows. They found a table hidden in a corner. Marcus pulled loose an empty chair, and Ruth sat down in front of a glowing fire, warming her hands. She settled back and crossed her legs, as Marcus ran his hands through his hair and asked her what she would like to drink.

He returned with their drinks and they sat in silence, enjoying the heat from the fire.

'Are you scared? I know I would be.'

'It's what I've trained for. I'm eager to get started, but I know the dangers. I'll be nervous for sure, but I'll be fine. Once I'm there, all the planning and training will kick in.'

'I know you can't tell me where you're going and I know it's somewhere in Greece, but what if something happens to you? I won't know.'

'I'm not planning on dying.'

'Marcus, don't say that. It's bad enough you're leaving me.'

'There are thousands of families and couples going through this. We're not the only ones. We're at war, Ruth. Bad things happen. People die, some get wounded, and some get captured. There's no point in hiding from the truth of it. I can't. Mentally, I need to stay strong. I've come to terms with the possibilities. Our training had a heavy psychological element to it. If I'm captured, I know what to say and what not to say. There are certain strategies and techniques that will save me if I get into a tricky situation. We've acted out possible scenarios and gone over them a hundred times. Mentally it was tough.'

'I don't want to know. I couldn't cope with that.'

'You're not making this easy.'

'That's because it's not.'

'I didn't mean it like that.'

'Then how did you mean it? Because from where I'm standing, it sounds like I shouldn't have any feelings.'

'I know how difficult this will be for you. Of course, I do. You'll have your family, your friends, your work. That's all I was trying to say. They'll be there for you when you need them.'

'That's the whole point, you won't be.'

'I know, but there's not much I can do about that. I wish there was. Believe me, if I could, I'd stay here.'

'Do you mean that?'

'If there was a way, don't you think I would have thought about it by now?' He had allowed her hope, but to believe in such an idea was preposterous to him.

'You said this was perfect for you. You had been specifically chosen because of your background and your fluency in Greek. I remember how much you went on about it and how much it meant to you. I'm not stupid, Marcus.'

There was a dry taste in his mouth, and he swallowed the last remnants of his pint. Marcus ran a hand over his chin.

'You're right I did, but now, now that it's imminent, the reality of it is different.'

He watched as she turned away from him. To his frustration, he found that his denial seemed unconvincing to her.

'Don't go tomorrow. We can leave Edinburgh. I have an auntie. She's dead now, but she lived in a remote cottage on Skye. She gave it to me in her will. We can go there. No one will ever know where you are. Can't you see? It would be perfect.'

'You're asking me to become a deserter. To go into hiding. I'd go to prison.'

'You won't be found. There's no one around for miles and I could go to Portree to get shopping and anything else we needed.'

'How would we pay for it?'

'I've got some money that I've saved.'

'And your job. What about that? You're not thinking straight, Ruth.'

'I'm frightened.'

Marcus suddenly sat forward in his chair. 'I am too, but not for me, for you. Even if I was not caught after the war, what then? What life would we have?'

Marcus looked at Ruth's hopeless face and he knew that if she looked at his, in her eyes, she would see the face of a coward.

Ruth scooped up her handbag and, in a hurry, she made her way out of the pub. The rain was but a drizzle as Marcus found his way out onto the street. He called after her, but Ruth did not turn around. Instead, he noticed she had already hailed a taxi, and he watched as she disappeared from him, never taking his eyes from the rear of the vehicle. Of all his mixed feelings, the one that rose to the surface was resentment. He was no longer in control of his life and, if terrible things were to happen, he would be alone. His heart felt heavy and adrift.

Corfu

1943

Stolen Happiness

'She left you.'

'Yes. She did. Since the war started, I've been back to Edinburgh a few times. We still see each other, but it's never been the same between us since that night.'

The house creaked in the silence around them.

When Helena finally spoke, her voice was but a whisper.

'I feel guilty for not feeling guilt.'

'Do you regret what has happened?'

She shook her head. 'No. Sometimes, I hope Vangelis does not come home. I hate myself for thinking like this. It's ironic because I don't want you to go. But you have to.'

'Then come with me.'

'What!'

'Come with me. Leave this place.'

'I can't.'

'You can.'

She shook her head. 'I can't. I can't leave Andreas.'

Helena's words fell like a hammer. Marcus held his head in his hands. He felt Helena's fingers run through his hair. When she leaned forward and kissed his hair, he closed his eyes, savouring her touch.

'You need to be loved, to feel safe, to have a purpose, to find meaning. With me, you would have all of these and more.'

'It's not that I don't want to. I want to with all my heart. There is nothing more I want in this world than to be with you Marcus, but it can never be.'

'And what will you do?'

'Try to make this house my home again.'

‘With all its memories, its ghosts?’

‘This is all I have.’

‘It would be like trying to rebuild on land that has been washed away.’

‘You have a funny way of saying things, Marcus.’

He tried to force a smile. ‘Yes. I suppose I do.’

‘Trust me, Marcus, it’s better this way.’

His smile shrank from his lips. ‘It doesn’t feel like it.’

‘We might only have tomorrow together or the day after. I want to live in the moment with you and not think about anything else.’

‘And I want to taste the deliciousness of you.’ Marcus pulled Helen towards him and, as their lips touched in a long, deep kiss, he felt like a balloon floating towards the sky.

She sat on the bed, a simple white dress draped over her knees, taken from the wardrobe where it had hung concealed for years behind her everyday clothes.

It had been her mother’s dress. The dress her mother had worn on her wedding day. Helena lost herself to thought, her mother walking to the entrance of the village church, where her husband to be waited patiently. In her mind, she pictured her parents exchanging the rings, and both sipped wine from the same cup, where the priest led them in the ceremonial walk, the dance of Isaiah, and blessed their marriage.

A sorrowful smile crossed Helena’s lips as she imagined wedding guests enthusiastically pinning money onto the dress. She now hugged it close to her chest. The dress signified the beginning of a new life, the prospect of children and family, and a long happy life together.

Unlike her father, at least her mother had lived to see Helena marry in this same dress and watch Andreas grow from a toddler into a boy. This, Helena was grateful for, as it gave her peace of mind, and yet the memories swelled her heart with her loss.

She bent forward and wrapped her hands over her head as a paralysing ache forced the breath from her.

Her love was a curse. It had taken everyone Helena had loved from her. There could be no other explanation.

She had stopped praying for them, and for God to have mercy on their souls. If there was a God, he had surely abandoned them all, just like he had abandoned and betrayed Greece and left it to the mercy of the devil itself. She, too, felt abandoned and betrayed. She felt no ties to the communists, the royalists, the nationalists, or the church. What had any of them done for her but cast their long and ugly shadow of division and deception? All stole her happiness and, from her, anyone she had ever loved.

And what of Marcus? This man had entered her life and given her so much. She felt fate had looked upon her. Their meeting was just a matter of time. For how else could it be? How could one describe such a thing?

And it frightened her. The sense of urgency to love and be loved, to touch and be touched, skin on skin, demonstrated an intimacy she had never known. With him, she had found a happiness that elated her into a state of mind she never thought possible. A quality of happiness she felt unworthy of, yet deserved. She dared to imagine a life with him, a life together. Another life. Another time together. It was a future they would not have. A future that was utterly impossible. She could not live a single day without him. That much, she knew. Yet, that was not how it would be and so they had lived each hour together as if it were their last.

She rose from the bed and carefully, with her hand, straightened the fall of the dress and gently hung it on the coat hanger. She brought the fabric to her nose and pressed her face against it, breathing its scent one last time and placing it back in the wardrobe.

She took a deep breath and closed her eyes, feeling exhausted and bewildered at how her life had altered. She fought back the tears because, if she were to let them fall, she could not imagine them ever stopping.

A Delivered Message

A boy had delivered the message. Only twelve, Marcus had thought. Helena knew him. He had been friends with Andreas. His name was Giorgos. He sat at the kitchen table, staring at Marcus.

Marcus caught Helena's eyes and her look troubled him.

'Marcus, this is Giorgos.' Helena's voice was shaking.

'Hello, Giorgos.' Marcus tilted his head, his forehead creased, as once again, he waited for an explanation from Helena, why the appearance of a young boy could derail her composure.

'I've never met an American before.' Giorgos' eyes were wide as if he were speaking to his favourite film star.

'He is from Scotland.' Helena corrected him.

Giorgos continued to stare at Marcus. 'You're not American?' he said incredulously.

'I'm afraid not. Sorry to have disappointed you.' Marcus grinned.

'Where is this place you come from? I've never heard of it.'

'It's a country that's part of Britain.'

'Oh,' he said, looking at Helena and visibly unimpressed. He reached into his pocket and pulled out a folded piece of paper. 'I've to give you this.'

It startled Marcus. He raised his eyebrows. The writing was Greek. *It is time for Aetos to take flight. Tomorrow night. 8 pm.*

He read it again. The finality of such few words caused an ache, a tightening that formed around him. It was going to happen. Until then, Marcus had had his doubts, and this had sat easily with him. He didn't want to believe this day would come. He had been dreading it and impatient for it.

'It's happening tomorrow night.'

She already knew. He could see that now. There had been an unmistakable sense about her posture, her voice, and her look.

'Can I go now?' Giorgos slid from the chair.

'You go straight home now, do you hear?' Helena ruffled his hair.

'I will. I promise.'

Marcus watched Helena close the door behind Giorgos. She turned and leaned against it. Helena could feel a light throb behind her eyes, the beginnings of a headache.

'How many of us have you hidden?'

'A few. The resistance has several safe houses all over Corfu and Vangelis was well thought of and trusted.'

'So, you knew when Giorgos arrived.'

She nodded.

'Why a child?'

'They often use children. It's better that way. The Germans will not suspect a child. If there was any doubt about the child's safety being compromised, they would call it off. It hasn't happened yet.'

'The boy has done this before?'

'Yes. We wait. They will come for you. Normally, there will be two men. You will meet them just outside the village, amongst trees. I will take you to them. You will leave and I will return home.'

'Where am I to be taken to?'

'I don't know. To a beach, an inlet maybe. Most likely there will be a boat waiting for you.'

Marcus felt a gnawing crawl in his stomach. 'I'm not ready to leave you.'

Helena put her hand to her chest. She bit her lips as tears welled in her eyes. She felt immobilised by the immensity of a force so overwhelming it crushed her. Helena felt rigid with shock and fear. Marcus moved towards her. She leaned into his chest and felt his warmth as he wrapped his arms around her. Marcus buried his face into her hair, inhaling her, the rich scent forcing an urgency upon him. He felt a sudden desire to touch her. He made a sound that was part hollow and part heavy. They had only one more day. He wondered if knowing this made it worse. It would have been better to have been told he was to leave suddenly, without warning. That way, it would spare them the agony of knowing, of waiting. The finality stung like a burn.

Helena had dreaded this day. Even though she knew it would come, she had forced it to the back of her mind. Denying the inevitable was not only efficient, but it had also been crucial to surviving each day. She wanted to scream. Andreas, Vangelis and now Marcus. She had turned the possibilities in her mind over and over. The happiness she knew with him was a gift she would always treasure, yet it too was a reminder of what she would not have, it would be taken from her, just like everything else she had allowed herself to trust and love. She had no words. There were no words. She knew what this meant. Life without him would be unimaginable.

She could see vividly the moment her world altered. A body shattered, blooded, and torn, spread lifelessly over the kitchen table. She was sure no one could survive such trauma. Inside, she urged him to live. It astonished her that, even then, the fluttering in her stomach was not purely physical, it was a deeper sensation; she did not imagine it, it was breathtaking.

They lay together in each other's arms. They spoke, but there were silences too, where they retreated into their thoughts. They listened to the radio, the gains and losses of both the German and allied armies. The levelled cities, the thousands who were now homeless, refugees adrift in their own country.

They smoked cigarettes and drank the last of the remaining wine. Marcus forced himself not to think of life without Helena, but his efforts were futile.

'You look a hundred miles away. Tell me what you're thinking?' Helena asked.

Marcus ran his finger along the curve of her hip, circling a small dark mole. 'The lost possibilities that could have been us.'

He traced his fingertips over her skin and between her legs. She felt the touch of his hand. 'There's nothing here for you Helena, only memories.'

Helena arched her back, pushing against him. She made a sound that infused him with a profound desire, but also, an overpowering sense of sadness strongly moved him. The thought of never being this intimate again with the woman he loved suggested a life he would never know.

Marcus rested his lips on the skin of her throat. 'Make new ones with me.'

She closed her eyes. 'I would if I could. I really would. All my life I've wanted this.' She turned her head and pulled him to her lips in a protracted kiss.

The Envelope

The time had come.

'Before we go, there is something I have to give you. Vangelis wanted to take some of it. He tried to convince me you wouldn't need it all or, in fact, even know if any of it was missing. I could not have stolen from you, because that is what it would have been. I was too proud, even though the money would have kept Andreas' stomach full for a long time. I was amazed at how much money Vangelis found on you. It would have kept us very comfortable for over a year at least.'

She pulled a white envelope from the drawer and handed it to him. 'I have kept it hidden all this time. It belongs to you.'

Marcus opened the envelope. He remembered now. Inside was enough drachmas to buy food and provisions for at least a year. He was astonished. After all he had been through, he had forgotten about the money. Maybe it had hidden in the far recesses of his mind as it struggled to process the damage and trauma his body had been through. He felt ashamed now. The money was to help him establish himself and live a comfortable existence amongst the poverty ridden and war-stricken populace.

Marcus pushed the envelope from him. Helena still held it and she looked at him as if he had finally gone crazy.

'I want you to have it. You deserve it.'

'As payment? Is this what you think of me?' She threw the envelope over the kitchen table.

He worried about her. She didn't eat enough and her face had thinned, her cheekbones were now prominent.

'Of course I don't think of you like that. But what good is the money to me now? It would mean a great deal to me to know that you will not starve. Give half of it away if you must, but keep the rest. I need to know you will do this.

Please, Helena. This is not about pride or principles, it's about survival.'

'It's too much.'

'There can never be too much. I won't take it. It will stay here with you in your house. One day, you might think differently. When there is not enough food on your table or clothes on your back to keep you warm in the winter, I know you won't starve. If I'm to leave you, I need to be convinced in my mind you can make that decision. It's very important that the money stays with you. It would mean everything to me.'

Helena looked at the envelope on the table, and then at the shapeless despondency on Marcus' face. She knew she would not win this argument. Also, Marcus was right. She had heard of the untold suffering on the mainland and in the cities. Starvation was like a famine that killed with viral proportions. She found accepting the money an intolerable necessity. This was not about morals or judgement or human obligation, this envelope served a different purpose.

She sensed his exhaustion.

'Very well.'

'Thank you.' It was at times like these, he cursed his survival.

Wreathed in darkness, the truck's headlights gleamed like the menacing eyes of a creature, stalking them amongst the trees. Helena touched Marcus' arm, and they stopped walking. Marcus could feel a pressure building in his chest.

'We wait,' Helena whispered.

There was a heaviness to the air and a scent of resin from the pines.

A door swung open, followed by footsteps crushing the earth beneath them. A figure emerged from the darkness. Instinctively, Marcus held Helena's hand. He had to touch her one last time. Something teased at the edge of his thoughts. Something was not right. Marcus assumed they would travel on foot, inconspicuous, hidden and camouflaged by the darkness of night.

A single truck travelling at night would stir the suspicion of every German patrol. He may as well have a target on his back.

Helena recognised the man. Even the beret on his head and the growth of his unkept beard did not disguise the fact he was one of the two resistance men who had visited her house when Marcus first arrived. The insolent one. And the feelings she felt for him that night surfaced again. She touched Marcus' arm, and he felt the curve of her fingers on his skin. He realised then the finality of the gesture.

Marcus took a step forward. Why haven't they killed the headlights?

'It is good to see you on your feet and alive.' Although he addressed Marcus, the man in the beret nodded a greeting towards Helena.

'What happens now?' Marcus asked urgently.

'My name is Panos. We will take you to a beach north of here. A fishing boat awaits you. A submarine lies a mile off the coast. You will be taken to it and your time in Corfu will be over. You will be taken to the naval base in Alexandria where she is heading.'

Panos extracted a cigarette packet from his jacket pocket, removed a cigarette, and offered it to Marcus. When Marcus shook his head, Panos clamped the cigarette between his teeth, the flare of his lighter flame brightening his face. He inhaled a lung full of smoke.

'What is the name of the submarine?'

'Why do you ask?'

'They are an interest of mine. They have always fascinated me.'

'Perseus, I think. Yes, I'm sure now, the name I heard was Perseus.'

'Really, I know it well. A metal cylinder with a crew of fifty-three and fourteen torpedoes diving to a depth of five hundred feet. Imagine that.'

'Better you than me. I prefer the ground beneath me. But then again, it is taking you home.'

'Thanks to you.'

'I can't take the credit for that.' He drew hard on his cigarette, his eyes suddenly weary, the confidence he exuded sinking from him. He stepped back. 'We need to leave now,' he said through tight lips.

It was then Marcus caught a shape, sliding silently from the cab of the truck.

He felt Helena's touch and lowered his voice to an urgent whisper, 'Stay behind me.'

Panos stared at Helena. 'Goodbye, Helena. We will meet again, I'm sure.'

She wanted to scrape her nails along his face. He belittled her. He frightened her.

Panos' hand flicked twice by his side and even though it was brief, Marcus knew it to be a signal. He motioned for Marcus to follow him. He looked around, his caution unmistakable.

Marcus took a step forward and, as he did, Panos was removing an object from his pocket. Marcus had expected this and already clamped his fingers around the pistol in his jacket pocket. In one motion, and to the Panos' horror, the pistol smashed into his skull and he stumbled backwards. His knees buckled, and he fell to the ground clutching his head, his hands already blooded.

Helena screamed, and Marcus thought it a reaction to the sudden violence, until he felt the air burst from his lungs as a fierce mass collided against him and, to his alarm, he was no longer in control. A dense weight pressed down on him. His mouth, full of dirt, ached and throbbed. The bone of knuckles drove against his face, and he felt his head splitting, a loud ringing filling his skull and, to his horror, his vision blurred.

The pistol, where was the pistol? It was no longer in his hand.

A hand arched, fingers clamped around a rock, a sickening thud, spurts of blood, the head jerked sideways and the weight fell from him.

Helena stood motionless, staring at her hand and the rock that tumbled to the ground, a deep red stain on its surface.

'I've killed him. Oh, my God, I've killed him.'

The crumpled heap at Marcus' side groaned and, as he pulled himself to his feet, Marcus cupped Helena's face in his hands. 'When he wakes, he'll have nothing more but a splitting headache.'

'He's not dead?'

'Unfortunately, no.'

Marcus scanned the ground until he found what he was looking for. He scooped up the pistol.

'The gun. You brought it with you.'

He remembered the old woman's words, *'In war, the luxury of choice is taken from us. If you must use it, it will be because you have to.'*

Marcus crouched next to Panos, if that was indeed his name, which Marcus now doubted.

'Are you working alone? Does the resistance know you were about to hand me over to the Germans?'

'Fuck you.' Panos scowled.

'Wrong answer.' Marcus pressed the pistol against Panos' knee.

'You wouldn't.'

'There's only one way to find out.' Marcus leaned his face close to Panos' ear. 'Tell me what I want to know or I'll put a bullet into your kneecap. In fact, I might cripple both legs. What good would you be to anyone then? By the morning you would have probably pissed yourself, or worse, shat yourself. Imagine being found like that.'

'You're full of shit. You haven't got it in you.'

'You're right. It would be messy.'

To Panos' horror, Marcus was now pressing the pistol against his temple.

'Maybe I'll just blow your fucking brains out and be done with it. You're beginning to piss me off, Panos. Oh, and by the way, I think you need to apologise to Helena.' In one swift movement, the butt of the pistol was pressing against his knee. 'If you don't, I'm definitely going to cripple you, and then I'll blow that tiny brain of yours out the back of your head.'

Panos' eyes were large and frightened, his confidence deserting him. 'Helena…'

Marcus pulled back the hammer.

'I'm sorry. I'm sorry. Helena, I didn't mean to make you feel… Vangelis was a good man and Andreas…'

He didn't get to finish his sentence. Helena grabbed a handful of his hair and slapped his face. 'I don't need your apology. You and your kind are nothing to me. I wouldn't lower myself.' She spat in his face and tears welled in Panos' eyes.

Helena turned to Marcus. 'What now?'

'We have to leave here. It's not safe.'

'What about these two?'

'Look away.'

'What?'

'Look. Away.'

She turned her head, just as two gunshots cracked the surrounding darkness and, as she flinched from the high-pitched screams, she felt Marcus' hand on her arm as he pulled her towards the truck.

'You shot them. I can't believe you shot them.' Helena felt sick.

'I didn't kill them. It gives us time. If they're lucky, they'll be found soon. If not, it's a long wait until the morning.'

'You shot them both… in the leg.' It was a thought that, when said out loud, would help to determine her own moment of clarity by processing the furious blur of activity that had just happened.

'I can't go back to the house, Helena.'

'Then I'm coming with you.'

'It's too dangerous.'

'What do you think that was? I'm not frightened for me. I'm frightened for you.' Her mind raced as she tried to think. 'There's a monastery along the coast. It will be safe. We need to go there.'

Marcus pulled on the steering wheel as the headlights lit the road ahead. On each side of the truck, darkness stretched before them, tenacious and formidable like walls.

The engine crunched as Marcus struggled to locate the correct gear.

'Left or right?'

'Left. Slow down, there's a lot of sharp bends ahead.'

She was right. He eased his foot off the accelerator.

'What has just happened?' Helena asked.

'There is no boat and definitely no submarine waiting for me.'

'How can you be so sure?'

'The submarine he called Perseus, it sunk off the coast of Cephalonia nearly two years ago.'

'He was going to hand you over to the Germans. They were collaborators.' The word stuck in her throat. 'But why? How could they do such a thing?'

'Money, the luxuries only the Nazis' could give them and, of course, the promise of being spared retribution.'

'One leg wasn't good enough. You should have shot both their legs,' she rasped in disgust.

'I've never shot anybody before.'

'Then there's nobody more deserving to be your first than those two pigs.' She thought for a second and then reconsidered. 'No, that's an insult to pigs.'

Just then, a deer, or an animal as big as a deer, Marcus struggled to tell, stood motionless in the middle of the road, staring at them. Marcus pulled the steering wheel to the left and, to his horror misjudged the width of the road. The noise was ear splitting as the truck buckled and snapped branches, its heavy wheels cracking and trampling undergrowth in the shadows. In desperation, the weight of Marcus' foot pressed the foot brake with such force, his thigh burned and ached. The brakes screeched and shuddered, kicking up showers of stone and dirt. And then, alarmed and panicked, he squeezed his eyes closed, as the form of a formidable tree trunk filled the windscreen and for a dreadful moment Marcus believed this was how he was going to die.

It had happened so fast.

Helena had screamed and, as suddenly as if he had just blinked, he was no longer in control. The noise and clamour, the crunch of metal and shattering glass, added to his sense of dislocation.

He turned sharply, 'Helena!'

She slumped forward, one side of her face swollen, a trickle of blood on her forehead.

'Helena!' he cried in desperation.

To his immense relief, she lifted her head. 'I thought we'd never stop,' she said through the pain. 'I'm alright, are you?'

'Better than the truck, it's going nowhere.'

His heart still thumped in his chest as he slid from the seat and, moving around the vehicle, he steadied Helen, who had tentatively slid from the passenger seat.

'Are you alright? Your head, it's cut.'

'It's nothing.' Her eyes were wide.

Steam hissed from under the buckled bonnet.

'How far is the monastery?'

'We can be there in an hour.'

For about twenty minutes, they sought the protection of the woods, swallowed by their density. They walked as soundlessly as they could manage, moving at a steady pace, until eventually Marcus struggled. He felt absurdly conscious of his inability to walk any distance, the pain in his leg disabling any stamina he had in reserve. Helena's look of concern only helped to stress his frustration with himself.

'We'll rest here for a while.' Although she was smiling, Helena could not hide the anguish in her voice.

Marcus lowered himself to the ground. He could not yet bend the leg in one full movement. It remained stubbornly stiff, much to his exasperation. He leaned against a tree, and his shirt, damp with sweat, stuck to his skin.

'Oh, Helena. You shouldn't be here with me. Since the day Vangelis cut me from that tree, I've done nothing but endanger you and changed your life beyond recognition. What have I done to you?' Marcus' face darkened.

'Stop it. I won't have you speak like that.' She walked over to Marcus and sat next to him. He shifted his weight, and she lay her head on his chest. Her voice was shaking, but she spoke. 'It'll be alright. Soon… Somehow… soon, you will be back home, and all of this will just be like a bad dream. There are others in the village who will look out for me. I will not be on my own. And anyway, the war will not last forever.'

Marcus leaned his head against the tree. He looked up towards the moon, a bright bulb in the night sky. Although she meant well, Helena's words could not dissipate his anger and his fear for her, that crawled within him like a slug. He knew he would have to leave her. And even though the most precious thing in all his life was leaning against him, his chest was tight. His departure from her life was just a postponement.

'Whatever happens, promise me one thing.'

She lifted her eyes to him. 'Anything. I'd promise you anything.'

Marcus smiled then, as her eyes caught his, and the love he felt in that very moment oozed from every pore of his skin that it hurt, it hurt more than he could ever imagine.

'Every night, look up towards the moon, and then remember, it will be the same moon that I'll be looking at too, longing to feel your touch and hear your voice.'

'Every night,' she promised.

He brushed a tear from her eye and kissed her forehead. The thought of keeping her safe was all that mattered to him. 'We have to keep moving.'

Soon, Marcus heard the distinctive and intermittent swish of the sea lapping against the shore. It brought images of lazy days, languorous and sultry, that stretched into the night. The broad expanse of St Andrews' beach snagged his mind. He loved his early morning walks, with the formidable cathedral's skeletal remains rising above the distinctive outline of the town behind him. He loved walking the length of the beach, especially when the tide was out, where the pristine sand stretched undisturbed for a mile or two, all the way to… It occurred to him he might never see such a sight again, but what had kept him going, even in his darkest times, was that maybe, maybe one day, he would walk along the beach with Helena. Such a thought was as precious to him as life itself. As his time with her moved from one day to the next, he had held on to it, even though he knew such a possibility was as far from his current reality and as unlikely as the war and all its suffering and death ending that very night.

A silver cone of moonlight shimmered in the placid waters of a bay, sheltered on each side by two lofty tree-covered hills.

'We're almost there. The monastery is at the top of that hill.' Helena pointed, and Marcus could make out tiny pinpricks of light on the summit.

'Don't worry, you won't have to climb all the way up there, there's a track that leads to it.'

Helena rapped her knuckles on the large wooden door to the monastery. They waited impatiently. A minute passed, then two. She struck the door several times with the heel of both hands.

Marcus frowned. 'What if there's no one here?' he asked out loud.

'It's a monastery. Where else would they be?'

Just then, they heard a key turning in the lock. Instinctively, Marcus' hand covered the handle of the pistol under his shirt.

'What time do you call this? We don't accept visitors at this hour.'

The heavy door creaked open, revealing a bearded monk, with eyes like coals and a scalp that looked like someone had buffed it smooth until it shone. He gazed at them expectantly.

'Forgive us, I know it's late, but this man is a British soldier who needs your protection and shelter.'

The monk pulled at his beard. 'That's an unusual request.'

'We don't have time to debate it.'

'Then you'd better come in.'

They followed the monk down a narrow corridor with several doors on each side. He stopped at one and, opening it, gestured for them to enter. The monk lit a candle that threw elongated shadows over the walls of the diminutive room. The room was windowless. This, too, emphasised its miniature proportions.

'We don't get many visitors. There is only this one cell that is not occupied. It's all I can offer you. It belonged to brother Manolis, who recently passed. God rest his soul.'

The room had a bed with a thin mattress and a single sheet neatly folded. The only furniture was a wooden wardrobe. Beside the bed, a crucifix adorned the wall.

'Morning prayers are at six. You're welcome to join us. After prayers, the Abbot will see you.' And, with a swish of his black robe, his footsteps retreated along the corridor.

Helena gazed down at the bed. 'I've never spent a night in a monastery.'

'It's a night of firsts. I've never shot anyone.'

'What's going to happen?'

'I don't know. That's the truth of it. If those two were working alone, they'll have to explain their wounds, and that won't involve mentioning me. If others are involved, we're still in real danger. Either way, I'm at a loss as to how I'm going to get off the island.'

'There's plenty of small boats, fishing boats. Maybe we can persuade someone to take you.'

'Where? I can't go to the mainland or Albania. I could, but what would the difference be? I'd have to walk all the way to unoccupied Europe. And there would be no one in their right mind who would put themselves at risk and sail a stranger halfway across the Mediterranean.'

In the dim light, he could see enough of her eyes to see the fear in them and the exhilaration of being safe gave way to despair.

So preoccupied had they been with their predicament, it took them by surprise to hear the soft murmur of prayers and of chants, voices that rose in unison. A performance of medieval tone, timbre, and melody. It seemed to encompass what was an audible orchestra of auditory perfection, mood, and peace.

Helena set the sheet on the bed. They lay down, their drained bodies welcoming the creak of the bed.

Helena's head rested on Marcus' chest. 'Their voices are beautiful. I've never heard anything quite like it. I could almost be in heaven,' she said, her voice drifting.

Marcus stroked her hair and, within a minute, Helena's breathing had deepened and he could tell she was sleeping.

It hadn't occurred to Marcus that their presence in the monastery was suspicious, and that tomorrow morning he may need to persuade the Abbot that he was who he said he was and not an agent of the Nazis.

Helena could not stay with him. His presence had put her in so much danger. All she was doing, by assisting him further, was increasing the possibility that when she went back to her house, the threat of discovery and constant danger would always hang over her. That was no way to live. He had grown used to being with Helena. She had been a constant presence in his life, a familiarity so precious to him, he could not imagine life without her. He depended on this woman so much that, without her, he was sure he could not muster the motivation to breathe. The thought of putting her life in danger shocked him, and that was the irony of it all. Each day, by staying with him, her life certainly was.

***

From the only window in the room, a bright shaft of sunlight caught a fresco of Christ gilding the wall in vibrant red, gold, and blue. Across from them, the abbot sat behind a large wooden desk. He had been writing on a sheet of paper and was nodding satisfactorily to its content.

The abbot was middle-aged, younger than Marcus had assumed. His beard erupted from his face and settled on his chest. He scratched the short wiry hair on his head with the end of the pen and asked them to take a seat. He scrutinised Marcus and Helena with a gentle smile. 'And your name is?' He directed his question towards Helena, his voice smooth, deep, and gravelly.

'Helena Bouzoukis, Reverend Father.'

The abbot raised his eyebrows. 'You are married. I see a ring on your finger.'

Helena shifted in the hard wooden chair. 'Yes. I am.'

'And who are you married to?'

'Vangelis Bouzoukis.'

'You are Vangelis' wife?'

'Yes.' She wanted to ask the abbot how he knew her husband, but the words would not pass her throat.

'We live in a small world indeed. Over the years, Vangelis has done some repair jobs here at the monastery.'

At the unexpected announcement of Vangelis, Marcus felt a small worm of jealousy. He knew his presence with a married woman would start an unwelcome interrogation and prying questions.

The abbot scratched his beard. 'Then where is Vangelis? Surely, he would not send his wife out into the night with another man, and a man wanted by the Germans. This is a peculiar situation indeed.' The abbot leaned forward and clasped his hands, now resting on the desk.

Helena knew an explanation was expected. 'Then, let me explain…'

Helena began at the beginning, from the moment Andreas told Vangelis he had found a man hanging from a tree. She did not disclose every detail. To Marcus' relief, Helena omitted to enlighten the abbot about how close they had become, nor did she speak of the love she now felt for this man, whose life was in the balance and at the mercy of this man of God and the church Helena had found to be a refuge frequently throughout her life. And now, she hoped with all her heart, it would continue to be so.

The abbot listened with an intent expression across his face. He did not interrupt Helena. He nodded occasionally, with an affirmative, 'uh, huh.' in a slightly raised tone that unnerved Marcus.

When Helena had finished, the abbot turned his gaze to Marcus. He spoke in broken English. 'My English bad, I try to speak.'

'I can speak Greek. It was the reason they chose me for this mission.'

The abbot nodded, visibly impressed. 'Yes. I can hear you speak our language very well. It comes as a relief to me. My English is bad, terrible. You are a British soldier, and you seek our help. You are here to aid the resistance in their fight against the Germans and the occupation of our country.'

'I am…' Marcus paused to find the right words. 'As Helena has explained, I didn't get the best of starts. I was supposed to parachute into a clearing and meet up with members of the local resistance group. Unfortunately, I landed in a tree and when I awoke my wounds were stitched and bandaged and I was being looked after by Helena and her family.'

The abbot's eyebrows furrowed. 'And what was the purpose of your mission?'

'Even though my mission was a failure, I cannot tell you that.'

'Why not?'

'I may have already been replaced.'

'So, what you are telling me is, it is quite likely there is already another agent who has taken your place, continuing where you have failed.'

Marcus flinched at the abbot's choice of words, yet he knew this was deliberate. It was intended to cause a reaction. 'I'd be surprised if there was not.'

'Doesn't this bother you? You are dispensable. Your value to your superiors has diminished. What makes you think they are even concerned about you? You'll already be forgotten about. You no longer have any value to them. You are as worthless to the allied cause as the flies are in this room.'

'It is the success and conclusion of our mission in this region that is of paramount importance to the war effort and its trajectory. That is the value of it. I'm just a cog in that machine who can be replaced at any time by another cog and another. Winning this war is what matters, not how we achieve it.'

The abbot smiled. 'Have you eaten?'

'No.'

Helena glanced at Marcus, obviously confused by the abbot's sudden departure from his line of questioning.

'Then let us have breakfast. I'm starving.'

They followed the abbot out of his room and along a corridor.

'What has just happened?' Helena whispered close to Marcus' ear.

'I think I must have passed the test.'

They entered another room where several rows of monks sat at benches, heads stooped and eating in silence. The abbot gestured for Marcus and Helena to sit and a monk approached, placing two plates of bread and cheese and two cups of water in front of them.

'Although we live a secluded life, we are not ignorant of the concerns of the world outside these walls.' The abbot touched Helena's hand. 'I cannot imagine your pain and suffering and what you have been through. If it can be of any comfort, and I hope it is, as a community, we pray for the souls of the little ones who lost their lives and were injured in the school tragedy.'

Helena swallowed; her throat ached, and she could feel her eyes sting. 'It is.' It was all she could think of saying.

'Your fluency in Greek was unexpected to say the least. How did you come to learn it?' The Abbott asked, chewing on a piece of bread.

'I'm an academic. I'm a better academic than I am a soldier. I resource and studying ancient Greek texts, especially biblical.'

The abbot smiled. 'You can read Greek as well.'

'Hebrew and Latin. It comes with the job.'

'My word. Your stay here is going to be an interesting one.' He wiped his mouth. 'We have a small library and some books I think you might be interested in. You're welcome to use it.'

'Thank you. I'd like that.'

'Then there is the question of you, Helena. In a way, it is easier with Marcus. As far as we know, no one knows he is here. But you conjure up many questions, the answers I am not sure of. What do we do with you? Is it safe for you to go back home? And what if you don't, then what? There will be suspicion. There's no doubt about that. People gossip and a missing woman whose husband has connections with the resistance will reach the ears of the Germans.' The abbot, undoubtedly perplexed, pondered the options.

'And then there is the question of what I see in front of me. Whatever has happened between yourself and Vangelis, it is plain to see you are no longer husband and wife, only in the eyes of the church. He has abandoned you. St. Paul refers to marriage as a "great mystery". The relationship of husband and wife is like that of Christ and the Church and yet some marriages cause more damage than good. These are difficult times; we have known nothing like it. What was once normal does not exist anymore. Life has changed beyond recognition. I can see what passes between the both of you. How you look at one another, how close you are. I'd have to be blind not to see it. Under the circumstances, I will not judge you.

The abbot took a drink of water. 'Last night, you shared the only available room we have. If you are to stay, this arrangement can continue.'

Helena had never heard a man of the church speak in such a manner. She witnessed the light of understanding in his eyes and, although her embarrassment lunged at her, his gentleness soothed it away and she felt aware of his extraordinary humility.

She recovered her composure and thanked him warmly.

He smiled. 'As long as it is possible, you have the protection of these walls.'

Under the eaves, swallows darted from their nests, swooping like graceful acrobats amongst the shade of the prunus trees. Twisting and darting over the small garden with its rectangular patches of vegetables and herbs, the swallows skirted the low wall where a precipitous drop met the cerulean blue of the sea below.

Marcus and Helena watched them, black shapes against the sky, their slender wings, long and narrow effortlessly gliding like ballerinas upon warm currents of air.

From here, they have seen most of the comings and goings of the three bays that stretch south below them. Some days, it is not uncommon to view a convoy of trucks ferrying soldiers, their helmets glistening in the sun's reflection.

At first, Marcus' heart was huge inside his rib cage as he waited anxiously, willing each convoy to continue its way and, as hoped, to pass the monastery. As the days passed and so did the trucks, Marcus found himself less vigilant, and casual with his diligence, until one time, he caught the glint of binoculars and a soldier training the lenses along the hills and shoreline. From then on, both he and Helena kept away from the edge of the perimeter wall and Marcus remembered the abbot's warning.

'A monastery will be the last place the Germans look for you. I emphasise 'last', which means they will come. You should understand this.' The abbot's voice still rang in his ears.

The monastery sat aloft an olive-wooded hill, whose rotundness and sharp gradient emerged from the sea with a Spartan air of impregnability. They had witnessed for themselves the spectacle of the sun melting into a scarlet and puce blushed horizon and, for a time, they adsorbed themselves in the luxury of such a sight that their imposed captivity, the ugly brutality and violence of war, the ever-present shadow of Vangelis, the constant threat of being discovered and the desperation of their situation fell from their thoughts.

Marcus delighted in these moments, never taking them for granted.

Each morning, when he had awoken in Helena's basement, he craved filling his lungs with air that was fresh and untainted from the enclosed and stifling environment that had become his world. It was a place where his mind longed for the colour of the sky, the contrast of shade, the bright tinge and quality of light and its ever-changing ambience. That effect can alter the heart and mind, but such influence was lost to him, and now it was found on a hill, in a place where he was, once again, hidden from the outside world.

It seemed to him he was forever in a constant state of disappearing. This time, it was different. It did not restrict him from the confines of four walls.

Around him were the visual revelations of a world he could not realise then. This new world was rich and sensuous. He could walk under the vast sky, marvel at the sea, its oasis of blue, inhale potent scents from the garden and the teasing aromas from the monastery's kitchen. His eyes could never tire of the whitewashed arches and walls and the domed roofed church. His ears never grew dull to the tintinnabulation of the three bells vibrating aloft in the bell tower that had become a landmark, reminding him that each morning granted him another day with Helena.

Mary Magdalene, Apostle to the Apostles.

The library was a place of silence and refuge from the outside world. Marcus was truly happy in the small space with its miniature window that framed the smooth cobalt sea and expansive sky. Not that it drew his eye often. Instead, the treasures of the books and manuscripts he found on the shelves preoccupied him. He felt alive and replenished. It was good to be amongst the theological mysteries, born from ancient minds, discussions, and debates. It was a place Marcus found illuminating with each new discovery and the treasures it gave up. He was a boy set loose in a toy shop.

On one of these visits, the Abbot brought Marcus' attention to a book he retrieved from a hidden panel in the shelves, bound in brown leather and decorated in golden lettering. With care, the Abbot placed it on the table and gently opened it, the leather creaking to Marcus' satisfaction. The book had been in the library since the monastery's construction. The abbot explained it dated back to the early church in the Holy Land, brought to Constantinople and believed to date back to the early 8th century.

'Is this book known to you?'

Marcus read the title. '*Mary Magdalene, Apostle to the Apostles*. No. I've never come across it.' Marcus' heart raced.

'It portrays Mary Magdalene as an apostle, but not only that, the author is quite clear, that she was Jesus' closest and the only one amongst all the disciples who truly understood his teachings. In that respect, it mirrors the Gnostic gospels and asserts her closeness to Jesus and the jealousy of Peter because she was a woman and one whom Jesus held in high regard amongst all the other disciples. It goes as far as suggesting that Mary Magdalene was the wife of Jesus.'

'How did it come into the possession of the monastery?'

'It's believed it was housed in the University of Constantinople and its Imperial Library and possibly before that, was amongst the remnants of the Library of Alexandria and part of its one hundred thousand volumes. It was amongst the artistic and literary treasures that were smuggled out of the city when it was sacked and fell to the Ottomans.

'It was brought to Greece by monks who were fleeing the great city and it has been encased in these walls ever since.'

'This is beyond anything I would ever have thought possible. I'd never in my wildest dreams thought I'd come across a book such as this,'

The abbot smiled knowingly. 'You can study it for only an hour a day. It's too precious to leave it out any longer in the natural light.'

'Of course. I understand.'

'Here.' The abbot handed Marcus a magnifying glass. 'Use this to appreciate the detail.'

Marcus held the instrument to his eye and leaned into the book. 'The illustrations are so detailed, and the colours look as rich today as when the ink was first placed on the paper. Just amazing. I haven't heard about this book. It obviously isn't catalogued.'

'It is just another book lost to history, except it isn't.'

'No. It's not. That's for sure.'

'You'll find some of the content, let's say, controversial. In parts, it offers a certain theological discussion that did not align with the church's teachings. It still does not. It proposes that Jesus had intimate relations with Mary Magdalene,

'Who is the author?'

The abbot scratched his chin. 'There has been a debate around that. Honestly, the church is not sure. It is influenced by the Gospel of Mary, which is the only surviving apocryphal text named after a woman.'

'I'm familiar with it.'

'Then you'll know it records the role of women in the early church. It was written at least a century after Mary Magdalene's death; it is *about* her. The surviving text comes from a fifth-century manuscript discovered in Cairo. If my memory serves me well, I think it was in 1896. Half the text in this manuscript no longer exists. However, third-century fragments of the gospel in the original Greek were discovered and published in 1938.'

'I've had the privilege to study the original fragments.'

'You have?'

'I was in Cairo as part of a delegation sent by the university.'

The abbot sat back in his chair and looked at Marcus and it was as if Marcus could read his thoughts. 'I know, I couldn't believe what I was looking at.' For a moment, he longed for those days. 'It seems like a different world. It was a different world.'

'One that I hope you will return to. Anyway, take advantage of this world.' The abbot gestured with his hand towards the book. 'Look at the opportunity it has given you.'

Helena rolled her eyes dramatically as Marcus, on his return, enthusiastically informed her of every detail and theological significance of his new find.

'My colleagues back in Edinburgh would give their right arm to spend an hour in that library, and here I am, ridiculously privileged to have its wonders at my disposal every minute of every day. God definitely has a sick sense of humour.'

'He does.' Helena's voice strained.

'I'm sorry, Helena. I've got carried away with myself,' Marcus apologised, guilt now hammering at him.

Helena inhaled a deep breath. 'I'm worried.' She flicked her hand through the air. 'We've been here on this hill for several weeks now. All I can think about is that my house has probably been burnt to the ground as a warning to others. It's my home. It's more than that. It's my memories. It's my only connection to Andreas.' She shook her head, trying to dislodge the image.

Marcus stepped towards her and pulled Helena's head into his chest. He caught the familiar scent of her hair as he kissed her head. 'Then, there is only one thing for us to do.'

At first, the abbot looked surprised. And then, incredulity etched across his face that not even his beard could disguise. It was inconceivably the most ludicrous idea he could imagine. In fact, he pronounced with an air of authority Marcus had seldom heard, 'It puts us all at risk. I cannot allow it.' And, with a wave of his hand through the air, as a final rebuke, he simply stated, 'It's unthinkable.'

'How can you just dismiss it like that? This is my home I am talking about. I need to know I still have a home. I've heard the Germans have raised houses to the ground.'

'I haven't heard of any such thing recently. There has been no report of such a thing. I'll get the local priest to check your house, Helena. That is the best and safest option under the circumstances. Wouldn't you agree?'

Helena turned on her heels and, striding towards the door, she flung it open. She spun round and faced them, a fire in her stomach flaming in her defiance. 'I do not need the permission of any man to visit my own home. I will go, with or without your blessing.'

The abbot sank into his chair with a heavy sigh, as Helena's heavy footsteps echoed down the corridor.

'She has a fighting spirit, Marcus. I like that, even though I'd prefer at this moment she did not. Never let it go out.'

'I wouldn't dare.'

Returning

The moment Helena saw her house, she knew they had visited. A cracked windowpane was visible. Even though the front door was closed, it showed the signs of being forcibly opened, and her garden had been ransacked of all its vegetables. She abandoned all discretion as she quickened her pace with a sense of purpose. She skirted a wall and followed a path. As she grew closer, fearing what she may find inside, Helena never broke her stride.

She stopped, and her hand gripped the door handle. The prospect of the unknown stood like a wall in front of her. She had to make a momentary decision. What if they were still inside? Through the cracked pane of glass, she glimpsed the inside of her house, feeling absurdly like an intruder. She could not imagine strangers in her house. The thought was abhorrent to her. Her heart pounded, her throat ached, her lungs were raw and bursting. With a tremendous physical effort, she kept from running away. Helena opened her front door and, for the first time in her life, she crossed the threshold with fear in her eyes.

She caught her breath.

Chairs had been upturned, crockery smashed to pieces on the stone floor. Her cupboards were emptied and stripped bare. They had toppled the heavy sideboard, lying like an upturned boat, its contents smashed across the stone floor in shards and fragments.

Helena stood in disbelief.

Strangers had defiled her home. Years of memories filled every room, good and bad, most precious, some despised. A life lived in these rooms, contained in these walls, was an emotional attachment beyond the meaning of words. It was in her bones and in her blood.

She knelt amongst the devastation, picking at the shattered remains of what had been the cherished ornamentation of a life full of simplicity. She fought off a strong desire to lie down.

She felt vulnerable.

A pungent stench grabbed her throat and a wave of nausea soared over her, and she swallowed and rubbed her eyes. It was then that the stark realisation hit her. They had urinated and defecated in the sink.

She felt violated.

Helena glanced around the room and she immediately drew her eye towards a photograph lying under the kitchen table. She scurried on all fours, like a lizard, and retrieved the photograph, still in its frame. She had discovered a streak of light in the darkness. 'Oh, my beautiful Andreas.' She hugged the frame close to her chest. It was then she noticed the opening, now exposed. They had found the basement. The unthinkable had happened.

She felt exposed.

Upstairs in her bedroom, the crunch of glass underfoot clawed at her heart. Her beautiful dressing table lay damaged beyond repair, the glass shattered. She gazed around her bedroom, numb and shocked. Helena's clothes lay thrown on the floor and over the bed. Her mother's dress still hung in its usual place but, like the long slash that split the wedding dress down its front it pierced her heart, the force of it bent her over and her cries, silent at first, muffled with her hand, could not dull the screams that came wave after wave. It was not just a dress; it was an entity with weight and texture; it was the only object of substance that bridged her loss.

Helena awoke to the sound of his voice. She thought she was dreaming, but when he touched her arm, she reached for him and he drew her into him, her skin warm and close.

'How did you get here so quickly?' Helena rubbed her eyes.

'By motorbike. It's ancient. It's been in the monastery for years. The abbot doesn't even know how it got there.

Anyway, I was as surprised as he was when it eventually kicked into life.'

'The abbot knows you're here?'

'He told me about the bike.'

For the first time that day, Helena could smile.

'The bastards. I'm so sorry, Helena.'

'It can all be replaced. I still have my house. Others have had their houses burned.'

Marcus surveyed the room. He knew she was being brave. Her fortitude amazed him and increased his hatred for the perpetrators.

'They know about us.'

'They found the basement.' Marcus wanted to turn back the clock. He should have left her. At least she would have been safe in her house, and this would never have happened. He blamed himself for the carnage around him. His stomach tightened, suffused with rage.

He crossed to the window. 'We need to go.' He stood tense and alert. Marcus had left the motorbike lying partially concealed in the long grass. He could still hear its rhythmical rumbling. He could not afford to kill the engine with the fear that it would not start again.

'Wait!'

Helena rushed to the wardrobe and reaching inside, she opened a concealed latch and pulled out an envelope. To his relief, Marcus recognised it. 'Thank God. At least they didn't find the money.'

'What happens now Marcus?'

'We need to go. You can't stay here. Take what clothes you need and lock the house up.'

He heard it escape her lips, a soft moan. He knew her intention, and it terrified him. 'I can't. This is all I have.'

'If this was the work of the resistance, your home is safe. You are Vangelis' wife, and this is his house. But why would they do this? It doesn't make sense. If it was the

Germans, we would be standing in the rubble and smoke of your house.'

'You think this was Panos, the bastard?'

'I could be wrong. All I know is you can't stay here. Look, we can tidy up and lock the house. You are valuable to him. He can bargain with the Germans and hand you over to them. We'll go back to the monastery.'

'He is right, Helena.'

Marcus' hand flashed to the handle of the pistol. Helena gasped and then her face broke into a wide smile.

'Christina! What are you doing here?'

'Since the night you left my house, I've been, at a distance, watching your home. Keeping an eye on it and the comings and goings… I saw Marcus.'

For the second time, this old woman had inadvertently, but with kind intention, chastised him. but

'Did you see who did this?' Marcus asked.

She nodded. 'Two men. One with a bad limp.'

'Panos!'

'The other spoke Greek, but with an accent. I think he was a German, but he was not in uniform.'

Marcus frowned. 'You're certain?'

'I've heard enough of them trying to speak our language to know how they sound.'

'Could you hear what they were talking about?'

She sighed. 'Not really. They were friendly with each other. That's all I needed to know.'

'That's it then. The Germans will look for us both. It was always going to come to this.'

'Listen to me, Helena,' Christina pleaded. 'You cannot stay here. You have to go with Marcus.'

Helena shook her head quickly.

'If you stay, you will certainly die. The reprisals! Remember the reprisals!' This time Christina was almost shouting.

'Christina is right. It is not safe anymore.'

The look on Helena's face was enough to kill him. For the second time, he was asking her to abandon the only thing left in her world which tied her to her past, the life she knew, and the child she loved and lost.

'They have taken my son,' Christina announced.

Marcus heard Helena's intake of breath. 'Dr Iannis.'

'He has been gone for several days now. I don't even know if he is still alive.'

Helena was horrified. 'Christina, I'm… so sorry, that's awful.'

To Marcus' astonishment, Christina's voice was strong and undeterred. 'Don't be. We're at war. We're all soldiers in our own way and we're all fighting for Greece. He knew the dangers and their consequences. As do you, Helena. As do you.'

Marcus reached out and gently took her hand. He looked at her hopeless face, her shapeless despondency, her sunken eyes, wet with tears and a look of confusion. And it killed him, for he was, in part, to blame for this.

She yearned for Andreas. Helena felt the air burst from her lungs, an outpouring of grief she could no longer hold back. Her entire body shook as she sank into Marcus' arms, the weight of her anguish crushing her over the death of her son, her beautiful and innocent Andreas.

A ribbon of memories flashed before her. Was it coincidence or fate? They had found each other among the saddest moments of their lives. When she first saw Marcus' broken body, a chill ran through her, but she knew even then. As Dr Iannis set Marcus' shattered bones and Helena cleaned the sutured lacerations, she prayed he would live. It was a reaction she now realised there was no control over. Before Marcus, her world sat on a pinhead, swaying from impossible decisions and the frenzy of her thoughts to the plausibility of acceptance. Her marriage had offered protection and attachment. Inevitably, there would be hard times. It was to be expected, after all. The trials of married life did not come with a manual. It was natural. Such judgement disturbed her, for she thought herself unable to affect her own life. She was caught in a loveless marriage, enmeshed in guilt and the need to protect her son.

In the beginning, she thought it would settle itself. Every couple goes through this. It was normal, she told herself. It would pass. Until she couldn't pretend any longer. They stopped talking. Yes, they conversed, but it was out of necessity, dispensed without feeling, devoid of detail. There was a distance between them, a barrenness of shared intimacies. Being loved and of loving ebbed from her like a river in a drought. They had both lost their way, each struggling to confront the ramifications that undoubtedly lay in front of them. She found to her relief that each passing month loosened her need for him as he became more detached, immersed in the guilt that ate at him. He considered himself worthless. The war had taken him from her. Like a spiteful lover, it drew him into the arms of the resistance and Vangelis relished its embrace. The call of the motherland was irresistible.

She remembered the moment of recognition on Vangelis' face. He knew. How could he not? Somehow, it made it easier for him to leave. It eased his decision. It gave him permission.

Within her heart, the choice was simple, but her head spun with its complexities. She craved to be free of the anguish and uncertainty. She needed the reassurance that Marcus felt the same and it left her breathless as each time, he reflected it with every word, every smile and spontaneous touch of his hand. It was literally breath-taking. It was bewildering. She could not help herself. It was as simple as that. She knew the treachery it entailed, but how could she deny what she felt? It left her breathless.

Vangelis had saved Marcus' life by cutting him from the tree and bringing him to their home. And in doing so, he had also saved Helena's life.

Most nights, when Marcus had lain in the basement still too ill to wake, Helena had sat alone with him and watched his face, and it amazed her to learn she grew to adore each curve and every angle.

It would be short-lived, that much she understood. She wouldn't be persuaded to leave with him. He had tried to convince her; how hard he had tried. He loved her, he really loved her and, in return, she loved him too. She knew that love was not enough, and all she would have would be her precious memories to immerse herself in. She hoped it would be enough.

Days had passed since her visit to the house. She lay on the hard mattress in the little cell, as the familiar scent of incense permeated the air. Helena found it impossible not to be moved by the deep and hypnotic incantations of the monks' nightly prayers. It was moments like these Helena contemplated the possibility that it was possible to believe in an omnipotent God. Then the stark reality of the grief and despair of her fellow villagers and countrymen struck her. All were under sentence of death. Why would a God of goodness not dispatch of such evil? Why would he allow such suffering upon innocent men, women, and children? Which side would he listen to when priests blessed their countries' armies in his name?

Helena bit the inside of her cheek. There had been news earlier in the day from the abbot. The Germans were now in the ascendancy and, throughout the island, the resistance cells were being dismantled and broken up with each new arrest and interrogation. The abbot advised them that, even though this was detrimental to the resistance's efforts to further the prospect of Marcus' escape, the abbot was confident it would now only be a matter of days. Word had reached him that his attempts at requesting the help of the church hierarchy in Athens had borne fruit. A British warship was in the vicinity and would pass Corfu, heading for Alexandria. It had been arranged that a local fishing boat would take Marcus off the island and meet up with the ship at a prescribed area and time.

Helena ascribed her nervousness to this latest development. It was finally happening, after all the waiting and uncertainty, enduring the agony of knowing there was no other choice, that eventually, he would leave her.

They had two more nights together. This slippage of time horrified her. Andreas surfaced in her mind as he always did. She needed to stay close to Andreas' grave and submit to the protectiveness her instincts craved, for she could not abandon her son. All her maternal feelings were against it. She despaired at the turmoil of her feelings.

She had been tempted many times to leave with Marcus. After all, the reward would be a lifetime together. Even if she could, it would be a selfish betrayal. She was trapped. Mostly, she was afraid of being alone.

The Abbot's words reverberated in her mind, 'If you love him, let him leave.' Helena could not help thinking, with the greatest reluctance, it was her only option. It filled her with a lurching emptiness, and she found tears filling her eyes. She had never known such vulnerability, this irreversible loss.

She knew it was him. She heard his footsteps coming down the narrow corridor, one heavier than the other, because of a slight limp. When Marcus entered the shadowy room, his eyes looked heavy and tired. She watched him cross to the washbasin. He unbuttoned his shirt, removed it, and washed his hands and face in the water. When he turned, she was sitting on the bed, her eyes fixed on him. She loved this man more than life itself. He had shown her a side of herself she thought had died never to be resurrected. He was her Christ, and she was his Lazarus.

Marcus moved from the basin and stood in front of her. Helena's face turned up anxiously to Marcus and, to her surprise, he was smiling. She opened her mouth to speak, but he put his finger to her lips and said gently, 'No more words.'

He cupped her face in his hands and knelt before her. He kissed her longingly, his hands now full of her hair, her fingers curling around his neck. Helena pulled him to the bed, her lips seeking his mouth once again. She felt his hands running the length of her body over her hip and thigh, his touch tender. His head moved to her throat, her shoulder and breasts, his lips feathery against her skin, his delicate touch sending lightning through her. Her hands ran through his hair as he kissed each inch of her abdomen and, when he touched her with his tongue, it felt as if he sought the very essence of her as every cell and bone awakened.

When he swelled and moved inside her, beneath his weight, she found his mouth again. The deeper they descended, she sank into the core of herself.

'I love you, Helena.' It was the most intimate of sensations.

Her breath came harder and she closed her eyes.

'Open your eyes. Look at me.' His voice was insistent with a slight forceful intent, fearful that the moment would pass.

Helena turned her head, and she fixed her eyes on him. She could feel the fluttering rising inside and sensed his gaze upon her. Her eyelids flickered and, desperately, she attempted to focus on his face. The elation from her love for him opened a depth of euphoric indulgence that previously she had never known. She raked her fingers through his hair and, when he sighed and called her name, she too called his.

At The Mercy of Circumstance

The sky was a dappled rose as Marcus rested a hand on the wall and looked out over the sea. The evening was warm and pleasing in the aromatic fug of the garden, where a monk filled a basket with herbs and vegetables. Light drained from the sky as a fishing boat carved its passage towards the shore, birds chasing the air above it. In such moments, Marcus thought it difficult to imagine the world was at war. It was a world he had experienced, with its bitter joys and contradictions. He gazed at the boat as it grew larger, and his stomach sank with the rapid way time was passing towards the inevitability that was now clear to him. He felt a sudden dragging inside.

Marcus heard footsteps and, as Helena walked towards him, he felt her watching him and the bliss it secured made him turn with a smile on his face.

'I thought you'd be out here.' She stood with him and watched the nightly display of glorious orange and fiery red that scorched the Ionian sky.

'I'm that predictable?'

'It's an attribute I like about you. It means you're stable and reliable.'

'Not boring and conventional?'

'No. You're certainly not that.'

'Good,' he said satisfactorily.

'What were you thinking about?'

'With each minute that passes, it gets closer.'

She was silent.

'The ship that will take me from you. It's out there somewhere.'

'I've tried not to think of this. I knew one day you would have to leave me, so I tried to live in the moment. It was easier that way. No. It was not easy. It was the better of the two options.'

There was a silence between them. Helena seemed to be lost in thought.

'I've often wondered if women had power, led nations and filled parliaments, and ruled as governments, there would be no more wars. We wouldn't carry our children in our wombs to sacrifice them at the altar of greed and hatred for those who didn't think like us or whose religion differed from ours. We would talk to each other and see the common good and celebrate what united us. That's what would be important, not what divided us. There would be no division, just a common humanity.'

'I'd look forward to such a time.'

'There's something I need to tell you, Marcus. It has troubled me these last few days, but I can't let you go without you knowing. It would be wrong of me. Unforgivable.'

'You're scaring me, Helena. What is it?'

'It is your right to know.'

'Know what?'

Helena put her arm around him and took his hand and gently placed it on her stomach. He looked into her eyes and found them literally breath-taking. 'You're pregnant!'

'I am.'

'My God!'

'I didn't want to tell you until I was sure, until there was no doubt. I couldn't let you go without telling you.'

'A baby!' He tilted his head towards the sky. 'I can't leave you now. I can't do this.'

'You must.'

'No. I can't. I won't.'

'You have no choice. We have no choice; it has been taken from us.'

'You have our child inside you.'

'That's why you will return after the war. We will wait for you.'

He would not abandon her. He was going to be a father. It was an exhilarating prospect, life changing and surreal. That he was speaking such words was incredible. He was in a state of shock. There was no other way to describe it.

He touched Helena's stomach with his palm. 'Hello, little man. Remember the sound of my voice and know I'll be talking to you every single day, no matter where I am.' He looked at Helena and stumbled over his words. 'I don't want to go.'

'I know. They are coming for you. You must.' A spasm of anxiety tempered her voice.

'I've just been told the most amazing thing anyone could be told and from this moment my life has changed and… I'm leaving you.' His face darkened. 'What kind of man does that?'

'One who wants to survive and grasp the opportunity to watch his child grow. I will not be responsible for your death. I have already lost a child in this war, and I will not lose the only man I've ever loved. Do you hear me? Do you understand me, Marcus?' Helena demanded.

He nodded. Marcus' head spun with exhilaration and dread; a cacophony of emotions that left him drained.

If he were to stay, what then? They would be in constant fear for their lives. The monastery could not hide them indefinitely. Heavily pregnant or with a baby, the prospect of evading capture would be slim. On her own, Helena would be just another Greek woman. The villagers would protect and shelter her and her baby. She would become invisible. As long as the Germans occupied Corfu, they would be forever hidden, moving from one safe house to the other.

Marcus gathered himself. 'Nothing will stop me from coming back for you. I don't care about my job, my life in Edinburgh. This is where I belong, with you, with our child.' His mind was working fast now. 'I can work for the museum in Athens, for the university, as well. It would be a coup for them to have someone of my standing in academia working for them. We could move to Athens and make it our home. We could be a family.'

His words excited and soothed her, subsiding the fear that lurked inside her. She, too, could imagine such a life. She dared to think it a possibility, but that was not now. How long would they be apart from one another? Separated by sea and land and events and circumstances out of their control. Absence and distance were real, not the promise of a life she could not comprehend. It was an untouchable existence, an unattainable reality. She wished it to be true with all her heart, but she would not hold on to it. The life she would lead when the war was over was not of this time, but the absence of Marcus was, and that forced a torrent of uncertainties upon her and, although her hands shook with the tremors inside her, the irresistible uprising of survival was absolute.

'There is a cost to life, and ours will be absence and distance.'

He took a deep intake of breath and kissed her on the forehead.

How long would the residual rapture of her company sustain him when he found himself confined to the constraints of Alexandria, or wherever his next posting would be? How many months and years would he endure the torment of not knowing if Helena was safe? She was pregnant, he reminded himself, as if he had just woken from a dream and discovered it was no longer a dream but real. His mind chased possibilities: being pregnant was not without risk. It could be inexplicably dangerous, not only for the mother, but for the child as well. There would be no way of knowing if mother and child were healthy, or indeed survived. He tried to think positively, to quell his fears, but the implications of being apart and separated by a war that had darkened the world for years, and maybe for years to come, fermented the anxiety in his thoughts.

Clamorous uncertainty engulfed him. They were all at the mercy of circumstance, he conceded.

Leaving

Marcus felt a hand on his shoulder. 'It is time.' The abbot smiled at him but could not hide the sadness in his eyes. Helena held his hand, and he felt her fingers tighten around his. Earlier, they had lain together for hours waiting for the light to fade in the room, knowing what the evening would bring.

As they stood below the belltower, each monk passed in solemn procession and wished him a safe journey. He felt a gnawing in the pit of his belly, and it was because there was no longer any question in his mind what he had to do.

A holdall was slung around his shoulder. Inside was the pistol and his cigarette case securely placed in an inside pocket. It was now the most precious thing he owned, as it contained a slight cutting of Helena's hair. Along with the pistol and cigarette case, wrapped and tied in leather, was the book from the library, *Mary Magdalene, Apostle to the Apostles*. The abbot was fearful that if the Nazis found it, the church would lose it forever and it would become another lost piece of stolen art and priceless literature to fill the coffers of the German elite. And the abbot's words still hummed in his ears, '*At least some greater good could come out of all this suffering*.'

Marcus did not have to be convinced. He knew its worth financially and historically. It was an academic treasure that had to be preserved. He promised the abbot he would secure the book in the care of the British Museum in London and, one day, after the war, return it to the monastery.

At the monastery gate, two members of the resistance, rifles dangling from their shoulders, both with a serious countenance that masked their heavily bearded faces, met them.

They progressed down the mountain at a rapid pace, the track lit by silver moonlight as the monastery shrank from view, swallowed by the dark with only the occasional and discernible flickering yellow light above them. The escorts had warned them not to talk. The only sound around them was the movement of their bodies, their heavy breathing, and unseen creatures scurrying in the undergrowth on each side of the track.

Once on flat terrain, they proceeded more cautiously, each step inching Marcus towards the beach and the boat that would take him from Helena. His stomach was hollow and nauseous. She was by his side, much to the objections of their escorts. They had mumbled their concerns to the abbot, but he, too, was adamant this was how it was to be. There was no other way. She had to see with her own eyes Marcus leaving on the boat, carried by the Ionian to safety, and one day make it back to Edinburgh. Helena could not live another day otherwise.

They crouched in the darkness behind rocks. Before them on the beach, and on each side of the inlet, two ominous hills rose from the sea like giants.

From his jacket, one escort pulled out a silver pocket watch and peered at its cracked screen. He leaned an arm on the rock and squinted into the darkness. The darkness seemed to amplify the rhythmic sound of the tide bubbling at the shore.

'There!' He pointed a long finger. Marcus could just make out the curved shape of a rowing boat and then the flash of a white light, then darkness, and then another flash.

Helena kissed him. 'Come back to me. I'll be waiting.'

He couldn't believe he was leaving her. His heart ached. He encased her face with his hands and stared into her eyes. He had to capture her face and take in every detail, imprint her permanently in his mind so she could never leave him. How he wished he had a photograph of her. He kissed her, never wanting to leave her lips.

'You must go,' the man with the watch urged him.

'I'm going now. I love you more than life itself.' He tried, but it was as if it paralysed his arms. He could not remove them from her.

'Helena! Tell him!' The panic in the man's voice was by now raw.

Helena pulled away from Marcus. 'More than life itself,' she repeated.

And then, heartbroken, he turned away from her. He ran towards the sea, his boots heavy in the sand. He clasped the bag close to his side. The water surprised him. It was cold, and it felt like he was wading through treacle. He thought he heard a rumble somewhere off in the distance. To his immediate relief the sea was shallow, just covering his thighs as he reached the rowing boat. A darkened figure called out a greeting and pulled Marcus into the boat. As Marcus sat, the man, probably only twenty Marcus thought, rowed.

'We will reach the fishing boat in about ten minutes.'

It was then Marcus realised there were tears in his eyes. The rowing boat was almost out into the open sea. Perpendicular cliffs stood like walls, waves lapping the rocks.

'Over there, look, the boat.' Marcus turned and looked across the dark water. The silhouetted shape of a small fishing boat hovered less than fifty feet away. He pulled the bag close to him and prayed this was not a mistake.

And then, towards the shore, he saw the headlights and shadowy figures jump from the truck. They disappeared, merging into the distance, and then reappeared, small and blurred. They seemed to float before his eyes.

Marcus felt his throat burn. He saw the flashes before the air splintered with the crack of gunfire. He could barely breathe. The moon appeared from a covering of cloud, casting an eerie light over the beach. A figure, not that of a man, but a woman; it was Helena. She ran towards the sea. The German soldiers had reached the sand and Marcus could not detect any movement from the cluster of rocks he had emerged from only minutes previously. To his horror, a soldier raised his rifle and aimed. Time slowed and Marcus' world stopped. His heart shattered. Helena fell forwards as if invisible hands had yanked at her, thrusting her body into the air as she tumbled and fell.

Marcus screamed her name and buried his face in his trembling hands. When he looked up, to his horror, two soldiers were dragging her body across the sand, and he could make out the lifeless shapes of two more lying near the rocks.

Edinburgh

2018

Atonement

Across the street, the sun teeters at the edge of the roofs, permeating the room in soft light, dispelling the opaque shadows. His eyes have become accustomed too. Jason has sat awake, sleep deadened by the constant activity in his mind.

At some point, he must have slept. As he tilts his mobile, the screen flashes a white light. It is seven in the morning. He remembers looking at his phone at four o'clock. Only three hours sleep. *'Time is all around us wherever we are.'* This has always been his reply when asked why he never wears a watch. It displays on our mobiles, on our laptops, on walls, on televisions, cookers, it's everywhere, it's always accessible.

And now, time has tapered to this single moment. The decision he is about to make has its beginnings in a place of yesteryear, its roots set amongst those whose lives have been lived, but are now alive and real, and as relevant now as they were then. They have become known to him, in a manner. Instead of being lost and buried in the past, they have become an integral part of his life. It is a connection that spans decades. It is the bond of what it means to be family.

Jason has spent the hours transfixed by the ghosts that stayed with him through the night. He contemplated it all.

He has contemplated the weeks Marcus spent in the basement, where with tenderness and patience, Helena selflessly attended to his wounds, waiting for the strength that, over time, would seep into his limbs, his bones and mind.

Jason recalled the sense of Marcus' life in Edinburgh tipping away from him, replaced by this woman with deep sad eyes, her hair thick and wavy, tracing his skin like the touch of feathers as she nursed and cleansed him.

At night, the silence around Marcus was so dense, it seemed the world had ended. And even during the day, like a thick blanket, the darkness was only dispelled by the light Helena's presence spawned.

Jason recalled Helena's entrapment in a loveless marriage by a husband whose eyes were blind towards her, whose mind cast her as fraudulent, whose guilt ate at him, and whose madness stole him. She was a shadow to him, as surely he was dead to her.

And unimaginably, amongst all of this, Helena lost her son, her little boy. How could she survive, her heart being ripped from her? How can anyone survive such a nightmare?

She came to realise she hungered to be with Marcus just as much as he craved to be with her. Yet, she could not leave her son for Marcus and the offer of a life of endless possibilities. Unhappiness was also a choice. Jason understands this now. It was the only one Helena could take.

Jason lets out a sigh and realises he has been holding his breath. He runs his hands through his hair and frowns. Stretching his taut arms and legs, he heads for the kitchen. A dull ache spreads along his forehead. He considers filling the kettle, but the feeling of grime under his clothes helps him to decide he is in more need of a shower than a coffee.

Showered and changed, he runs his hand over the cover of *Mary Magdalene, Apostle to the Apostles*. Bubbles rise in his stomach. The colours are as vibrant as the day the monk etched them onto the paper. He was not sure how these things had worked. Had it been a collaborative effort? Or had one individual painstakingly spent weeks, or months, applying the inks? It is a work of art. He holds the book and his smile curls. *Literally, the weight of history in my hands*, he tells himself.

Even after his shower and coffee, his head was still foggy, his headache continuing to gnaw at him. His flight was at three in the afternoon. He would try to catch some sleep then.

Jason isn't sure for how long he will be gone, but he packs a light bag. He finds a box delivered by Amazon a few days previous. He is glad he hasn't thrown it out. The book fits snugly into the box. Jason slides the box, with the book, into his hand luggage. It will stay with him for the duration of the flight.

It is still early. He has three hours to spare. He looks out of the window and inspects the sky. It is cloudy, but there is no sign that it is about to rain. I need a walk, he tells himself. His flat is part of a building on Sandport Place that exemplifies the recent regeneration of Leith. Its reputation as a place of poverty and prostitution, and the harsh side of life, has been erased from its streets and character. It is now a vibrant area brimming with delis, café bars, and restaurants.

Jason heads over the bridge that straddles the Water of Leith. He turns left, ambles along the cobbles of The Shore, where he takes a seat outside Toast, his favourite place to eat breakfast. He orders an egg benedict with smoked salmon and a black coffee and watches the reflection of the buildings opposite in the placid water.

During the war, Marcus was several years younger than Jason. It is a fact that has made Jason not only admire the resolve and strength of character Marcus displayed, but wonder how he would have coped with the physical and psychological rigours of being wounded, near to death in a country at war, in a small windowless room, relying on the charity of strangers for his every need.

Within a few moments, Marcus' world shrank to just four walls. The low ceiling had become his sky, the world he knew suddenly beyond his reach. Jason tried to imagine not being able to see the sky, and breathe the air around him, and hear everyday life. All were so familiar, all had become so mundane. Most of the time, his mind did not even register the sensory pleasures around him.

There is fear and there is a fear that is so raw that brutalises every waking hour. What thoughts must torture the mind, knowing that life could end at any moment? Each morning, Marcus opened his eyes and must have wondered if that day would be his last. The possibility of being discovered, tortured, and shot would have been a constant torment. Jason has tried to comprehend how this would feel, and he has concluded he cannot give it suitable justice of thought. It is too far removed and beyond anything he has ever experienced or known.

A shiver comes over him.

How can he even manage to consider such an existence, when he does not even know what it means to be alone and vulnerable? The world is not closed to him. It is open and instantly available with a single tap: friends, family, news, media.

And what of the book? This was Marcus' world. The ancient penetrating the present. Jason would give anything to understand the unfamiliar alphabet and to read it. Although he is careful when handling the pages, he feels an undeniable guilt when doing so, as if he is encroaching upon its secrets without the permission to do so.

He is familiar with the Mary Magdalene that Catholicism portrays, the brief mentioning of her, but this version portrays Mary as an apostle, as Jesus' closest and most loved disciple. She is the only one amongst his followers who really understood his teachings. There are also suggestions that she was Jesus' companion, she and Jesus were in a relationship and, possibly, she was the wife of Jesus.

There is a sense of urgency. What did all this mean? Did understanding the past help us live better lives? Is this why he feels so compelled to deliver the book to the monastery? It is his attempt to numb the pain, to dull the grief and loss. Is this all about Jason? Is this his personal atonement, just like the Ian McEwan novel he feverishly devoured when at university?

He wants to stop the noise screaming in his head; the anger at himself, the self-hate, the resentment at what he had done and what he should have done. A veneer of normality, of smiles, laughter and humour is the public persona he projects. It is a natural performance, but it is a performance all the same. He is an actor of convenience; he has told himself. When the curtain falls, and he is alone, the dark shadows descend and engulf any slither of rational thought and a relentless weight pushes down on him, his lungs gasp and the ache in his stomach rushes upwards and grips his throat.

His mobile buzzes and Rachel's name appears on the screen.

'Hiya, Jason.'

'Rachel!'

'When are you off to the airport?'

'Soon. I'm just getting something to eat.'

'Nice. Where are you?'

'I just nipped along to Toast.'

'Let me guess, egg benedict and smoked salmon?'

'I know. How sad am I?'

'Nicely predictable, I would say.'

'It's a nice morning, and I needed the fresh air.'

'You, okay?'

'I'm fine.'

'You're crap at lying, Jason.'

'Ach. I'm just… I've just been thinking about a few things, that's all.'

'If it's about what I think it is, you can't keep it bottled up. That's not healthy.'

'I know, I know. In fact, I'm going to collect my repeat prescription after this.'

'Good. Remember to take it with you. It helps.'

'I won't forget. It's at the top of my list,'

'You don't make lists, Jason.'

He laughs then. 'Well, if I had one, it would be the first thing on it.'

'I've not told you, but I think you're doing a superb thing.'

'I hope so. It feels right, and that's what's important. I'd give anything to read the book, just like Marcus.'

'You would?'

'You sound surprised.'

'It's not your usual thriller.'

'No, but it's thrilling to know I'd be reading a book that was written nearly eleven centuries ago and it's not a copy.'

'It is pretty mind-boggling.'

'To think I'm touching the very pages the author wrote on and touched himself is surreal. I'm scared that I might mark it, or, God forbid, rip it, so it's packed securely in my bag.'

'In your suitcase?'

'No. My hand luggage. I'm not letting it out of my sight. If I need to go to the toilet, it's coming with me.'

'What about going through security with it? What if you get stopped and they search your bag?'

'They won't. On the scanner, it'll look just like a normal book.'

'Well, make sure there's nothing else in your bag that will make them want to look. All your liquids should be in 100ml bottles and…'

'I know, Rebeca. Don't worry. I'm sure it'll be fine.'

'Remember to phone.'

'I'm not moving there.'

'Just phone me. Promise?' Her voice hardens.

'I will. Promise.'

'Good.'

For the first time, there is a silence.

'There's one more thing.'

'Yes.' He stretches the word.

'I'm pregnant!'

Corfu

2018

A Fortuitous Encounter

It has been two days since he arrived. The calm and blue sky has not changed in that time. On the journey from the airport, the taxi driver informed Jason it had not rained for two months.

From the balcony, he sips the last of his water and gazes out over the plush landscape of knotted forests. Green as far as the eye can see, swathing the bank of hills that tower towards the sky.

Back in his room, he places the book in the small safe sitting behind the glass sliding doors of a fitted wardrobe. He closes the safe door and applies the code, checking that it is securely locked. Satisfied, he heads out, along the corridor where large ceramic pots stand like sentries, then he emerges into a large and airy reception area, with its plush leather sofas, glass top tables, and floor to ceiling windows. The receptionist is talking into the phone but still manages a smile as Jason passes through.

A patched stone drive leads from the hotel to a narrow road and a cluster of restaurants and café bars, and, further along, amongst the trees and well-kept gardens, the plush two to three-storey sparsely populated hotels and apartments.

The morning air is already warm, the air fringed with heat, as Jason walks the slight gradient that leads towards the outskirts of the village.

On his way, he passes the timeworn walls of a church and belltower, a graveyard with dilapidated headstones, leaning with age and demise. The village clings to the hill in a maze of narrow lanes and streets, barely wide enough for single vehicles to manoeuvre hesitantly along.

He wonders how much has changed since Marcus' time. Suddenly, he is aware his breath is tight in his throat, and his heart is pounding. He is amongst the very streets and lanes Helena called home.

A group of children head towards him, heavy rucksacks bulging with books strapped to their backs.

Free from the confines of the classroom, they are exuberant, chatting and smiling amongst each other. A playful skirmish between two boys grabs the attention of the others, who become vociferous in their encouragement of the unfolding spectacle. Jason smiles at the pretend bravado and, although he can't understand their words, it sounds light-hearted, jovial teasing, all accompanied by spirited pushing. The others continue to spur the two boys on, laughing and smiling as they do so. Some girls shake their heads, unimpressed with these juvenile antics. They hurry past Jason without giving him a second glance.

Andreas would have been the same age as these children. It is a thought not lost on him. In their history lessons, did these children learn about the horrors and suffering of war? Did they know it visited their village and scarred the lives of every family? Had they been told the story of the school bombed by the Nazis? A meaningless termination of life where death was the only figure that drained years of happiness and purpose.

It occurs to him then that Andreas' grave would be in the church graveyard. All the children were buried there. Jason has already passed the church. He turns and heads back down the street. Jason sees the belltower first and then the walls of the church come into view. He quickens his step. When he reaches the entrance to the graveyard, he pauses, his enthusiasm suddenly dented. It occurs to him that the inscriptions on the headstones will be written in Greek; he will only recognise the numbers of the year. Then again, the year of birth and of death should make it easier for him to discern the age. The self-congratulatory smile that crosses his face swiftly disappears as he pauses on the verge of the graveyard. He swallows the last remnants of gratification as the symbol of Helena's grief and pain is about to become not just words written on a page but a real, ever present and tangible entity.

The cemetery looks cluttered with headstones but, as he moves closer, he can see it is set out in a uniformed pattern. He feels an edge of trepidation accompany him as he moves methodically from one grave to the next, scanning each headstone. He wipes beads of perspiration from his forehead when it dawns on him that Helena's grave may also be here.

Would the Germans have allowed her to be buried in the cemetery? Jason thinks not. They shot her whilst she was aiding the enemy. She was an example of what happens to those who help the allies.

An uneasiness rises inside him at the thought of what might have befallen Helena. He hopes that her body was handled with care and respect. Christina would have done everything she could to make it so.

In the centre of the cemetery, there is a bench beside a tree and, needing to escape the sun, Jason seeks the shade. He settles himself on the bench and straightens his back. He notices a posy of flowers recently placed in a vase. Although most of the graves are old, it is heartening to know that those still connected to them care for some.

Jason clasps his hands together and frowns. It sickens him to think there might be no evidence that a woman gave her life in such tragic circumstances to aid her country's fight against the evil that had consumed it and possibly wiped out all memory of her. As would have been the fate of thousands just like her, Jason considers for a moment.

He wonders if Marcus was ever tempted to return to Corfu. As far as he knows, he never did. Jason can understand why. It would have been too painful.

He is staring at his feet when a shadow appears on the ground. He lifts his head to find an old woman standing in front of him, her head bent slightly as she studies him. She is dressed from head to foot in black and leans at an angle on her walking stick. Her face is lined, yet her eyes defy her age, a blue, so striking Jason feels he could be looking into a cobalt sea. She has the face, he thinks, that can keep a secret.

'Kalispera.' She gestures to sit.

Jason shuffles along the bench to make space. He smiles awkwardly, not knowing what else to do.

She steadies herself with her walking stick and, stiffly, she lowers herself onto the bench with a deep sigh.

She turns and smiles. 'Einai zesto simera.' (It is warm today.)

'I'm sorry. I can't speak Greek.'

'I know some of the English. My daughter and grandchildren teach me.'

'You speak it well.'

'I come every day. My husband, he is just over there.' She points an arthritic finger towards a corner of the cemetery. When Jason looks, there is no one there. And then it occurs to him, this is where her husband is buried.

He nods.

'I sit every day. There is only me sitting under this tree.'

'Would you like me to leave?',

'Oxi! You stay.'

They sit in silence, then the old woman says, 'Strange. Someone so young sitting amongst the dead.'

'I was looking for someone.'

'Who?'

'A young boy. He died during the war.'

'The war?'

'The Second World War.'

She looks puzzled. 'Why do you want to find this boy?'

'It's a long story. My great grandfather knew him.'

'This was a long time ago.'

'Yes. It was. The boy was a pupil at the school. It was bombed during the war, and he was buried here in the village.'

'I remember.'

Jason's eyes widened. 'You remember?'

'I was born just before the war. As a child, I remember people talking about it. Your great grandfather was here during the war?'

'He was a British soldier.'

'Did he tell you much about the war?'

'He was injured, and a family hid him in their home. The boy I was looking for, he was their son. That's why I'm here in the cemetery. I've been looking for him but, I can't read the writing on the gravestones.'

'I will help you. What is the name of this boy?'

'Andreas Bouzoukis.'

She leans on her walking stick and pulls herself to her feet. 'Come. Let us find this boy, Andreas Bouzoukis.'

She shuffles from grave to grave, at times, she shakes her head. Sometimes, she says the name of the occupant, especially if she knew them, and she tells Jason a little about who they were.

After a while, she stops, and her mouth declines at the corners. Jason scans the writing on the weather-beaten surface of the headstone. It has faded, but it is still legible. Amongst the Greek lettering, Jason recognises familiar shaped letters of the alphabet, but it is the date his eyes train towards 1936 and 1943.

'We have found your boy.'

'Is there a woman's name too?'

'Oxi. Just the boy.'

Jason feels exhausted with emotion. He thinks of Helena, and here he is, standing in the footprints of time, where she stood, wrapped in her grief and bewildering pain.

With her head bowed, the old woman mumbles in Greek, and Jason thinks she is unwell. Then he realises she is reciting a prayer.

'O God of spirits and of all flesh, who have trampled down death and overthrown the Devil, and given life to thy world, do thou, the same Lord, give rest to the souls of thy departed servants in a place of brightness, a place of refreshment, a place of repose, where all sickness, sighing, and sorrow have fled away.'

Once finished, she makes the sign of the cross three times.

Jason breathes in tightly and wonders when the last time was that a prayer floated over Andreas' grave.

'Thank you for that.'

'It is a prayer for the dead.'

'I'm not religious and I don't know what you said, but it felt very poignant.'

'This word I don't know.'

'It means I found it emotional.'

'Ah! I see. Cemeteries have that effect on people.'

'I suppose they do.'

'When I was young, I thought I was going to live forever. Look how wrong I was.' She laughs. 'I will be in this place soon.' A defiant smile flashes across her face. 'But I will try my best to keep out of it as long as I can.'

'For some, the clock stops ticking forward. Some are young forever, like Andreas and…' Jason's heart stutters in his chest. The weight of guilt, now so familiar, is still unnerving to him.

The old woman looks at him, and she can see it swimming in his eyes. Something painful, a confession perhaps. He keeps his secret, and she can see his reluctance to offer an explanation. He drops his gaze, takes a deep breath and sucks it back inside him.

She leans more heavily on her walking stick, inhales a low, unsteady breath and watches as Jason's eyes travel the dry earth, and she can see them being caught by something. She glimpses briefly silver as Jason scoops a chain from the ground.

He inspects the chain, running it through his fingers. A link has broken. He bites his lip. 'It's broken, but it looks like it can be easily fixed. There's a cross as well. I'd hate to think it had some sentimental value to the owner.'

'I'm not on Facebook, but my daughter is always talking about the Facebook groups that are about Corfu. There's even one for the village. I could ask her to mail a message that you have found a necklace. Maybe the owner will see it?'

Jason smiles.

'Is this funny?'

'No. Not at all. It's called a post not a mail.'

She waves her hand dismissively. 'Ah. It's the same thing. The world is getting smaller, and the years have passed like months. What do I care what it is called?'

'It's a good idea. In fact, I could join a few groups and pages and send out a few posts myself.'

'Even better.'

'I'll mention I was with you if that's okay?'

'It won't make any difference.'

'Why not?'

She looks at him. 'You don't know my name.'

Jason sucks in his breath. 'What was I thinking?'

She opens her hands in shrugging dismissal. 'It is okay. I did not tell you my name either. My name is Effie.'

'And I'm Jason.'

'I like this name.' Effie looks at him almost clinically, inspecting his face. 'It suits you. You look like a Jason.'

‘I’ve looked like this all my life, so I think I look like a Jason too.’

They both laugh.

‘Thank you for helping me find Andreas.’

‘I’m glad I could help.’

Jason thinks about asking Effie if she knew Helena. After all, when she was a girl, the village would have been a close-knit community where everyone would have known each other’s business. Effie gave no inclination that she recognised Andreas’ surname Bouzoukis, and anyway, Helena was already dead when Effie was a young girl. She would have said if she had known her.

‘It’s time for me to go. I hope you enjoy your stay. Have you any plans?’

‘I’m thinking of visiting the monastery tomorrow.’

‘You will like the views of the bay and the sea up there. It gets busy with tourists, so go early.’

‘I will.’

‘Adio. (Goodbye) Jason. There are few young men who come here on their own. I’m sure you have your reasons.’ Effie rubs the base of her back and there is a pause, in which Jason could have replied, but he holds back. After a moment’s awkwardness, Effie smiles warmly. ‘I hope you find what you are looking for.’

He catches something in her eyes and, in that moment, he knows there are some things worth holding on to.

Jason watches Effie shuffle along the path and he wonders if it is with the wisdom of age, or did she see something in him she recognised, his thin and unconvincing veneer of protection?

Edinburgh

An Echo of Years

The haar had engulfed the streets of Leith, rolling in from The River Forth, like heavy plumes of smoke, diffusing lights and traffic as its wetness seeped through pedestrians' clothes and hair, dissolving familiar landmarks and buildings in its weighty silence.

'I can't see a bloody thing,' Jason complained as he cautiously steered into Leith Walk.

'Slow down. There's plenty of time. I don't have to be there until seven.' Melissa spoke without lifting her eyes from the screen of her mobile phone. 'I've just messaged Julie.'

'Jesus, I've never seen it like this.' Jason turned off the radio.

'Hey! I was listening to that.'

'I can't concentrate with Beyonce continually telling me she's a single lady.' Jason shook his head. 'When do you need me to come for you?'

'It's fine. Julie's dad is coming to pick us up and take me home.'

'What time?'

'Ten. And Dad knows, he said it was alright. We're just having a pizza, we're not hitting the clubs.'

Jason laughed. 'You wouldn't get in, anyway. Even with all that makeup on.'

'I look eighteen, and anyway, even if I got asked my age, I've got fake ID.'

'And how did you get that?'

'A girl at school. She's in sixth year. Seemingly, her brother gets them.'

'And I bet he doesn't just give them away.'

'Don't tell Dad, Jason.'

'I should, but I won't.' He turned and smiled at her, and she too was smiling, and suddenly he was overcome by a protective warmth. His little sister had grown into a young woman, and he felt he was seeing her for the first time.

A Land Rover filled the windscreen. And he would never have thought it possible, but in that instant, real time paused around them, grinding to a halt. Just for a second.

And then, everything changed.

The impact was sudden, unstoppable.

The crunch of compressed metal violent and excruciating, like a bomb exploding.

Instinctively, his foot stamped on the brake and, as the steering wheel jerked, the windows shattered around them, spraying shards of glass inward and a rush of freezing air across his face.

Apart from the deep cut across her forehead, she looked peaceful and still. She could have almost been sleeping.

He reached out to touch her, but the airbag wedged him stubbornly to the seat. He screamed her name. It was an echo that would haunt him over the years.

Corfu

A Question of Burden

He joins several Corfu Facebook groups, including a Facebook page dedicated to the village. He posts he has found a necklace in the village cemetery, uploads a photograph of the necklace, and invites the owner to personally message him.

That evening, Jason takes a walk along a stretch of beach near to where he is staying. It is a natural bay sheltered by two forested hills on each side. He sits on the sand and watches as the waves tumble gently on the shore. Above him, the moon rises with crimson incandescence and to his right, on the crest of the hill, the milky lights of the monastery look warm and welcoming in contrast to the apprehension that is building inside him.

He does not know if this is the actual beach where Marcus escaped Corfu. If it was, then this was where Helena was shot. Marcus recorded little detail about the location, other than there being two hills on each side. There are many similar beaches of that description in and around this area of the island. It is impossible for Jason to know.

A sudden rush of pity overcomes him. Jason takes a deep breath and covers his mouth with his hand. The past has imitated the present, and two lives have imploded. Marcus' loss has touched Jason. Both traumatised by witnessing the death of someone they loved and both had to live with the guilt that has gnawed away at them every day since. Holding onto all that bitterness, anger, and that regret must have been suffocating for Marcus, just as it has been for Jason. They have both suffered bone deep grief. Jason has tortured himself with the responsibility of his sister's death, just as Marcus had done with Helena. This has been both their nightmare, and this has been their connection.

Jason lifts his head and stares out into the bay. What is it he is expecting to find here?

Tomorrow he will go to the monastery. He will return the book and it will be over. The book will have returned home where it belongs. While Jason was considering this, he heard a throng of people sing Happy Birthday in the taverna just off from the beach. It was then he remembered how significant tomorrow was. When he had read Marcus' journal, he discovered Marcus had spent his birthday in Helena's basement. It had been during the early days of his recovery from his injuries.

When Jason decided he was going to travel to Corfu and return the book, Marcus' birthday was only a few weeks away. He knew then he would visit the monastery on that day. It would be a fitting ending to the book's return and the perfect birthday present.

Jason has decided he will buy freshly made bread, some cheese, tomatoes, and olives. That morning, the lady who manned the reception recommended the village baker. 'You can't miss it,' she proclaimed. 'You'll smell the bread before you see the shop.' And she was right.

As Jason crosses the narrow street on the environs of the village, his eye catches a man further ahead, who steps onto the street without checking for traffic. Jason recognises the sign above the door the man had just vacated, showing he had just visited the village doctor.

Well dressed and old enough to be Jason's father, this is not the reason he holds Jason's interest. Jason recognises the stiff posture, the blank expression. At this moment, this man inhabits another world. He has turned inwards and is alone with his thoughts.

Jason continues to scrutinise him as the man approaches an attractive woman sitting at a table outside a café opposite the doctors. She addresses him in English, and Jason recognises a Greek accent, and it surprises him to hear the man's reply. It is a Scottish accent. 'I'm fine, Elora. I told you so.'

He watches as Elora sweeps a Baku straw hat from the table and holds it to her chest before placing it on her head. Her words were now inaudible to him, apart from hearing her call the man by his name, Brodie. She reaches over the table and gently touches his arm, and Jason can see her relief is palpable.

When he has bought his groceries and is once again outside, Jason passes opposite the café. The couple have gone, and Jason was sure the man called Brodie had been economical with the truth. Whatever that truth may have been, and for whatever reason it was not told, Jason has already seen him carry the weight of that burden.

Something is Changing

He can feel the weight of the book in his rucksack as he begins the climb up towards the monastery. Jason is sure the tarmacked road would have been nothing but a dirt track when Marcus and Helena made their way along its steep gradient.

Today, the trinket shops and the small church at the foot of the hill are bustling with customers. Around him, the air is thick with European, Russian and American accents. It seems like the rest of the world has converged around this tranquil bay.

He feels like he is walking on the back of a giant snake as the road coils around another blind corner, bursting with wild trees of every description, olive trees, and efficient stone walls that keep the road clear of nature's debris.

He rises above the bay, and the view is indeed magnificent in his eyes. It takes his breath away. Behind the whitewashed facades and terracotta tiles, colossal hills, saturated in thick green forests, rise like giant stepping stones towards the vast crystal blue sky. Below him, Jason peers at the turquoise bay, lapping the sands of the beach like a graceful masseur and he believes there is no better place to be. Everything is well in his world.

The pristine white walls of the monastery confront him as he rounds the last bend. Close to the gated entrance, several cars sit and above the large door, in between two flagpoles, a fresco of Mary with a baby Christ sitting in her lap, looks down upon Jason.

A placard announces the visiting times, and Jason is early. If it is at all possible, he would prefer to miss the throng of tourists descending upon the monastery. There is no telecom to speak into, so he raps the wooden door with his knuckles, hoping it will attract the attention of someone on the other side. He waits. Silence. Again, he knocks on the door, this time more forcefully. He slides his rucksack from his back and holds it in front of him, like an offering.

'Jesus, I'm actually here,' Jason whispers to the door in front of him.

The rattle of a bolt sliding, and the disgruntled emissions vented in Greek, straighten Jason's back.

The heavy door swings open, revealing an irritated bearded monk brushing flour stains from his black habit.

He points to the placard and sounds off a volley of sentences, and, although unintelligible to Jason, the international body language of disgruntlement communicates perfectly.

'I'm sorry. I need to speak with someone, the Abbot maybe. I have something that will be of great interest to him.'

The monk stops brushing his habit and, exasperated that Jason is still standing in front of him, he places his hand on the edge of the door and peers at the placard.

'Visiting time starts at ten o'clock.'

Jason turns to see a uniformed man, a parking attendant? Or a ticket collector? He is unsure. Jason is just relieved he can speak English.

'I don't want to visit the monastery; I need to speak to someone with authority.'

The man nods his head, evidently surprised at Jason's request.

'Can I ask why you need to speak with someone of… authority? You are sure you don't want to see the monastery?'

'No. Well… maybe after, I suppose.' Jason holds up his rucksack. 'I've got a book that I'm returning to the monastery.'

Again, another surprised look. 'Why would you have a book that belongs to this place?'

'It's a long story. Look, I'll show him the book.'

Jason unzips the rucksack as the man speaks to the monk.

'He thinks you are mad,' the man says matter of fact.

'Maybe I am,' Jason says, as he slides the book from the protection of the bag. He holds it upright for the monk to see.

The monk steps forward and peers at the cover, and a tangible mix of excitement and astonishment infolds his face. He enthusiastically crosses himself three times and ushers Jason towards him.

The man smiles. 'It seems you are not mad after all.'

The monk gestures for Jason to follow him, his habit flapping at his ankles, as he hurries under an archway decorated with vines. Jason passes a black and white cat sitting contented in a cardboard box beside large vases and pots that erupt in a medley of vibrant colour. They approach a belltower, and he recognises it from Marcus' description in the journal.

The monk waves Jason forward and they enter a door that Jason must duck under and then he finds himself in a corridor that leads to two doors, a chair beside each one.

The monk shows for Jason to sit and disappears through a door. Jason noted, at some point, he must have returned the book inside the rucksack. He can't remember doing it.

A few moments later, the monk returns and shows Jason into a spacious room. A man sits behind a large dark wooden desk and, as Jason enters the room, he rises and walking around the desk he extends his hand. 'I am the abbot. My name is Athanasios and yours?'

'Jason.' The abbot's good command of English is a comfort to him.

'Please Jason, take a seat.'

Jason sinks into the chair and immediately feels the tension ease from his arms and legs. As the Abbot sits opposite him, Jason notices he has short silver hair and a thick wiry beard. His eyes are a startling shade of blue and he examines Jason over the rim of the small reading glasses perched on the end of his nose. His hands sit crossed in his lap and, if he is at all unnerved by Jason's sudden appearance, he contains it well.

They study each other silently and then, in a soft voice, he asks, 'I believe you have something to show me. A book.'

'I do.'

'And how did you come by this book?'

'It was my great grandfather's. It did not belong to him, he was… he was its custodian.' The choice of word pleases Jason. He is sure it would please Marcus too. He holds the rucksack tighter.

'So, your great grandfather did not ow. Hen this book?'

'No. He was merely looking after it. As he promised he would do.'

Athanasios scratches his beard. 'As he promised he would do?'

'Yes.'

'This book seems to have a mysterious history. We both know why I'm asking you these questions, Jason. It's important to know why, after all this time, you have decided to return the book and, as of yet, you do not seem to be offering an ulterior motive to do so. Which so far is an agreeable position. Am I right?'

'I'm not interested in a reward. This is not about money; this has more value than any amount of money could ever have.'

Athanasios leans back in his seat. 'According to brother Theofanis, the book did not look like a forgery. Of course, it could be, but then it still does not answer how it is in your possession and how you knew to come to this monastery, of all the monasteries you could have gone to in Greece? We are not the most significant. And how did you know to come to Greece? As you can see, I have many questions. So, I'm intrigued to know your answers, Jason.'

Athanasios sits with his back to the only window in the room. Jason thinks this odd, as the view is stunning, like a painting on the wall that frames the horizon parting an indigo sea and azure sky.

'I know how it must look, and believe me, I've tried to think of the best way to explain it, but I keep coming back to the reality of it, which is, there is no short answer. Since we're in a monastery, I'd assume time isn't an issue, so I'll tell you everything I know.'

Jason discloses how he discovered his great grandfather's journal and narrates the events in Corfu that led Marcus and Helena to the monastery during The Second World War and how Marcus gained the book, *Mary Magdalene, Apostle to the Apostles*.

Occasionally, Athanasios nods, smiles, and pulls his beard, but he doesn't speak. Once finished, Jason takes the book from his rucksack and places it in front of Athanasios, who clears his throat and, with a finger, slides his glasses up his nose. He lays his hand on the book and takes a deep breath.

'It has been passed down to every Abbott how the book was given to a British soldier who was also an academic to save it from the Nazis. We have always hoped one day it would return home and here it is in front of my very eyes. You have done a beautiful thing, Jason. We shall be forever indebted to you.'

'It's Marcus you should be thanking. He knew that if he gave it to any museum, you would never get it returned, so he was the keeper of the book, and he always hoped that the book would be returned to the monastery. Today would have been his birthday.'

'Then it is a fitting present indeed.'

'I'd like to think so too.'

'During the war, it had to be hidden. But not so today. It will be the centrepiece of the library.' The Abbott takes off his glasses and wipes his eyes with a handkerchief. 'Stay for lunch, Jason. Would you like to see the library?'

'I'd love that. I know it meant a lot to Marcus to have free access to its books. When I read about his time spent there, it jumped off the page.'

Athanasios holds the book in his hands and carefully opens its pages. Jason watches as the Abbott's eyes fill with wonderment and his face lights up. 'It's a miracle.'

Jason spent several hours in the library. He didn't read any of the books. The closest he got was to brush his fingers along their spines that filled the bookcases like bricks in a wall. He sat at the table that stood in the middle of the room and his mind pictured Marcus reading avidly and scribbling frantic notes on a writing pad.

He wondered if the library had changed over the decades, and he hoped it hadn't. The air was thick with the scent of must and old books. It would have been a place Marcus would have been happy in and fulfilled. Even after all he had been through, and what he knew was about to come. Within these walls, Marcus could escape the complications of the world, the horror, the brutality, and buffer the hatred and madness with the silence of books and ancient gentle minds.

It is here Jason feels closest to Marcus; it is amongst these books he is understanding the lure that has brought him here. This is as much about Jason as it is about bringing the book back to the monastery where it rightfully belongs.

Jason needs to feel liberated from the guilt. He needs to find the courage to forgive himself. Jason longs to shed the pain that is a reminder each day he killed his sister in a car crash on a foggy night in Edinburgh. Blame crushes him. It seems a lifetime away, and yet, it seems only yesterday.

He is trying not to let go, but he is already forgetting the details of her face, the particularities of her smile and the sound of her voice.

There is a blank space in his life. It should fill with the memories of a teenager growing into a young woman, experiencing the thrill of nights out, passing exams, going to college, university, a first job, her first love, becoming responsible for the decisions she makes, making choices that will shape her life…

He needs to fill that blank space with acceptance. He yearns to be rid of the weight of anguish and the constant over thinking: what if he had taken a different route? Would she still be alive if he had driven slower? Or had not been so desperate that instead of stopping, he went through a red traffic light?

After leaving the monastery with Athanasios' sentiments of gratitude still echoing in his ears, Jason sits on a low stone wall, looking out over the bay below him. The sea is a translucent sheet of glass sprinkled in turquoise and shades of the most striking blue, he thinks, that could only be drained from the sky.

The light is different too, bathing everything in a silvery white, or is it the vibrance of the verdant hills that gently slope towards perpendicular cliffs and dark mystical caves? Whatever it is, it fills Jason's eyes with a perfection he has rarely seen. The bay is sheltered by a narrow inlet between two hills that slope into a sapphire sea with tinges of emerald and deep ultramarine, where shaded patches appear like one giant aquatic map stretched out along the shallow seabed.

He feels different. Something is shifting. The air is warm and infused with the scents of pine, jasmine, lemon and rosemary. Like incense in a church, it permeates the ether around him.

He has done a good thing, of that he is sure. He could feel the wave of excitement, like a tsunami, sweep through the monastery as he sat down to eat lunch with the monks and Athanasios, who stood in front of them, holding the book high above his head, like a trophy for all to see. Some monks clapped enthusiastically whilst others blessed themselves and Athanasios beamed like the sun.

Jason's thoughts turn to Marcus as they often do, and he has an impression of Marcus smiling approvingly.

He has not felt this happy since the accident. It is life affirming. It has been years since he has felt this good about himself and, until now, he has always told himself he doesn't deserve to, but not today and it is life giving.

The thought of leaving, so soon after his arrival, leaves a pang echoing in his chest. There is no obligation to book a flight to Edinburgh, at least not just yet.

For the first time in years, he is feeling optimistic about the days in front of him. He feels unusually calm and something else that is more potent; he feels connected.

The next day, after breakfast, he is sitting under a parasol in the gardens of his small hotel. He has just spoken to Rachel on his mobile and informed her of his visit to the monastery and of his decision to stay a few days longer than he had planned when he checks his messages.

There is a personal message on Facebook. The necklace! After yesterday, it has slipped his mind. He opens the message and reads it.

He sets the mobile on the table in front of him and sits back with a self-satisfied smile. He may have just found its owner.

An Invitation

It is her airy smile that does it. Warm and captivating, it enamours him to her. She is sitting with her leg crossed over the other, her hands resting in her lap against the fabric of her beige dress that shows off her slim figure. He knows it is her from the profile picture on Facebook. She is sitting at the table with a man and, to Jason's surprise, he feels a stab of jealousy.

She looks up at him as he approaches the table, her chestnut hair floating across her shoulder.

'Hi. I'm Jason. You must be Thea.'

That smile again.

'Jason. Please take a seat. Would you like a drink?'

He lifts his hand. 'I'm fine, thanks.' He sits down, pressed into a slight unease. 'I recognised you from your photograph on Facebook.'

'Did you? I keep meaning to update it. This is my brother, Nikos.'

'Oh! Hi Nikos,' Jason says, and he is immediately aware of the relief in his voice. Nikos raises his hand in acknowledgment.

She pulls her hand through her hair. 'I'm so glad you found my necklace; it was a present from my mother. I've worn it for years. It was like losing an arm when I discovered I'd lost it.'

Jason hands the necklace to her, and she immediately puts it on. 'Thank you. Thank you, so much.'

'My pleasure.'

'Who are you here with, your wife, a girlfriend?'

'I'm on my own.'

'Oh!'

'I know. I keep getting funny looks from people in the hotel.'

Thea laughs.

'I wasn't expecting the English accent.'

'We're from Slough. We're over visiting family.'

'Our grandparents came to England in the 50s. We're born and bred in England, but Greek all the same.' Nikos' sombre face breaks into a smile.

'My parents have a villa about a ten-minute drive from the village. We use it as a base to visit relatives, but I'm staying in Corfu Town this time. The villa's nice, but there's always someone visiting. This time, I decided I'm having sometime to myself as well.'

Nikos sighs. 'Unfortunately, I didn't have Thea's foresight.'

'My hotel's small. It's a family run business and very quiet.'

Nikos smiles. 'Any rooms left?'

A waiter hovers nearby. 'Are you sure you don't want a drink? I'm having another,' Thea asks.

'Actually, I think I might.'

'Then it's on me. It's the least I can do since you found my necklace.'

Jason is about to protest, but Thea is already speaking to the waiter in fluent Greek.

She turns to Jason. 'What would you like?'

'A lemonade.'

'Nothing stronger?'

'Just a lemonade, thanks.'

'It's my birthday, so I'm having a wine.'

'Happy birthday.'

'Thanks. I can't tempt you?'

'Honest. A lemonade will be just fine.'

She touches the necklace. 'This is the best birthday present I could get. Thank you.'

'I'm just glad I could find you.'

'That's the power of social media,' Nikos says. 'There's some good that can come out of it. I think Facebook gets too much bad press. The media need to acknowledge the good it has done.'

'I think it's the media that has too much influence and power.'

'I wouldn't argue with that,' Nikos says and lights a cigarette. He offers one to Jason, who kindly refuses.

'Come tonight.'

Jason looks dumbfounded. 'Where?'

'I'm having a party at the villa. Some family and friends. I'd love it if you could come. You must. That's if you have got nothing else planned. After all, you gave me the best present ever.' She thinks for a second. 'And of course, you can bring someone.'

'It's just me.'

'That's right. You said.'

'I'm not the best of company.'

'You're doing okay so far,' Nikos says with a smile.

Thea takes a drink and looks at Jason over the rim of her glass. 'Come for an hour at least. If you feel uncomfortable, you can leave. I won't take it personally.'

'I won't know anyone.'

'Believe me, you'll know everyone's life story before the end of the night. You're in Greece.' Thea smiles. 'You haven't said yes.'

'I haven't said no.'

'So, you'll come then.'

'I'm thinking about it.'

'God. It's like watching verbal tennis.' Nikos chuckles to himself. 'I think I've just invented a sport.'

'Seven o'clock?'

'I'll need the address.'

Revelations

Jason can't believe he accepted Thea's invitation. It was an impulsive decision. He can't deny he is glad, because he would like to see her again, but the thought of being at a party and not knowing anyone doesn't fill him with confidence. In fact, the opposite is true. The thought of it now fills him with dread.

He won't go. There, he has decided. And she won't miss him. He only met her today. She was just being kind. She probably felt obliged to invite him because of the necklace.

He checks his watch. Five o'clock. He should get a shower and change for dinner. He'll visit the restaurant at the beach, the one he went to last night. The food was excellent.

He opens the balcony doors and steps out into the late afternoon sun. There is something about its warmth on his face that is inevitably therapeutic and satisfying. So, why is he already feeling a pang of regret?

When the taxi drops him off, he is facing the impressive facade of a large villa and, behind him, the sea glitters in the soft light of the fading sun. He can hear a pulsating beat and the chatter of guests and amongst the twinkling lights that adorn the trees, people sit at tables and already, the party is well under way.

'Jason. You came.' It is Nikos striding down the path towards him, drink and cigarette in hand. The welcome enthusiasm in his voice is clear and it is enough to tame the worm of apprehension in Jason.

'I wasn't expecting this. What a lovely place you have here and you couldn't buy that view.'

'I know. It's special, isn't it? Let me get you a drink. I hope you're hungry. There's plenty of food. Our cousin is a chef in Corfu Town, and he's put on quite a spread.'

She is wearing a cornflower blue skirt and a white blouse cut low at the neck. She has on the minimum of makeup, which Jason approves of. He detects that in conversation, she lightly touches her necklace. It is a habit he finds endearing.

'Look who I found.' Niko pats Jason between his shoulders.

'Jason! I'm so glad you came.'

Taken aback by the genuine delivery of her sentiment, Jason gathers himself. 'I was just saying to Nikos how beautiful the house is.'

'I can't take the credit for that. Mum and dad built it and over the years extended it. They didn't want to be a burden to the family every time they visited. It gets used at least six months of the year. Mostly in the summer.'

'I'll get you a drink.' Nikos offers. 'What's your tipple? There's plenty of lager, Greek, Spanish, German and gin, vodka. Maybe you're a whisky man?'

'Just a lemonade for me.'

'Starting off slow. I like your style. Do want ice with it?'

'Perfect.'

'You don't drink, do you? There's nothing wrong with that. Actually, it's quite refreshing. Like the lemonade I should imagine.'

They both laugh and Jason can feel himself relax in her company.

'That's the problem I used to… a lot.'

'Oh! I see. You don't have to explain yourself, Jason. I wouldn't expect you to. That's your business.'

'It's okay. It was a long time ago.'

He finds it easy to talk to her. She tells him about her family, their move to England and, even though she was not born in Greece, they spoke the language in their house and the food on their table was Greek.

Jason's normal inhibition, his default concerning his past, lies dormant within him. He speaks about growing up in Edinburgh, his days at university, his job and his sister: the accident, his guilt and regret, and the depression he has endured for years. It astonishes him how easily he can open up to her.

'The problem was and still is, I blame myself…' He looks away. He has divulged far too much. What was he thinking? Christ, she'll be wanting to run a mile now. 'If I'm honest, I don't know why I've told you any of this. It's your birthday. I'm sorry. Maybe I should go.'

Thea touches his forearm, and it feels like electricity on his skin. 'Stay. Please stay. I can't understand what you must have gone through. I'd be a liar if I said I did, and it would only belittle the courage it took for you to tell me.'

He shrugs. 'I find it easy talking to you.'

Speaking of the accident has never been easy. The hard truth has fortified his deepest feelings, shifting and realigning his life. He finds he can speak with her without embarrassment or restraint and, to his relief, the complexity of his guilt is dissolving.

She is smiling and still touching his arm and suddenly they are both aware of it. Reluctantly, Thea drops her hand.

'I thought the drink would make it better. It didn't. I have some good friends, more like family, really. If it wasn't for them, I don't think I would be here today. They persuaded me to get the help I needed.' He doesn't elaborate further.

'I'm glad you're still here today, Jason, and that you chose to come to my party.' For the first time, there is a silence between them.

'Are you hungry?' Thea asks.

'Now that you mention it, I am.'

'I'm starving. Let's get something to eat. I've got a ferocious appetite.'

'I wouldn't want to keep you from your guests.'

'You're not. Look at them. I doubt if it mattered if I was here or not.'

There is indeed a copious amount of food. Various salads, bread, olives, and dips. Silver trays line a long table, filled with moussaka, a spiced lamb bake, chicken souvlaki all heated underneath by gas rings.

Thea hands Jason a plate as they take their place in the queue.

The woman in front of them speaks to Thea in Greek and Jason's eye wanders around the extensive garden. He can see musicians sitting on high stools. Amongst their instruments is a Bouzouki, a Kithari, the Gaida Kavala, which to Jason's untrained eye looks like the bagpipes, a violin and a handheld drum. The Bouzouki player begins a riff, his fingers sliding gracefully but also intricately along the neck of his instrument. Then, his fellow musicians accompany him, forming the backbone and rhythm, complementing the melody that entices several women and a young boy to hold hands, held high with sweeping steps and swaying hips in a graceful and unified line.

A faint breeze brings warm moist air from the sea, soothing the flushed skin of those still dancing as Jason and Thea sit at a vacant table. Nikos brings Jason his lemonade and, as he and Thea eat, he knows he finds everything about her irresistible and he wonders what they are heading towards.

Thea smiles. 'I don't know your surname. You haven't told me what it is.'

'I haven't?'

'I would have remembered if you had.'

'Lavigne.'

'That sounds rather exotic.'

'Not really, it's French.'

'France can be exotic.'

'I've never thought about it in that way.'

'Look at Monaco and Nice. That entire area is like a different country. It's on the doorstep of the Mediterranean.

The south of France has a certain feel to it, don't you think?'

'My dad's family is from that area. Near to Nice.'

'There you go. The exotic Lavignes' from Nice.' She laughs then, and he delights in just being with her.

'I've been to Edinburgh a few times. I love it. It's a beautiful city.'

'Where is your favourite place in Edinburgh? A bar? A restaurant? A particular area?' he asks her.

'I love walking up Calton Hill. The view of the city is amazingly panoramic. You can see the coast of Fife over the River Forth and even the bridges on a clear day.'

'You know your geography as well.'

'Does that surprise you?

'Not everyone would know that.'

'My dad loved golf. And every year he took us all to St Andrews. He played golf, and we spent most of our time on the beach with mum.'

'That beach is amazing. It can get windy at times.'

'I know. It used to rock the caravan.'

'Oh! The hill.'

'That's the one.'

'I know it well. I know it's a cliché, but it really is a small world.'

He fills his fork, and as he is chewing his food, Thea smiles at him and raises her glass.

'To Edinburgh, and us.'

He reaches for his glass and clicks the rim of hers. 'To special moments.'

She gazes at him. 'To special moments.'

'I was up Calton Hill just a few weeks ago. I saw a couple getting married. There were about fifty guests standing in a circle and the bride and groom were dressed in what I'd describe as period clothes. Like that series Outlander. It was definitely a humanist wedding. They were repeating their vows and you could tell they were personal to them as a couple. It was quite beautiful. And then, quite bizarrely, an old double-decker bus, just like the ones you used to see in London, dropped off another wedding party. They all got their photographs taking by a photographer with Edinburgh as the backdrop. It was quite a surreal moment.'

'Have you ever been married?

'Not even close to it. What about you?'

'Closer than you, it would seem. It was a few years ago now. I'm glad I found out what I did when I did. Let's just say I got a fortuitous escape. I found out he liked to share it about. Not a good idea when he tries it on with your best friend.'

'As you said, a lucky escape.'

'For the two of them. They eventually married and were divorced within a year.'

'Wow! Your best friend did that?'

'I didn't appreciate it at the time, obviously, but, in hindsight, she did me a huge favour.'

'Ouch!'

'Yeah. They got what they both deserved. From then on, I just concentrated on my business. It was a lifesaver. I kept myself busy. If you were to ask my friends, they would say I married my business instead.'

'And what is it you're married too?'

'Restaurants. I have three, and I'm opening my first in London next month.'

'Let me guess, Greek restaurants.'

She smiles. 'Of course.'

'That will definitely keep you busy.'

'It does. That's why I enjoy myself when I'm here. It's the only place I find I can relax and not always think of work.'

'Just sometimes.'

She laughs. 'You're getting to know me. But I'd love to be able to spend more time in Corfu. Maybe one day.'

She takes a drink. 'What about you, Jason? What's it like working in the financial sector?'

'It's pretty boring really, but it pays the bills. Edinburgh isn't the cheapest place to live.'

'I know. I thought about expanding north, and Edinburgh was my obvious choice, but the business rates were almost on a par with London.'

'Where did you have in mind?'

'We looked at St Andrew Square and George Street.'

'That figures.'

'I know. They're quite prestigious areas. There was a smaller place on Rose Street, but it didn't fit my business model.' Thea dabs her mouth with a napkin and Jason can't help but gaze at her. He wants to linger in this pleasing sensation, but reluctantly pulls himself away.

'The food was delicious.'

'I wanted Stephanos to be the chef at my new place in London, but he is happy in Corfu Town, as is his wife, and why shouldn't they be? Money and prestige don't bring happiness, that can only be found in the simple things in life. Look at that sunset. Money can't buy that beauty. It is given to us freely, so I respect his decision. We all need a life that is worth living.' For the first time since he met her, Jason detects a trace of sadness. It is short-lived.

'Tell me, Jason.' Thea is curious. 'You found my necklace in the cemetery. What were you doing in there?'

He smiles. 'I could ask you the same question?'

'I have family buried there. Every time I visit Corfu, I try to leave some flowers.'

'I was looking for the grave of a young boy who died a long time ago.'

She inclines her head. 'Now I wasn't expecting that. Maybe some macabre interest in old graves, but certainly not that. Why?'

'It's the reason I'm here.'

Just then, an older woman pulls Thea from her seat. The woman speaks rapidly in Greek and laughs. Thea is standing now and beaming. She turns to Jason.

'Seemingly, it's bad luck not to dance at your own party.'

'You better go then, not that you have a choice,' Jason smiles as the older woman is enthusiastically pulling Thea by the hands.

Jason feels irritated. He wants to tell her, but the moment has passed. The garden is lit in a glow of bulbs dangling from branches like ripened fruit. The placid sea, so radiant earlier, is a bluish black in the luminous light. He gazes at Thea as she dances. Her attraction is overpowering. What has just happened? What did she see in him? He swallows his misgivings and taps his feet to the music. By now others are dancing, but Jason finds it difficult to take his eyes off Thea.

'It is you!'

Jason turns and the last person he expects to see is lowering herself into the chair next to him.

'Effie!'

'I'd ask for a dance, but my feet refuse to do what my brain tells them these days. I never thought I'd see you here.' She looks at him and her face breaks into a smile. 'What a lovely surprise.'

'The necklace belongs to Thea. As a thank you, she invited me to her birthday party.'

'I'm an old friend of the family. Her grandmother and I were friends when we were girls and, when she left for England, we stayed in touch.'

She taps her feet to the music. 'I'm so glad to see you. I have some news for you.'

'You do?'

'Yes. When I left you at the cemetery, I found out about the young boy's mother, Helena. We have our very own village historian, Spyros Tsolia. If there is anything he doesn't know about the history, traditions and folklore of the village, then it is not worth knowing.'

'I see.'

'I have some wonderful news for you, Jason. She didn't die.'

'What!'

'Your Helena. When she was shot, she was not killed.'

'But that's impossible. This man has got the wrong Helena.'

'No. It is the one you told me about. Spyros told me she was the mother of the young boy whose grave you visited.'

'Andreas.'

'Yes. The one I showed you. There is no mistake, Jason.'

It is unbearable. The shock strikes him like a punch to the stomach. He tries to make sense of it with the facts he knows; the facts written by Marcus' own hand.

'Marcus saw Helena running down the beach. He heard the gunshot and he saw her fall. The Germans dragged her body towards the truck. She was dead.'

Jason frantically searches Effie's face, willing her to say *Yes, you must be right. She was dead.*

Effie's smile turns down at the edges. 'No. He was wrong. After the war, she stayed in the village and then, in nineteen fifty-two, she and her husband emigrated to Australia.'

'Her husband?'

'Yes.'

Jason can't say the name. Already, the implications fermenting in his thoughts. A rapid, sudden heat rushes over him. His face darkens a little.

'What was the husband's name?'

'Spiros called him Vangelis.'

At that moment, the magnitude of Effie's words pummels him.

'Jason, are you unwell? The colour is draining from you.'

'Marcus lived the rest of his life believing the Germans had killed Helena and he had witnessed it with his own eyes. That was why he never returned to Corfu.'

'I'm so sorry, Jason.'

He breathes in deeply, shocked and suddenly exhausted.

'I need to go for a walk, Effie.'

This is incredible, he tells himself. He is struggling to take in the implications as he walks aimlessly along a dimly lit track.

It was through Helena that Marcus had seen a way to rise above the indecisions and injuries of the life that waited for him in Edinburgh. With her, he could survive the destruction his choices would make, to choose Helena over Ruth, to plan for their future together. On the night of his escape, they had made love for the last time and, as they both lay in bed within the sanctuary of the monastery, the most exhilarating feeling of love poured from him.

Years later, Marcus wrote in the journal, it was the happiest he had ever been. During the years that followed, he had to reinvent himself, reattach himself to a life without her presence, where the light dimmed and his capacity to love was unfulfilled and restricted, knowing half of his soul had died on a dark and lonely Corfu beach.

Jason doesn't know how long he has been walking. He can no longer hear the music from Thea's party. He recognises some buildings and the houses he is passing are familiar to him. Jason is now on the narrow lane that leads to his hotel, streetlamps are more frequent, and he can hear the gentle swell of the sea on the beach.

He looks up decisively at the restaurant that overlooks the beach. He is not ready to be amongst people. His head pulses and, when he thinks of the trajectory of the lives of Helena and Marcus, a dull pang echoes through his chest. He now doubts Helena, and his grip on who he thought she was is slipping.

Jason feels his feet sink into the sand and wanders close to the surf. He takes off his shoes and steps into the sea, feeling its caress and gentle reprise on his skin. He has only visited the beach at night and never during the day, preferring his own company. Now, alone with his thoughts, it brings little consolation.

Jason finds it incomprehensible that Helena and Vangelis were together again. He had obviously returned after the war. Had it changed him? Was he no longer the man that left her? Did she take him back upon his return? Or did she wait for Marcus, who, believing he had seen her killed, had no reason to go back to Corfu?

And what of her circumstances? It is impossible for Jason to even consider her state of mind. She loved Marcus. That is not in doubt. The Nazis would have ravaged Corfu. Poverty and starvation were widespread amongst the populace. Vangelis would have offered Helena safety and stability in a time of fear and uncertainty and Marcus' absence.

Once the war ended, Jason wonders how long Helena waited for Marcus' promised return? How practical would waiting indefinitely for Marcus have been? She would have been holding on to the hope that Marcus had survived the war. His nonappearance would only have confirmed her worse fears he had not.

She knew with all her heart he would not have lied to her. She also knew how much Marcus loved her and that he would have sacrificed everything to be with her again. Marcus promised her a new life, one in which she would never again have to suffer the physical and mental scars she had endured. He would have given her the stars if he could. He would have died for her. And so, Jason can only assume Helena waited for Marcus for as long as she could and, in his absence, she grieved for him. The dark logic of despair motivated her decision to take Vangelis back.

The irony is implicit.

Marcus thought he had witnessed Helena's death; the gun firing, Helena's limp body falling and being dragged along the sand. Ever since, he had lived with the soul-destroying consequences.

It would have crushed Helena to have known this. And now it makes sense. Both Helena and Marcus thought each other dead and there was no other choice on their parts but to live life as best they could. Their futures would be forever apart.

An Unexpected Development

Jason awakes the next day to a text from Thea.

Effie told me a little about your great grandad and the woman called Helena. Life can be so unfair. If you need someone to talk to, I'm all ears. I hope you enjoyed the party. Effie had more to tell you, so she confided in me and asked if I wouldn't mind telling you, which I didn't, of course. We can meet up today as I am leaving for London tomorrow.'

He reads the message again. He regrets leaving the way he did, and he deserves her silence, however he is elated that Thea thinks otherwise. And for all that, he is eager to know what Thea must disclose. Knowing that she is leaving the next day makes it even more urgent that he sees her again.

He always knew. The second his eyes fell upon her in the square and she looked up at him, he had lived his life at that specific moment. The thought of Thea leaving and never seeing her again only confirms the swell in his heart is real.

The sun is already warm on his back as he places his cutlery on the empty plate and drains the last of his coffee. He dabs his mouth with a napkin, slides his feet into his flip-flops, and checks his phone.

Thea has replied to the text Jason sent her asking to meet in the square at ten. She wants to meet in the cemetery. This surprises Jason. He feels himself aching to see her again.

Thea is sitting under the tree in the middle of the cemetery and talking into her mobile phone when Jason strolls towards her. She stands and he can see something is irritating her as she walks amongst the headstones, her hand looping through the air in wide gestures. He hesitates. Jason feels conscious of himself and fiercely regrets walking into this situation. He suspects that his timing has placed Thea in a quandary, and all he wants to do is recoil from the intimacy of it. He can hear the strain in her voice but cannot decipher her words. Jason sits on the bench, out of sight, and waits.

When Thea finally appears, her face is flushed. 'I'm sorry, Jason. I had to take that call.'

'It's not a problem. Is everything okay?'

Thea shakes her head and frowns. 'Not really. We're behind in getting the restaurant ready for its opening date. A rival has poached my manager and we have a burst water pipe from the offices above us. It has brought a section of the kitchen roof down. It's a disaster. Thank God I'm leaving for London tomorrow.'

'Will you get it all sorted before your opening?'

'I hope so. The roof can be fixed this week. It'll take a while longer to get a manager, I'm afraid.'

'Hopefully, it will be the right person this time.'

'There's not much loyalty in the restaurant business just now. Everyone is chasing money and we pay our staff above the average for the industry. I've got people who have worked for me since the day I opened my first restaurant. Enough about me. How are you?'

'I'm sorry I left in the way I did.'

'Don't be. Effie told me all about it. It must have been a shock for you. But there's more.'

'It can't get any worse.'

'Effie told me that the man Spyros did some more research and discovered where Helena lived, and the house is still standing today.'

'That's amazing.'

'I know.'

'Oh my God!'

Thea is smiling. 'I know.'

'I have to see it.'

'Effie thought it would be a good idea if I took you to the house.'

'But why did you want to meet me here in the cemetery?'

'I'd love to the know the whole story about your great grandfather and the woman Helena. That's why I wanted to meet you here. I'd like to see the little boy's grave.'

Thea sits beside Jason and tucks a stray hair behind her ear. He tells her of the young man who fell from the sky and into the heart of a young Greek woman. When Jason has finished, Thea wipes the tears from her eyes. 'Life can be so cruel.'

'It can be, but the time they spent together was the most precious time. It was a gift that life had given them. They found what it meant to truly love one another. How many people can say that? I think that was what sustained them when they lived all those years apart.'

'I hope Helena was happy. She deserved it.'

Jason smiles. 'Let me introduce you to Andreas. If my bearings are right, he should be just over here.'

More Than a Space

The houses and buildings of the village have thinned out, leaving the narrow-shaded lanes behind, and opening into wide spaces as Jason looks around, dazed by the brilliant light and Thea by his side. Around them, the air is heavy with the purity of earthly scents and the scattering of wildflowers and herbs.

Can this really be the house? And would there be anything inside that would suggest it was so? The rational part of his brain knows that the odds are stacked against it, but the emotional seal on his heart is certain, as something teases at the edge of his memory.

At some point, the walls of the house were white. They now sag with paint that flakes and cracks, spreading like roads on a map. Blue faded shutters lean offset, at the mercy of hinges that are rusted and bent. Jason's stomach sinks as the gaping hole in the roof exposes rib like rafters where birds sit pruning feathers, unperturbed. The garden is overgrown, suffocated with weeds the size of small trees that strangle and entwine themselves around a fence, no longer upright, but broken. Against one wall of the house, a bench sits buckled, rotten and splintered, disintegrated with time. Around its legs, pots lie scattered, cracked, and weathered; their colourful contents long decayed into the ground where they fell.

As the sun spreads shafts of golden light over the hillside, it covers the house in a tawny hue. And the thought of what happened here within its walls, and what Marcus would have thought if his eyes were to befall on such abandonment, dissipates Jason's happiness with such a heavy heart that it forces him to gasp for air.

They walk towards the house in silence. And as they approach the front door, Jason's mind races with the details of Marcus' journal. He gazes at the dilapidated bench. And to know this was where Marcus and Helena sat when the day grew dark was a significant moment. It was now no longer just words that told the story. From this moment onwards, the journal had become a living entity, forming images in his mind so distinct they appeared in front of his eyes.

He pushes the front door. He is taut with a strange mix of excitement and trepidation. The door is stiff on its hinges, so he applies more force. He steps across the threshold and his shoes crunch with the dust and grime underneath them. The air is thick and stale and, around them, a dull shadowy light obscures the house.

Thea throws open the windows and shutters and light streams into the house, illustrating how tired and ramshackle it has become.

Jason inhales a deep breath and his brow furrows. He wasn't sure what he'd find, but it certainly wasn't this. The stone cladding floor is awash with bird droppings and grime. Red spray-painted graffiti swathes the walls. A staircase that leads to the upper floor looks fragile and ready to crumble. Empty bottles of vodka and beer, juice cans and cigarette butts lie strewn across the room. Mould infested tins and cartons obscure the surface of a table, a tabletop large enough to accommodate the body of a man to rest upon.

Could this be the very table Vangelis and Petros laid Marcus upon and where Dr Iannis and Helena stitched and cleaned his wounds? If it was, to see it now, punches a hole in Jason's chest.

As he walks around the table, he traces his fingers along its surface and deliberates the marks scratched into the woodwork. Could a young Andreas sitting at the table doing homework or eating dinner have made these? Such a prospect pleases Jason, although he assumes Helena would have not been as accommodating. He smiles at the thought, as it brings a much-needed air of domestic intimacy to the house that was once a family home.

Jason sets his lips together tightly and looks around in disbelief at what has become of the house. 'Did anyone live here after Helena?'

'Effie said that after Helena left for Australia, the house had several occupants. The last owners never actually moved in. It was bought by a German couple. I heard they had plans to renovate the house and hire it out as a holiday home.'

The irony is not lost on Jason. 'They must have had a change of mind. This place has been unlived in for years.'

'I expect it's still owned by them. In the state it's in now, they'd struggle to sell it.'

Jason's eye slips towards a door at the far end of the room. He picks his way through the surrounding disarray.

He knows that when he opens the door, there will be a staircase leading to a basement.

He steadies himself against the wall to his right and takes each step cautiously into the darkness of the basement below him.

'Are you alright down there?' Thea asks.

'If I could find a light switch, I'd feel much better.'

Suddenly, he hears a click and, above him, a naked bulb flashes with light.

'The light switch was by the door.' Thea says, as a matter of fact. 'I'm surprised the electricity is still connected.'

'Thanks,' he replies sheepishly.

'Anything of interest?'

It rises in his chest like smoke, an impression of reverence that is sensed when entering a place of wonder.

He stands still, rooted in the moment.

Jason struggles to comprehend. He is in the very place Marcus lay for weeks, where Helena nursed him and where their hesitant beginnings grew into a love that neither could deny.

He crouches and lays his palm on the stone floor and, if he tries hard enough, he can hear Marcus and Helena, words of affection, whispered like a soft breeze. A rock lodges in his throat and tears well, as he wipes them away.

'Are you okay?' Thea asks as Jason emerges from the basement.

'I am now.'

'I take it there wasn't much down there?'

'That depends.'

'On what?'

'Some places are more than just a space… much more.'

Thea holds out her hand. Jason watches her face, her lips part as if to speak, and Jason feels a compelling urgency and places his hand in hers. It is warm as her fingers curl around his. Stirred by her gesture, he steps closer to her.

With Thea's lips tentatively close to his, Jason's churning emotions want nothing more than to indulge in her. They stand for a moment. She feels his hand now in her hair and with Thea's breath warm against his mouth, he can feel the fullness of her lips. She sighs, each savouring the intimacy and, when he presses against her mouth, their kiss is tender and protracted.

He is holding her face in his hands, both staring into each other's eyes. Nothing needs to be said.

Jason watches Thea as she takes a sip of wine. He regards her, the way an artist studies his painting. Can knowing someone for such a short time, only a matter of days, constitute being in love with them? If he never saw her again, how would this leave him? It is a prospect he does not want to consider. And so, that is his answer.

It is extraordinary how he feels. Over the past few days, he is amazed how she slides into his thoughts effortlessly and, when he is with her, he cannot feel the ground between his feet. He has known nothing like this. It is unimaginable to think she captures him in this way, just as Marcus would have been with Helena in this very place. He closes his eyes briefly and considers this.

'What are you smiling about?' Thea tilts her head in semi-humorous enquiry.

'Was I? I didn't realise I was.'

'Well, you were. It wasn't just any old smile. It was what I'd call an indulgent smile.'

'I didn't know there was such a thing.'

'There is. I've just told you.'

'Then there must be. I believe you.'

Jason draws a circle on the tablecloth with his finger. 'If you must know, I was thinking about us. Well, mostly you, really.'

'Oh, I see.'

'And now you're smiling.'

'I suppose I am.'

'So, we make each other smile.'

'It seems so.'

He can see in her entire demeanour she, too, feels there is something happening between them. How far are they prepared to go?

'This was the last thing I was looking for.'

'You're regretting what happened earlier?'

'No. That's not what I'm saying.'

'Then what are you saying?'

'My life is complicated. You've no idea. I shouldn't be in Corfu, really. I should be in London getting ready to open a restaurant. There's too much going on with the business, and in retrospect, I was mad agreeing to come. I must have had a moment of weakness and Niko persuaded me. This wasn't supposed to happen. You weren't part of my agenda.'

'And that's problematic?'

She puts her hand on his arm. 'That's not what I mean.'

He drops his gaze to her hand. She has not removed it. Instead, her fingers glide softly over his skin. It is a lingering endearment. 'The timing could have been better. I'm leaving tomorrow and… let's just say, I won't be working nine to five. Once the restaurant in London is up and running, I won't have much… me time.'

'I get that. Don't worry. It shouldn't be any other way. You've only known me two minutes.'

'I'm not explaining myself very well. I don't want it to be just this between us. I'd like there to be more. I want to see you again and I think you feel the same.'

A nervous elation comes over Jason. 'I do and I'd like that. I'd really like that.'

'So would I.'

'I wasn't sure if you'd want to see me again, especially after I told you about… my past.'

'Not everyone would have been so honest. I think that tells a lot about the person you are. It must have been difficult for you to share how your sister's death has affected you. I really respect the fact that you told me.'

'I've never been that honest with anyone about how it has changed me. It felt easy telling you. And that on its own was a strange reality to me. The accident and her death reshaped the person I thought I was. The experience of it has endured so long, it felt like it was separate of time, it was permanent, it didn't leave me. It has always stayed with me. It has felt like an unending present, but that is changing now. It was easy to tell you because you made it that way. Even now, speaking like this, with you, was something I never thought I'd be capable of.'

'I don't know what to say.'

'Then don't say anything. I can't explain it, but I feel it, if that makes sense. I've felt so guilty for years and that centred me on all the negativity of my thoughts and emotions, sometimes without even knowing it. People have tiptoed around me for that very reason. How sad is that? Now, I feel rescued.'

'You feel rescued… by me?' She stumbles over the words.

'To some degree I do. But really, when I think of the essence of it, it's more like a sense of place. I've never been to Corfu before, so I had no idea what to expect or what it was going to be like. When I saw the village and walked through it, I felt this incredible ambience within me. The only way I can describe it is, it felt like I was being held.'

'This experience has really changed you, hasn't it?'

'It's like I've come home. I feel connected to this place. I think being in Corfu is just the beginning. It has been a reprieve from being the person I'd become. I know it sounds weird, and normally I'd be the first person to say that such things are nonsense, but I can't deny it. I can't belittle it. It is so much bigger than me.' Jason smiles awkwardly. 'Enough about me. What time is your flight tomorrow?'

'Five o'clock. Although I need to be checked in by three. What about you? What are your plans?'

'I've achieved what I came here to do. I'm not sure. The last few days have been like an emotional rollercoaster. It's a cliche, but true. I've flipped from being extremely happy to disbelief and sadness and back to happy again.' Jason answers after a sombre moment of reflection. 'Before I came, I just booked a single flight as I didn't know how long this was going to take or how it was all going to turn out. I suppose I need to think about booking a flight home.'

'You seem hesitant about that.'

'Mixed feelings. I'm not sure,' he says truthfully. 'I'd like to stay a little longer. I'm here now. I should make the most of it. I've heard Corfu Town is nice. Maybe I'll head over there.'

'It's nice. It has a colonial feel to it. Its history is fascinating. If you like castles, well actually they're fortresses, whatever you want to call them, it has two.'

'I was brought up with castles. We have quite a lot of them in Scotland, you know.'

'I know, actually. One thousand and sixty-three and half of those are uninhabited.'

'Wow! That's impressive.'

Thea grins mischievously. 'It would be if it were true.'

Jason shakes his head. 'You were so convincing. That's quite scary, you know.'

Thea laughs. 'I need to get back to my hotel in Corfu Town. My luggage won't pack itself. Why don't you come with me? I'll show you around and be your guide for the rest of the day.'

'I'd like that,' he says cheerfully.

'If you like museums, there's the Archaeological Museum and the Byzantine Museum. Also, if churches are your thing, Saint Spyridon Church is worth a visit, but if you ask me, a visit to The Church of St Nicholas of the Elderly is a must, it is much more intimate and it is my favourite in the whole of Corfu.'

'The Church of St Nicholas it is then. I like the sound of the Byzantine Museum too.'

'There's also the fortress where the views of the town are spectacular.' Thea sighs, as she manoeuvres her car into a parking bay in front of her hotel that has an uninterrupted view of the sea. 'But I'm being over enthusiastic, aren't I? We don't even have a day together.'

The mention of the little time they had remaining deflates Jason. It is a reminder of how he feels about Thea, even though he has not had the luxury to get to know who she really is. None of that matters. His heart speaks a different language.

'We'll just make the most of the time we've got,' Jason says, unbuckling his seat belt. Thea delves into her bag and plucks her lipstick from its confines. She angles the rear-view mirror, and expertly paints her lips red. Thea smiles as she feels Jason watching her. He leans into her and kisses her cheek, tracing his lips along her skin until he finds her mouth and feels drunk with the taste of her.

He holds her hand as they stroll through hushed narrow streets decorated with wrought-iron balconies that thread through the old town. Thea takes Jason to one of her favourite restaurants, Skalinada, for a late lunch, then to The Church of St Nicholas where his eyes open wide in appreciation at the painted ceiling and myriad of frescoes that line the walls and marble altar in brilliant colour. Thea lights a candle and crosses herself three times while Jason stands back at a respectable distance.

When they are outside, he looks at her quizzically. 'I was surprised when you lit a candle. For some reason, I didn't think you practised your faith.'

'Whenever I'm in the Old Town, I always make it a habit of mine to visit The Church of St Nicholas and light a candle. My grandmother is to blame. She would bring me to the church every time we were in the Old Town. I think because the church is so small it didn't dwarf me, and I felt comfortable in it, and it was my grandmother's favourite church. I've got some wonderful memories of spending time here with her. I'm fortunate I've still got my parents.'

'Mine died a few years ago.'

'Oh! That's dreadful. They must have been young?'

'They were. Thankfully, Mum had passed away before the accident. It was bad enough watching Dad trying to cope. That didn't help me, it only added to my nightmare. I find that hard to accept. I know he didn't blame me; it was enough that I blamed myself.'

'I can't imagine how that must feel.' She squeezes his hand. 'What would you like to do now? We could go to the Old Fortress. You'd love the views,' her soothing voice announces. 'Or… we could go back to my room?'

He looks across the room. It is spacious and modern with a large flat screen television on one wall, a king-sized bed, and double sliding glass doors that open onto a balcony and breathtaking views of the sea.

Thea slides her feet out of her sandals and draws the heavy curtains, muting the light in soft shadows. She crosses the room and lays her hand on Jason's chest. There is a silence between them, and then Jason smooths back a strand of hair from her face. Instinctively, Thea raises her head slightly as Jason traces her cheek with a finger, faint but precise. He slides it gently across the membrane and fullness of her lower lip and his heart leaps as he watches her mouth open, tentatively enclose around the tip of his finger and slide along its length. The warmth is immediate as her tongue moves in fine delicate motions across him and then his mouth is on hers in a pairing of sensuality and pleasure, and it astonishes him how quick they are alone in a universe of their own making.

They lie naked, face to face, on the bed. Jason touches her face as if to make certain she is beside him. He kisses her on the mouth and, reaching with his hand, feels the fullness of her breast. He slides his hand along her stomach, a feathery touch that descends along the curve of her hip and when she moves her leg for him, he finds her and the sound she makes is exquisite to him; it catches in his chest and nothing else matters but this.

He gasps as she reaches for him, encasing him with each tender stroke. Her lips are almost touching his, her breath warm and soft against his face and then gently she kisses him full on the mouth. His fingers move inside her and stir a warm, liquescent sensation that spreads through her stomach, and she gasps and calls his name.

Her tongue licks across her lips as she guides him towards her and, when he enters her, it fills him with the most astonishing sense of elation; he never wants it to end. He is a willing captive in the rapture of her touch. It swells his heart with a feeling so exultant, so pure and intense. It is a love he has never known and scares him to know such closeness. To experience such conjoint intimacy takes the breath from him. He feels the convulsions build inside her and he, too, can't hold himself back any longer, and when she cries out, she holds him tightly to her. And in that moment, he wants to weep.

The fading light slips in through the window as Jason contemplates every angle and curve of Thea's face. He has been watching her sleep and, when her eyelashes flicker, he wonders if she is dreaming. He wants to slide his hand through her hair but fears the touch will wake her and he has not had enough, not just yet, of absorbing every detail. Her expression is enviably content. She rolls onto her side and opens her eyes. Her face brightens.

'It wasn't a dream,' she says softly, not taking her eyes from him.

'It wasn't.' Jason leans into her and kisses her forehead. He smiles. 'See, I'm real.'

'How long have you been watching me?'

'Not long. Just a few minutes.' He hesitates and gazes at her. 'I've never felt like this before, Thea. I'm in love with you.' There is no longer any question in his mind what he must do. 'I can't let you just fly back to England. The thought of never seeing you again is absurd to me. It's too much to even consider. It scares me to think you might just walk out of my life and I'll never see you again. I can't let that happen.'

'And it won't.' She reaches with her hand and, with the back of her fingers, she strokes his face. 'The second I saw you, when you returned my necklace, I knew even then. You stopped my heart and, when you spoke, your words were like a defibrillator; I felt incredibly alive, and I just wanted to spend as much time as I could with you.'

'You did?'

'Why do you think I invited you to my party?'

'Ah! I see,' he says sheepishly.

Thea sits up and swings her legs off the bed. 'Why don't we freshen up and go out for some dinner. You can have a shower.'

Jason arches his eyebrows. 'We can both have one… together.'

They are sitting outside in a narrow lane. Around them, several other diners are enjoying their evening meal with the ebb and flow of conversation filling the sultry night air. Above them, tall Venetian buildings spire towards a streak of night sky, their walls brushed with the silver illumination of the moon. They go through ordering their meal without paying much attention to the menu. It feels ordinary but it is not. The waiters shift from table to table, taking orders, and disappearing into the main building, reappearing again carrying trays of food and drink. Jason moves the cutlery nervously.

'If you're okay with it, once everything settles with the new restaurant and I've got a bit more free time, you could come down to London.' She cups her hand around her wine glass but does not drink from it. 'That's if you're able to.' She looks at him across the table. Her heart inflates with a neediness she has not known since she was a child.

'Nothing will stop me from seeing you. I don't think I could stand it otherwise.'

He is dreading tomorrow and, torn between the relief that he will see her again and the agony of filling the time in between until he does.

'There's always FaceTime. We can speak to each other every day.'

'Seeing you but not being able to touch you and inhale you will be a torture.'

'It will be one that we'll both have to endure. It will only be a few weeks at the most. I want to have you all to myself. There's so much I want to show you. I've a flat in Kensington. We can go to the theatre, museums, take long walks, eat out and I might even cook you the occasional meal, Greek cuisine, obviously.'

'You never mentioned a flat. You must spend a lot of your time in London. I didn't think you stayed there.'

Thea drinks a mouthful of wine. 'I did. But I don't spend much of my time there. Not so much now.'

'So, I'm a little confused. Was this recently? You said you lived in Slough.'

'It was a few years ago.'

'Before the restaurants, I'm imagining. This is your first one to open in London.'

'It was.'

'Did you live long in London?

Thea nods. 'Five years.'

'That's probably long enough for anyone. Edinburgh feels like a village compared to London. I've never much cared for it.'

'It's like any other city. It has its good attractions and some not so good. At the time, it was the place to be and work.'

'What did you do?'

'I was in advertising. Our clientele was mostly in the media, music, business, that sort of thing. Our offices were in the city. We worked hard and played hard.'

'So, what happened?

'It was a crazy time. The pace of life was a hundred miles an hour. And there were always temptations. It came with the territory. Parties, business events, it felt like, if you wanted, there was this social conveyer belt of drugs and drink, an unwritten rule in your job description, you know.'

Jason tries to imagine this other Thea.

'There were trips abroad, Europe mostly; Paris, Berlin, Rome. A different language and scenery but the conveyer belt was international, it kept on rolling.'

'And that's when I met Jeff.'

Unease beats in Jason's heart. Why is he so surprised? Already, he is jealous of Jeff. Jason feels like her words have sucked the air from his lungs.

'Delightful, delectable and charming Jeff… and terminally ill.'

Jason's resentfulness dampens. This he isn't expecting.

'He was a client of the advertising agency. His company had a turnover of tens of millions a year. He was one of our most valued clients and he was lonely and had six months to live. His wife had died several years ago. They had no children, and he had no extended family. The loneliness of our lives drew us to each other.

'By then, I hated my job and the life I was leading. I wanted to… I wanted to follow my passion, but had always been too scared to throw caution to the wind. I was afraid of throwing it all away. The prospect of failure intimidated me. I had all of this energy and ideas on how I could make my passion for Greek food become a viable business opportunity. In a business sense and on a personal level, I had no idea how to express this. Jeff made me believe I could do anything I wanted to. He stripped away my self-doubt. He was attracted to me because he knew I was unhappy and, before he died, he wanted me to become the person he saw I was capable of becoming.

'We saw each other twice a week. Initially, just for coffee, then he took me to his favourite restaurants, the theatre and the cinema. He loved European films, especially French films. He opened my mind to new possibilities. I told him about my love of food, Greek food and how it had always been a dream of mine to not just have my restaurant, but to have a chain of them. And he said to me, what's stopping you and I said, I am, and he said, I believe in you.'

Thea's eyes brim with tears. Jason hands her a napkin and she dabs each one. 'God, I must look a mess. My mascara will be everywhere. I probably look like Alice Cooper.'

'You don't and your eyes are just fine, honest. Jeff sounds like a really nice guy.'

'He was. He was one of life's gems.'

'The way you talk about him, you must have loved him very much.'

'I did. I loved him for the man he was. He was sensitive but also single-minded, and he exuded an easy-going charm.'

'He sounds perfect.'

She looks at Jason and is suddenly overcome with panic. 'But as a father figure. You weren't thinking… you were, weren't you?'

'Well, yes. What other way was I supposed to think?'

'Oh, Jason.' She reaches over the table and holds his hand. 'It was never like that between us. Jeff was old enough to be my father.

'In the end when he died, it was quick, thank God. He didn't want people feeling that they had to visit him when he was in hospital. He said he would have hated the attention. The last time I saw him, we went out for dinner, and by then he didn't have an appetite, but although he ate very little, he wanted it to be just as it had always been. He died the next day, in his sleep, and I never had time to say goodbye. Thinking back, he knew. I've heard people know when their time has come. It's like a sixth sense. The last thing he said to me was, the perfect life is an illusion. Even with all his money, it was a lie. He would give it all away just to live another day.'

Jason squeezes her hand. 'I'm so sorry, Thea.' He feels an impulsive surge of impotent pity and affection.

'It doesn't end there. I got the shock of my life when I found out I was a beneficiary in his will.'

'Really!'

'Yes. He left me a note. Just a few lines. It read simply, *Chase your dream. Remember, I believe in you.* He left me two million pounds.'

'Jesus! That's a hell of a lot of money.'

Thea draws in a breath. 'There was a condition that went along with it.'

'A condition! What do you mean?'

'The money couldn't be spent on just anything. The way it was set up, monies would only be released for a business venture.'

'I see. That's incredible.'

'Without Jeff, my life would be completely different. I know how privileged I am because of his money, but it was through my determination, passion and belief in my business plan that I am where I am today. It was difficult; I certainly wasn't an overnight success. There were times I thought I was deluding myself. I had to dig deep into my psyche.' Thea pauses for a moment, deep in thought. 'And you know, even with all that money, it could have gone spectacularly wrong. I am who I am because of him, and I remind myself of that every day.'

He looks down at their hands. Her fingers are warm and entwined around his and a nervous exhilaration comes over him and panic seizes him. *I've just met her, and tomorrow she will be gone.* They exchange a look. She holds his gaze, and she seems to sense his sadness. Her eyes are like a pool, and he can see his reflection in them just as the air catches his chest. Time is moving forward like the tide, and she is slipping from him with each passing second. Thea will leave him. There will be no reprieve. It was decided before they met.

And in that moment, it occurs to Jason he is reliving the torment Marcus must have experienced when he knew he had no choice. He had to leave Helena. Jason finds this strangely comforting; such a reaction leaves him uneasy and perplexed. Why would he feel like this? But when he considers this, to his relief, he is satisfied with his conclusion. Marcus' journal is no longer just an account his great grandfather had written. Jason can now relate to the emotional whirlpool Marcus and Helena must have inhabited. Living under such immense strain, it destabilised everything for them.

Jason finds it incredible. After three generations, he is breathing the same air Marcus breathed here in Corfu, and incredibly, he is experiencing similar heartache and emotional conflict. He is walking in Marcus' shoes.

Jason looks at Thea intently and breaks the silence between them. ‘I love you, Thea. I love you more than life itself. I can’t explain it. I’ve only known you a matter of days, but I feel I’ve known you all my life. I don’t pretend to understand that. It’s extraordinary, and it is incomprehensible, that’s all I know.’ Looking into his eyes, Thea knows he means every word and when Jason leans over the table and kisses her on the mouth; she too cannot explain it. She has fallen in love.

Edinburgh

2018

Three months later

In a lifetime, this can only happen once. Like a birth, like a death, it is unique; he cannot separate himself from what he feels. It is part of him, like the blood that flows in his veins, like the air that feeds his lungs, he needs her. It binds him to her like he has never felt before. Their union is a mystery to him.

Without her, he just existed. He had lost his way. He walked the streets of his life, bewildered and alone, turning inwards to the seclusion of his thoughts, a place that haunted him.

Without her there is nothing, only emptiness, and he fears that place, the void that waits.

A concentrated shift is taking shape. In his mind, he has captured the moment. He can vividly picture another life. A life where he is happy. A life where their love is unconditional, it is faithful; it permeates every aspect of their life together.

He has known her intimately. With her, he will never feel lonely. His love for her feels like a bright light, forever undimmed.

That last night in Corfu Town, after their evening meal, they made love, and in the morning after breakfast, Thea left for the airport. Jason did not go with her. Travelling with her to the airport felt like an unnecessary prolongment of what was going to be an inevitable tearful separation.

Instead, Thea dropped Jason at the bus station. He held her in the car and ran his hand through her hair. What more could they say that hadn't been said? His last memory was watching her car swing around a street corner and disappear from him.

Jason sips his coffee. Above him, the sun is mottled in cotton clouds that reflect a calm mirror image on The Water of Leith.

He sees her walking towards him. Rachel is talking on her mobile and when she reaches Jason, she kisses him on the cheek without interrupting the flow of her conversation. She sits opposite him and crosses her legs. Jason raises his cup, and she nods and smiles. He orders her an Americano and another for himself and a slice of carrot cake. Rachel often enthuses it is the best carrot cake in all of Edinburgh.

She places her mobile on the tabletop. 'Sorry about that. It was the office. I can't even go out for lunch without there being something that can't wait for an hour and needs my immediate attention.'

'It's okay. I got you your favourite cake.'

'You know me so well.'

'You've told me often enough.'

'It's like wine. You get your good and bad and, when you find a good one, you stick with it. There was this café bar in London, a Lebanese couple ran it and their carrot cake was to die for as well. I think I must have put on a stone in a week. I had one every lunchtime.' Rachel scoops a piece of cake with her fork and savours the taste. 'God, it's like an orgasm.'

Jason laughs. 'I hope you're not going to do the When Sally met Harry scene?'

She throws her head back and laughs. 'You're quite safe. I'm not going to embarrass you.'

He leans back in his chair and smiles. Pleased. 'Good.'

'How are you feeling? I hope you're taking it easy.'

'I am. Look, I've got a bump now. It's really happening.' She places her hands on her stomach.

'How many weeks are you?'

'Eighteen weeks. I've got my first scan tomorrow. I'm going the whole hog and getting the 3D video.'

'I've heard they're amazing. You'll have to show me. And the father, is he going too?'

'He's been a bastard. He's been one of the biggest mistakes I've made. I don't need him. I can do this on my own.'

'You never told me his name.'

'He's a business associate in London. I would see him when I was down there. We've been seeing each other for a few months… were seeing each other. He's married.'

'Rachel.'

'It's fine. I'm over him. And if there's one good thing that's come out of it is this little one.' She pats her stomach.

'So, you're going all the way?'

'It was a shock to start with, I won't deny that, but I've got used to it now. I'm going to be a mother. I like how that sounds. And anyway, it's about time I grew up. And you will be great too, Uncle Jason.'

Jason laughs. 'I'm flattered by your confidence in me.'

'How was London?' Rachel asks, while spooning carrot cake into her mouth.

'You mean… Thea.'

'Well, yes.' She wipes some crumbs from the corner of her mouth. 'Obviously.'

'Fine. We're fine.' He gives a smile of self-satisfaction. 'The restaurant has been an amazing success. In fact, she's thinking about opening a second one in London.'

'You're hiding something from me. I know you too well, Jason.' Rachel sounds wounded.

'I'm… I mean, we're going back to Corfu.'

'A holiday?'

'Not exactly.'

Rachel smiles and looks at him directly in the eyes. She can see Jason is enjoying this. 'What do you mean?'

'We've bought a house… Helena's house.'

London

2018

Two weeks earlier

It is a bright morning and Jason and Thea are eating breakfast on the roof garden of her flat with views overlooking the London skyline.

'Are you sure about this?' Jason asks, a smile hovering at his lips.

'I know what it means to you. When you saw how dilapidated the house was, I could see how devastated you were. It was in such a deplorable state.'

'It would take an awful lot of money.'

'Jason, it's not as if I can't afford it. And besides, the house deserves it. It's part of the history of the village, and it needs to be preserved. It needs to be lived in again. I'll get the best builders and tradesmen in Corfu to work on her.'

'How do you go about buying a house in Greece… In Corfu?'

'Don't worry. I've already contacted our family lawyer in Corfu, our accountant, and the bank. My lawyer has already approached the German owners and they are happy to sell.'

'Really?'

'Yes, it's really happening. You think it's a good idea?'

'Thea, I can't believe it. How long will take?'

'I can't foresee any problems. The owners are just glad to get the house off their hands. At the least, six, maybe eight weeks.'

'It's as simple as that. As short as that.'

'As long as there are no unforeseen circumstances, which I'm sure there won't be, they're desperate to sell.' Thea pauses. 'I've been in touch with the building company who built the villa, and they could get started pretty much straight away.'

Jason looks at Thea in bewilderment. 'I can't believe you would do this, for me.'

'If you're happy, I'm happy.'

Jason embraces her. He pulls away and looks into her eyes.

'I can't have you shoulder all the expense. I've got money from the sale of mum and dad's house and their estate. I'll contribute my share.'

She knows that look on his face. There is no point in trying to persuade him to back down. 'If that's what you want. But I'm paying for the restoration.'

'Six weeks is not a long time.'

'I think it would be good if we went before then. I've asked my lawyer to draw up a pre-contract agreement. It needs to be signed by us and the current owners. It commits both parties to an agreed price and agreed completion date. We're required to pay a ten per cent deposit which will be held in trust by my lawyer until completion. And we need to be present for the signing of the contract for the house. It's advisable. While we're in Corfu, I'll get in touch with the architects, and we can draw up some plans.'

'You've really given this some thought.'

'We can stay at the villa. Once the building work starts, we'd be close enough to the house to oversee the work.'

'You can't be that long away from the business.'

'There is the internet. I'd be contactable every day and there are Zoom calls. If I need to go back to England, it's only a four-hour flight at the most.'

'There's my job as well. I can't take much more time off.'

'I was thinking about that. Why don't you come and work for me?'

He tilts his head. 'And do what?'

‘I’m looking for a partner. Someone who has experience with the money side of things. Someone with a track record of working in finance on a global scale, you know, keeping the business in a healthy financial position. I need someone I can trust. Someone who can work closely with me.’

‘How close?’

She pulls herself up against him and puts her arms around him and he knows that expression in her eyes. ‘Is this close enough?’

Corfu

2018

Home

It has rained for three days, the late November sky dark and angry; and Jason feels he could almost be in Edinburgh. It is an unaccustomed sensation feeling chilled in Corfu. Jason has always imagined it being warm all year long. It hasn't occurred to him it rains and gets cold in the winter months. He has always imagined the picture postcard image, but that has now been reassessed. In the main living area of the villa, there are electric heaters, strategically placed for optimal effect.

Thea is standing at the floor to ceiling window, an arm wrapped around her waist, hugging her long cardigan to contain its warmth. She looks out over the garden and speaks into her mobile phone.

'So, you will be back at work tomorrow. That's good. I don't want to get too far behind. Hopefully, the covering is still attached to the beams on the roof. The worst of the storm has passed, going by the weather reports.' She listens and then nods in agreement. 'That's good to hear. We'll be there about ten. So, I'll see you then.'

She turns to Jason, who has not understood a single word as she has spoken in Greek. 'Everyone will be back tomorrow morning, the joiners, plasterers, and electricians. The weather is going to clear, so it's all hands on deck.'

'It was a stroke of luck. They managed to get most of the new tiles on the roof. Did the tarpaulin hold out?

'They checked it this morning.' She smiles. 'The house is dry and still standing.'

'I can't believe the amount of rain we've had.'

'How do you think Corfu is such a green and lush island?'

'Yep, I get it now.'

By the early afternoon, it has stopped raining, and the sun is illuminating the grey metal clouds in golden yellow light drying the last raindrops on the flowers and leaves in the garden. Thea is sprawled on one of the large white leather chairs, reading a book and chewing her lip. She drops the book into her lap and looks across the room. Jason is scrolling through emails on his mobile.

'I wish I could write like Liane Moriarty. Her books just immerse you in her characters' lives; you become invested in them within the first chapter.' She thinks for a moment. 'I haven't seen you read a book. You don't read much, do you?'

'When I do, it's usually a biography, but not often. I should read more.'

'I think my love of reading came from my English teacher. I remember him saying the written word is the most powerful medium we humans have invented. It can change the way you think, it can alter your beliefs and values. It's true. Books can influence you in a way that they can change our perspectives, our emotions; they become our friends, helping us to analyse and observe the world around us. Mostly, they have the ability to transform lives.'

Jason thought for a moment, then perched himself on the edge of the chair. He gazed at Thea with an expression of sudden realisation and his eyes widen.

'And change them forever. If I hadn't read Marcus' journal, I wouldn't have come to Corfu and been able to find the way to put my grief and self-blame to rest. I wouldn't have found your necklace and, most importantly, I wouldn't have met you. You're absolutely right. By reading the journal, I rediscovered the things I'd lost and was reminded of who I really was. I couldn't have done any of that without reading the journal but, most importantly, without you, Thea. I am who I am today because of you.'

'I don't think so.'

'Well, I do. Believe me.' Jason looks at her steadily and the gratitude he feels is overwhelming. 'I've thought about this. I dread to think about where I was heading. I wasn't in a good place, Thea. Nobody was responsible for the turmoil inside me, nobody invented it, I did. I was angry. I was wounded. I hated myself for what happened. I blamed myself for my little sister's death.'

The glow in his eyes deepens with emotion and his voice is soft with affection. 'But meeting you turned my world upside down… in a good way. I had become so judgemental and unforgiving of myself, I was drowning. I didn't ask to be so fucked up. I was lost. I was desperate. I didn't make myself be that way, this man, consumed with hate for himself and enraged with the world around him. There were times I felt the urge to take a drink. Just take one and numb the pain, just one. It won't harm you. Each time I pulled back, but it was getting harder to do so, and then you stopped me dead instantly with that radiant smile. Finding your necklace beside Andreas' grave was my saving grace. It led me to you. I've said nothing to you because I was scared that you'd feel the pressure of it and by revealing the truth, I'd be destroying my one chance of finding happiness and the joy of being with you.

'Finally, I can let go of the past and embrace the future, our future, you and me, and that feels so liberating. So, when I say, you have saved me, Thea,' he takes a gulp of air to fortify himself, 'I mean it with all my heart.'

Thea can see he means every word, and she is moved, but unsure how to deal with Jason's candid revelation. She can feel the sting of tears in her eyes when Jason moves towards her. He kneels by her chair. With a delicate touch, he traces her cheek bones and runs his fingers along the line of her jaw and then, leaning into her, he kisses her mouth and, closing her eyes, Thea pulls him towards her.

The next morning, they stroll hand in hand, with safeguarding steps, avoiding the tan stained puddles that colonise the potholed track leading to Helena's house.

The intimate natural hues of the hills and pines surround them in an abundance of earthly aromas and, with each passing minute, the air grows warmer, fresh and anew. Overhead, the sun dissipates the cloud cover and, much to Jason's relief, he can feel its heat on his back.

As they walk, he is accompanied by images of their lovemaking; they slide effortlessly into his thoughts, the tentative brush of skin against skin, the explicit pleasure, taste, and ecstasy.

There is a sense of urgency around them. 'If we get a few weeks of good weather, the house should start to take shape.'

'Now that the new roof is on, it shouldn't matter so much about the weather. There's lots of work to be done inside. I can't wait to see it taking shape,' Jason says happily, and it makes Thea happy to see him this way.

Coming towards them, Jason can see a woman and a dog. The dog's tail is wagging like a fan behind it and the woman is wearing a wide-brimmed hat and carrying a lead loosely in her hand. The dog runs towards them, and the woman calls out in Greek. When it reaches them, the dog rubs its body against Thea's legs, its tongue glistening as it hangs from its panting mouth. Thea bends towards the dog and runs her hand over its head. 'Hello, boy. You're gorgeous.' She smiles at Jason. 'I just love a Golden Retriever. They're so friendly.' She tickles the dog's ears, and Thea's eyes widen in delight. 'Oh, you like that, don't you? Yes, you are a beauty.'

The woman approaches them and immediately apologises. ‘I’m sorry. He thinks everyone is going to feed him.’

Thea smiles. ‘A typical retriever.’

‘He certainly is. Friendly and always hungry.’ She slips the lead in her hand over Jasper’s head. ‘Come on, Jasper. It’s nearly your favourite time of day, lunchtime.’ She smiles at Thea and Jason. ‘Nice to meet you.’ And then they both head off, Jasper’s nose nuzzling her hand.

As they walk on, Jason stops suddenly and turns to look at the woman and dog, who are now a considerable distance from them.

Thea watches Jason. ‘What is it, Jason?’

‘I knew she was familiar to me. I just couldn’t place her. I’ve seen her before, in the village with a man. He was Scottish, and he called her… Elora. Yes, that was her name, Elora.’

As they approach the house, Jason takes a breath and gradually exhales. Two vans are parked next to the house and already the house is a hive of activity. A cement mixer, a trestle, stacks of wood and a wheelbarrow. Scaffolding surrounds the exterior of the house. A stalky man with a silver beard appears at the door, wiping his hands on his overalls.

‘Angelo.’

‘Thea. And this must be Jason.’ He offers his hand and Jason shakes it. Angelo’s grip is strong and assuring. ‘Please, come inside.’

As they move into the house, the transformation astonishes Jason. What was once filthy with grime and dust, where plaster peeled from graffitied walls and bottles and cans littered the stone flagged floor, now is a space that is rejuvenated and cleansed. Gone is the stuffiness and airless oppression he felt when he first entered the house all those months ago. And, although it is still a work in progress already, Jason can imagine how it will look.

'As you can see, you still get the feel for the open space the house would have had. This part of the house will have the kitchen and be the living space. I wasn't sure if it would be at all possible but, as you can see, we have kept the original stone floor and brought out its original colour. Over there, where the fireplace was, we have installed an Aga to keep the original features where possible, as I think it is important to maintain the historical aspects of the house. It will please you to know that even with the recent bad weather we are still on course to finish on time and on budget. The basement was in an awful state of disrepair. There was a lot of dampness on the walls. We're in the process of stripping it back to the bricks. When doing so, we found something unusual.'

'Oh! What was that?' Thea asks.

'Behind one of the bricks there was a small space where we discovered an old tin and inside the tin was this envelope.'

Jason hasn't noticed the envelope, but Angelo has been holding it all this time. Angelo hands Thea the envelope. Thea looks at Jason and she can tell intrigue and apprehension seizes him.

From somewhere upstairs, someone calls for Angelo's attention. 'I'd better go. I'll leave you to look around.'

The light in the house is muted because the electrics are still not complete. 'Let's go outside,' Thea suggests.

Once in the garden, Jason notices a bench by the side of the house. It is new and is standing against the house in the same spot where Marcus and Helena would have sat at night.

'I remembered you told me they used to sit here under the cover of night to allow Marcus to escape the basement and breath fresh air. It was to be a surprise.'

'It still is. And a most welcome one.' He kisses Thea on her cheek. 'Thank you.'

They sit down, and Thea turns the discoloured envelope in her hand. She offers it to Jason. Hesitantly, he takes it from her, and placing under his nose, he takes a deep breath, inhaling its smell. It has obviously been there a long time.

'Are you going to open it or just smell it?'

He glances at her and then looks down at the envelope. It could be nothing, he tells himself, and then it could be everything.

He slides a finger under the flap and gradually lifts it, exposing the contents inside. He removes several sheets of paper, neatly folded in half and, when he unfolds them, the sight of the Greek handwriting squeezes his heart. In the years to come, he will never forget the exhilaration that bubbled inside him as he peered at the neat handwriting before him, longing to discern its meaning, the identity of the author already known to him.

Thea takes the letter from Jason and searches his face. 'Are you ready to hear this?'

Jason takes a breath and slowly releases it. With a mix of anguish and anticipation, he replies. 'There has always been something missing, and I think it is about to be revealed. We owe it to her.'

Thea clears her throat and begins.

You said you would return, and I believed you then as I believe you now. You held my heart in your hands and, after all this time, still do. There is not a single day that passes from the sun rising to its setting that I don't think of you. How could I not, my darling? You were the air I breathed that filled my whole being with life, with hope, with joy and with the most unsurmountable love I never dreamt was possible to feel and to know.

I thank God every day for you coming into my life. You were a light in my darkness, and you are still there, my love. You have not faded, and I am comforted by it.

I know now you are at peace. Only death could have kept you from me. I have cried rivers of tears for you. I have fallen into the depths of despair. And I have grieved for you. I hope they returned you to your family. Your absence has been a torture, worse than anything the Germans could have ever inflicted upon me.

The night you left, I was shot, but only wounded in the arm. They took me to a camp and I spent several months locked away from the sun and sky or any other human voice except that of my captives. Their inquisitions fell onto deaf ears. No words of betrayal spilt from my lips. Even when my body was beaten and starved of food and my mind was not my own, I kept your name from them. You were like a ghost to them.

And during that time, a seed was growing silently and steadfastly. In the safety of my womb, a precious life was defying all the odds.

I was consumed with the most incredible joy and happiness. A part of you would always be with me, even in death. But an all-consuming sadness, a reminder of what should have been also flattened me.

Your daughter is Carissa. I named her after my mother. Every time I look upon her face, I see you reflected in her eyes. I see you in her smile. You would be so proud of her. She is perfect. She is the embodiment of our love.

When the Germans left, I had nothing. I had no one except our darling daughter. I spent the long winter months in the house, just the both of us, and only went out to buy what food there was on the empty shelves. The Germans had taken the animals. There was little meat and only the vegetables that the garden would grow.

There was one saving grace. I still had the money you gave me. Remember, I kept it under the floorboards. You were insistent that I took it, and it was a godsend. It saw us through the winter and the summer, but eventually it dwindled.

That was when Vangelis returned from fighting on the mainland. The war had changed him. Vangelis was a different man than the one that had left. He begged me for forgiveness. He assumed our daughter was his, and I, with no means to provide for her, with only the certainty of poverty as an assurance, led him to believe she was.

Forgive me, my darling. I live with this every day, but I will do anything for her, and many children had died from starvation and disease. The country was on its knees, and Vangelis was my only hope.

It is not perfect between us, but it is a life that we have and, without Vangelis, we would have surely been at the mercy of others. I had one choice and one choice only and now Carissa has a life, she has a future, and it was the only thing I could give her, something we both dreamed about but would never have.

Vangelis has secured passage to Australia. It is a country I know nothing of, but he tells me it is a land of opportunity, jobs and stability. The year is 1952 and Greece has changed since the war, but Australia is a country like England and there are many Greeks leaving their villages and towns to make a better life for themselves. Carissa is strong willed and determined; she also has a love of books and of learning. She is her father's daughter.

I long to feel your arms around me, and I know I will when God decides it is time. We will meet again, my love. I have always loved you, my beautiful Marcus.

Thea drops the letter into her lap and wipes the tears from her eyes, and Jason can see his own feelings mirrored in her face as he draws the air over his teeth.

He has spent a long time wondering who Marcus was, who Helena was, and how their short time together changed both their lives forever. If he was to come to any conclusion and retract meaning from it all, they epitomised what it meant to be human, to love unconditionally, theirs was a life of understanding, of passion, and forgiveness. They chose, however improbable it was, to commit themselves to each other in the face of adversity and to the detriment of their own wellbeing. They did not give up on each other as they faced the pain of separation together and, even when the cruellest blow struck, theirs was a love worth holding on to.

Jason thinks of Helena and Marcus sitting together under the camouflage of the night sky, exactly where he is sitting now. He can't contain his happiness; it surrounds him and radiates around his heart in a rush of contentment and belonging. He takes Thea's hand and, closing his eyes, he inhales the surrounding air. He is home.

The End

Other books by Dougie McHale

I hope you enjoyed my writing. If you would like to read more of my books you can view them all on Amazon at the links below.

Amazon.com
Amazon.co.uk

Connect with me at my website, on Facebook and Instagram. I'd love to hear from you.

Acknowledgements

Heartfelt thanks to Sheona, my wife, for her continued support and constant encouragement. Thanks to Tracy Watson, Maggie Crawshaw, Anne Clague, Lisa Richards and Dilys Killick. As my advanced readers they have given me invaluable feedback on all of my novels. Finally, as always, I am indebted to Katrina Johnston for her editorial skills, advice and time.

About the Author

Dougie lives in Dunfermline, Fife, with his wife, daughter, son and golden retriever.

Beneath a Burning Sky is his sixth novel.

Thank you so much for taking the time to read my novel. It really does mean everything to me. My novels are inspired by my favourite city, Edinburgh and my passion for Greece, her islands, people, landscapes, sea, light and ambience, all of which are important themes and symbols in my writing.

My books encapsulate themes such as love, loss, hope, coming of age and the uncovering of secrets. They are character-driven stories with twists and turns set against the backdrop of Edinburgh and Greece.

I never intended too, but seemingly, I write women's contemporary fiction and since 95% of my readers are women, I suppose that is a good fit.

Since all my books are set in Edinburgh and Greece, you will not be surprised to know that I identify with a physical place and the feeling of belonging, which are prominent in my writing.

Edinburgh is one of the most beautiful cities in the world, it is rich in history, has amazing classical buildings, (the new town of Edinburgh is a world heritage site) and it also has vibrant restaurants and café bars.

Greece occupies my heart. Her history, culture, religion, people, landscape, light, colours and sea inspire me every day. There is almost a spiritual quality to it. I want my novels to have a sense of time and place, drawing the reader into the social and cultural complexities of the characters. I want my characters to speak from the page, where you can identify with them, their hopes, fears, conflicts, loves and emotion. I hope the characters become like real people to you, and it is at that point, you will want to know what is going to happen to the characters, where is their life taking them in the story.

The common denominator is, I want my novels to be about what it means to be human through our relationship with our world, our environment and with each other. Most of all, I want them to be good stories that you, as a reader, can identify with and enjoy.

Printed in Great Britain
by Amazon

24573555R00155